THE AGE OF
WONDER

Also By Michael Grieg

A Fire In His Hand

Poems: "Guide to the City"

THE AGE OF
WONDER

A Novel by

Michael Grieg

DONALD I. FINE, INC.
New York

for V.I.

Copyright © 1988 by Michael Grieg
All rights reserved, including the right of reproduction in whole or in part
in any form. Published in the United States of America by Donald I. Fine,
Inc. and in Canada by General Publishing Company Limited.

Library of Congress Catalogue Card Number: 87-46030
ISBN: 1-55611-072-3
Manufactured in the United States of America
10 9 8 7 6 5 4 3 2 1

Library of Congress Cataloging-in-Publication Data
Grieg, Michael.
The age of wonder.
I. Title.
PS3513.R657A7 1988   813'.54   87-46030
ISBN 1-55611-072-3 (alk. paper)

This book is printed on acid free paper. The paper in this book meets the
guidelines for permanence and durability of the Committee on Production
Guidelines for Book Longevity of the Council on Library Resources.

"You Make Me Feel So Young" by Mack Gordon and Joseph Myrow copyright © 1946 WB MUSIC CORP. Renewed. All rights reserved. Used by
permission.

"Merlin" by Geoffrey Hill from *Geoffrey Hill Collected Poems 1986*. Copyright © Andre Deutsch Publishers. All rights reserved. Used by permission.

Sometimes a man seeks what he hath lost; and from that place, and time, wherein he misses it, his mind runs back, from place to place, and time to time, to find where and when he had it . . .

—Thomas Hobbes, *Leviathan*

ONE

I went to the Garden of Love . . .
And I saw it was filled with graves,
And tomb-stones where flowers should be . . .
　—William Blake, *The Garden of Love*

1

Some weeks after he left the paper, where he had mostly been doing obits the last year, he found himself bringing the dead back to life. His father, dead almost fifty years, was first.

There was no trick to breathing life into the dead. There was no need to consult books on necromancy, witchcraft, the innumerable reprints now that deviltry was fashionable. It had nothing to do with mixing strange ingredients Safeway didn't sell, spider's legs and toad's blood, or digging up bodies, or uttering incantations. All that was necessary, he discovered in time, were a few facts, some imagination, a little faith and the need, the honest need, to raise the dead. Also, it helped if your life was falling apart.

Once he caught on, he heard the voice of Ben Dorn, fifty, balding, lying under a red woolen blanket in the back room of an apartment on Davidson Avenue in The Bronx, his hazel eyes closed, asleep forever until his sixty-two-year-old son summoned him back to life.

In the beginning, when Nathaniel Dorn first thought of reviving the dead in all their reborn innocence, he had no luck. He was sitting in the chlorinated warmth of his hot tub, looking out from the deck at the freeway commuters inching home.

A wisp of out-of-sortness settled on his mood. He wasn't

feeling as fortunate as he had every reason to feel. There was nowhere he had to be. No obligations to anyone except for his son living in the unit downstairs. He had been helping Stan go to computer school ever since the stabbing made Stan close up his car repair shop. His support would end once school was over.

Why, Nathaniel thought, he had every right to feel as carefree as a schoolboy, even more so; that was the kind of retirement he wanted, the ability to be a kid again, an experienced kid with resources and without concern. There was nothing he had to do. He could easily do anything he wished, anything he could afford. And yet, and yet there was this wisp of uneasiness. He could do anything about most everything except what to do about the woman in his life, now out of his life, maybe temporarily, maybe not. Already, he felt himself half in mourning for her, half in rage.

He thought of his dead wife, Rachel. Gradually, as he and Gloria Dell had gotten closer before their estrangement, Rachel had begun to fade from his mind. He had felt the mourning was over. Now her image returned, as dark in her looks as Gloria was light. He wished he could talk to her. She would know what he should do about Gloria. Rachel always spoke her mind.

What made it even more painful was that Gloria lived close by on the hill, three blocks away. During their separation he would see her car or her dog near Asimakopolos, the busy Greek restaurant, or Good Life, the community market, or The Daily Scoop, the ice cream parlor, or Klein's, the deli, and he would feel obliged to look away to avoid an unwanted confrontation. Potrero Hill was like a small town, with its own neighborhood newspaper, *The Potrero View*, an enclave set in the heights minutes south of downtown, a neighborhood that wasn't on the way to anywhere else. A visitor had to want to go there or belong there to be there.

"No matter what," Gloria had said, "we'll be close neighbors."

Gloria Dell, 797 Rhode Island Street, San Francisco, Ca. 94107. Three blocks away, *neighbors* . . . The word resounded in his mind, *naaaayyybuuurrrrs*, like the heavy lid of a tomb shutting tight.

"A fair weather lover," he would say, embittered by the enforced vacation from each other Gloria had proposed. Her decision had disrupted his retirement plans when he needed her most. And he would be harsher sometimes. "The bitch, she's a bitch, a gentle bitch but a bitch, a snow queen bitch," he complained to their therapist, Hilda Kaddish. "She's a passive aggressive depressive, growing more hysterical by the minute."

Nathaniel saw Kaddish every Thursday, the day after she saw Gloria who, yes, he did love, after all, perhaps. Gloria, he recognized, had every quality of grace, peace and quiet he wanted for himself even though she didn't seem to want him anymore, whether or not she called it a vacation from each other. Whatever she called it, it was crazy-making. It was making him crazy.

In calmer moments, less hysterical himself, he would think: *She's had an attack of feminism. She's suffering from a post-menstrual identity crisis. Feminism must be fucking up her mind. Why does she have to read those books and attend those meetings? Doesn't she have enough to do with all her good causes on behalf of this and that? Why doesn't she just stick to reading mysteries and attend to me?*

Then he would catch himself, the reflected glimmer of his self-serving condescension toward her. No, what Gloria was

11

doing in her own work with Kaddish was admirable. She was struggling to build her own strength, to overcome the emotional disasters of a loveless childhood and a couple of failed marriages. Helping others and reading murder mysteries was a relief from therapeutic strain. Her attempt to unburden herself was a noble struggle at her age, and he admired her for it. He did, he did.

Rachel Dorn, be my witness, I have nothing against women's equality and a woman finding herself. I'm all for a woman with a mind of her own, he assured himself. *Rachel would not have had it any other way . . . Why, I read Mary Wollstonecraft even before Rachel, even before there was a feminist movement, and I did my share of cooking and keeping house and caring for the kids during thirty years of marriage. I encouraged Rachel to go back to college and build a career of her own. And I believe, heart and soul, in Gloria's right to be herself, to make her own choices. Only why does that have to exclude me?*

And, in the early morning hours of his retirement, awakened by uneasy dreams, he would touch the pillow next to him, in the king-size bed, find her head not there, and call out, "Gloria, oh, Gloria . . . It's my own doing. My craziness. Who would want to stay with someone like me? I'm so meddlesome. I can't relax. I have to put myself forward all the time, feeling I have to give you permission to be yourself . . . Nathaniel Dorn, even my name sounds heavy. Dear Gloria, why can't I be gentle like you? Gentle!"

At the sound of his voice, Golem would bound from the closet where he slept, leap on the bed, perky Golem, redolent with ass-shit dog smell, licking his face. "Well, I have you, Golem," he would say until the massive shepherd began nosing his way under the blanket to his crotch. "Oh, get out of here, into your closet!" he would finally shout, trying to shoo the beast away. "I'm going to have to cut off your nuts if you don't stop this shit."

Gloria had suggested he get Golem neutered. "He's too much," she said. "It's impossible to hold on to his leash. He's so eager to get it on. One of these days he's going to pull your arm out with his virility. Think of your heart, Nat. It's a terrible strain."

The SPCA had cut rates for senior pet owners, she told him. Cut rates for castration—the pun made him wince and smile at the same time. But he held back from doing what she suggested, the surgical sedation of rambunctious Golem who was given to humping chair edges, table legs, knees, whatever he could get his hindlegs into.

Golem was much like him, he decided. They were both so intense and intrusive. In a way, he knew what Gloria meant when she would decry his intensity, yes, what amounted to an addiction to her.

Gloria had insisted on the vacation from each other after he had let his son Stan stay in the apartment. She felt a foreboding that Stan, who had been on drugs, would return to drugs.

"Stan's going to school," he said. "He's got his life to live, and we've got ours."

He had asked Gloria to marry him; instead, she said it was time they separated for a while and had more time for themselves. With retirement, he had all the time in the world.

But all he could think of was that he was losing her. The terrible irony of it all, his asking her to marry him and she responding with an insistence on more privacy, made him tremble with indignation, even now. Almost as soon as the enforced vacation began, he started calling her.

"Can't we postpone this thing?" he would say. "It's not a good time for me. I've got so much on my mind, what with Stan. First the stabbing, now I'm not feeling well."

"You'll survive," said Gloria, whose own health was shaky. A mysterious allergy, a virus, whatever it was, had been clouding her mind.

One specialist thought it might be a form of encephalitis, and until the condition began to improve he had a foreboding that he might lose her, as he had his wife. Now, he feared, he might lose her anyway. "Gloria, let's talk about this so-called vacation."

"Nat, we agreed." And she would hang up.

He would call her back. "You hung up on me."

"Yes," she would say. And she hung up again.

He called her back. "It's me, Gloria."

"Yes, I know."

"Look, Gloria, I'm sixty-two. I don't need you hanging up on me. Please don't hang up on me."

"Look, Nathaniel, I'm sixty-six, and I'm busy. Please don't call me back unless it's an emergency." And she hung up. She had called him Nathaniel, a formality that coldly told him how angry she was.

And she had hung up three times on him. On Nathaniel Dorn, lately Nat Dorn of the San Francisco *Standard*, masterful phone man at the paper, an expert on a slow day for news, known for his skill in manipulating hard-nosed cops and politicians into giving him info they had sat on for weeks, was losing control. He felt frustrated. He felt sick.

It qualified as an emergency, he decided. "My heart doesn't feel good," he told Gloria after waiting two hours before calling again. "I'm getting stabs of pain." An enlarged prostate was also giving him trouble. "It's getting harder and harder to pee," he said, courting the sharing, the intimacy she wanted to put aside.

"See a doctor, Nat," she said. "Take care of yourself." She was not without kindness. She had called him Nat, but she had hung up, and he felt sick, sick of himself, after the call.

Increasingly, like Gloria, he found himself unbearable; he also wanted to be free of his own intensity, the flame in him that was consuming the butterfly aspect of his soul. When he told his therapist that, she snorted. "Be sensible, Nathan," Kaddish said. "Don't put yourself down. You'll make yourself sick with that kind of thinking. The flame is also you."

Those first days after leaving the paper he bought more food at Safeway than he and Golem and his ancient cat, Gamel, could eat in a month. He cleaned the house, even under the kitchen sink, although his cleaning woman, Mrs. Finney, was coming the next day. He went through his mail, a month's mail he had neglected while at the paper because answering was too much like work. He took clothes to the cleaners, weeded the backyard garden near the fig and apple trees, washed normally smelly Golem, drained the hot tub, refilled it, and made a backup address book in case he lost it.

In the days that followed, he did most of the things he usually avoided.

He underwent a medical checkup. Months before, his complaints to Gloria of not feeling well had been justified; the specialists decided he had a leaky heart valve that might have to be replaced by a plastic contrivance, a diagnosis which had hastened his retirement. The checkup also revealed he had an enlarged prostate that accounted for impeded peeing, a sure sign of male aging. In addition, he was more than ten pounds overweight and his blood pressure was up. Type A to a T.

He joined a health club.

He telephoned his brothers, Lonnie and Paul, and, except for Rita, his sisters, Helen and Jill, all back East. They were surprised to hear from him after all these months. He told them about his heart and his retirement, but not about Gloria. He mentioned to Lonnie, a retired engineer, that he was thinking about buying a personal computer to write a novel, maybe a family saga, *their* family. But maybe not. After all, he said, he was beginning to enjoy his retirement too much to spoil it by getting busy on a big project like a sprawling saga. They were glad for him, they said. That's it, Nat, enjoy life, you've earned the right.

Nathaniel knew what they meant by earning the right. They weren't just thinking of all the years he had put in on the paper. They were also thinking of how he had carried on after the death of a wife, the worry over an adult daughter who remained unmarried and, worse, the burden of a son who had been on drugs and, God forbid, might still be on drugs.

Lonnie asked the inevitable. "How's Stan?"

"Oh, fine," he said. He hoped Stan was fine.

"No more problems?"

He hadn't told them about the stabbing. Well, it was old stuff anyway. "What problems? Stan's doing all right. He's going to school now."

"That's wonderful," Lonnie said. "Maybe now you can enjoy life."

* * *

16

Nathaniel tried.

He went through his address book and began calling friends, some from far back in his past and a continent away.

One of them was Stanley Lee, Stan Lee, old friend from school days in New York. Rachel and he had named their son after him, the first black he had known from the heart out, sharing enthusiasms of radical ideas and girls, *Don Giovanni* and Chinese food. They had once identified so much with each other's verbal shafts and shortcomings of character that they would call out to each other, "How's my white Stan?" "How's my black Nat?" Only time and a continent, San Francisco at one end and Brooklyn at the other, had kept them apart.

"Hey, how's black Nat?" he asked as soon as he heard Stan's voice across the distance. It took a while before his old friend knew who he was. They had not spoken to each other for months, not since his son's stabbing, Stan's namesake. A crisis or a stab of nostalgia would sometimes, over the years, prompt him to call his old friend.

Within minutes, they were freshmen again, sharing now the intimacies of life after sixty. Stan was older and had retired a year before from his job as a race relations investigator for the government.

"Hope you do better than me, old buddy, with this retirement," Stan said. "So far, for me, it's too much drinking, too little loving, and too much getting on my kids' nerves." Stan paused. "How about you, Nat?" he asked. "It's always good to hear your voice, especially with you picking up the tab. That's a luxury for we fixed income types . . ." He heard Nat boast that his retirement money was princely, that he had gotten *The Standard* to put him out to pasture alongside a palace, "socialism for the old." There was a sadness in his old

17

buddy's voice, Stan felt. "You or the family in some bad trouble?" he asked.

For a moment, Nathaniel thought of telling Stan about his troubles with Gloria. But Stan would call him a fool for letting himself be pussy-whipped. He would probably sing a snatch from the *Don:*

Eh via, bufone, sentimi, amico: va che sei matto, va chei sei matto, va che sei matto, va chei sei matto, matto, matto, matto!

Oh, come now, clown, listen to me, friend: don't be crazy, don't be crazy, don't be crazy, don't be crazy, crazy, crazy, crazy!

In his mind's ear, he could hear Stan's jubilant baritone, friendly and mocking.

And then Stan would bring up Rachel, a one-in-a-million woman old Stan had adored and how Nat couldn't expect a truly sweet substitute, not in one lifetime. "No, no bad trouble, Stan," Nathaniel said. "I got the time now to call old friends, so I'm calling...Any chance of you making it out this way?"

"Not much chance," said Stan. He had a new woman in his life, with a seventy-eight-year-old demented mother given to fits of kleptomania who needed special care. He was helping with the psychiatrist bills. It was tapping his resources and he was even reduced to smoking cheap cigars. "Save your money, Nat," Stan said. "At our age you never know when some emergency will strike. And, Nat..." Stan paused.

"Yes?"

"Remember what the *Don* says: *E tutto amore...It's all love. If you're true to only one, you're cruel to all the others. I feel so much love in myself that I love them all, and since women don't understand these things...*"

Nat finished the line: "*...they call my natural goodness deceit...*"

"You got it, buddy," said Stan. "Hey, whatever's bugging you, try and lighten up ... As the *Don* would say, 'What the hell!'"

From the earliest days of their friendship, Stan had enjoyed the idea of assuming the mantle of the *Don*, relishing the reputation of at least 2,065 conquests. Beneath the disguise, Nathaniel knew, lay the ludicrous melancholy of Stan's incredible self-admitted difficulty in achieving erection, especially with black women. It was incredible to him, early on, that Stan would share so intimate an embarrassment with him, and out of mutual embarrassments their friendship had grown despite the long distance of space and time.

Then Stan was gone, and he was alone again with his plans.

Nathaniel put aside plans to buy a computer and start a novel. Computers would come down in price. Besides, he had not yet received his first Social Security check, although he was not wanting for money. There was his Guild pension check, modest but helpful; and he had his savings, his IRAs; he would have the rent from the apartment downstairs once his son was on his own; he had the house next door that he and Rachel had bought ten years before and fixed up to rent out or sell, and he was thinking now of selling. Adding it all up in his mind, he realized he could buy that computer if he really wanted to, and he could easily afford a trip around the world to forget Gloria, if it came to that. But it was just as well to be a little cautious about where the money went. His retirement income made him comfortable, but the money wasn't inexhaustible.

At such moments, when concern or lack of concern over money intruded, a sour aftertaste of materialism would prompt him to look for a sheaf of unfinished poems, phrases, images that he had put aside during his years of newspapering. He had once, in his early manhood, before the children came, published a small book of poems and he had a small reputation that went with the book. Now that money was no great concern, he felt the time was right to stitch the disparate lines together. And, inspired momentarily before putting the sheaf away, he began a poem about being sixty-two:

> *I'm still a baby shuddering to be born*
> *at sixty-two. I want to laugh . . .*
> *Where is that damn serenity of rumored inheritance?*
> *Instead, I've got soiled shorts, frayed socks,*
> *and nubby memories I've half forgot.*
> *Instead, I feel the birthpangs of soul, of heart,*
> *held back by glib illusions and compromise.*
> *I feel the promise of so much waiting to take form . . .*

He liked what he had written. It was a bit glib, but he liked the promise the words carried. He put the poem aside to await further inspiration.

At other times he felt he had enough of words, what with more than thirty years in the newspaper business, not counting his efforts at freelancing and poems and trying to write fiction. At the least, he figured, he had averaged 500 words a day, the least. Say, 300 days a year, thirty years . . . He got out his pocket calculator. That was 4,500,000 words, maybe more like five million words. *War and Peace, Remembrance of Things Past*, plus *Ulysses*, several times over.

Maybe it was time, he thought, to learn another kind of language. He thought of enrolling at the Community Music

Center and learning to play the piano. He thought of joining
the Art Institute and taking a life drawing class. He envied
Gloria her talent as an artist, the way she drew like a bird
takes to song. She could also play the piano, not inspired, but
she could play. Vivaldi, even Bach, even Mozart. He envied
her her comfort at the piano.

Gloria could fill her time without any trouble, without
him. She had her drawing, her music, her aerobic class and
her good causes. She was also learning Spanish. One afternoon a week she worked as a volunteer art teacher at La Casa
de los Niños, a shelter for disturbed children at the Latino
edge of Potrero Hill on 24th Street. And then there were her
visits to her married daughter in Marin.

She had time for drawing, her piano, aerobics, learning
Spanish, teaching art to disturbed children, a grandchild and
a therapist. No wonder she could do so easily without him,
he thought, when, tired of trying to be carefree, he felt the
chill of loneliness.

Maybe he ought to find a good cause himself, he thought
without enthusiasm. Maybe some publicity work for the
children's shelter or something else worthwhile . . . Then he
thought of all the begging goodwill handouts he had rewrit-
ten in a lifetime of newspapering and quickly discarded the
notion. No, he was weary and wary of good and lost causes.
Confronted by an appeal in the mail, or someone asking on
the phone or at the door, he would overcome any promptings
of conscience by telling the callers he was a senior on a fixed
income.

"Someone's making a buck out of this," he would tell
Gloria. "They have nothing better to do than to tap into our
collective sense of guilt to line their own pockets. Well, not
from Nathaniel Dorn, not this old investigative reporter."

"Don't become a crabby old man," Gloria told him. And she managed to get him to make small contributions to her good causes. In her presence once, unasked, he made out a check to Amnesty International to show that his old liberal heart was in the right place. And he had even put on a Santa Claus suit for a celebration at the disturbed children's shelter.

"There, I've done my good deed for the rest of my life," he told Gloria. "A Jewish Santa Claus, handing out boxes of crayons to little Latino loonies."

Gloria had poked him playfully in his thickening Santa Claus midriff.

Between tasks to fill the time and plans and fits of inspiration, Nathaniel relaxed by reading the paper each morning, from beginning to end, although he had taken a solemn vow at his retirement party never to read the damn *Standard* again. The obits were of particular interest; he studied every word, looking for errors, and was pleased that first week to catch a mistake in the obit of a minor city official with whom he used to play poker. "You'll have to have someone redo it," he told an assistant city editor that morning by phone. "That'll be more attention than old George got during his whole official life." He could hear the resentment to the pesky duty in the editor's voice. "Nat, do me a favor and stop reading the paper."

There were also some important things he did, or thought of doing.

Passover, that springtime housecleaning of the Jewish soul, was a week off, a good time to clear things away, to start his new life. He began throwing out the unwanted memorabilia of thirty years of family life, stuff that had accumulated before his wife died eight years ago. He rented a dumpster from the Scavengers and started to extricate himself from the debris of the past.

"Bravo!" exclaimed Hilda Kaddish, his therapist in misty Colma, a stone's throw from the cemetery. She had been through every new therapy enthusiasm as one of Fritz Perls' cohorts at Esalen before settling on a mix of Gestalt and anything else that worked.

In the unorthodox way of some California therapists, Kaddish had become more than a therapist. She was something of a Dutch aunt, if not a Dutch uncle, who, on occasion, might bawl him out for doing something crazy and self-destructive.

In a typical flare of unorthodoxy, she had told him he was crazy for giving Stan the apartment in his house—and rent-free yet.

"You're too nice for your own good and his good," Kaddish told him. "I'm warning you, Nathan, you're making it easy for him to go back on drugs. Be smart. Kick him out of the house."

Nathaniel defended Stan. "The kid's trying. He goes to school. He's really trying."

"Be smart, Nathan."

He looked at her and shook his head. For all her insights, he thought, she just doesn't understand the need of a son for a father and a father's need for a son. Only someone whose own father died so young, when they were both young, could understand.

"You're talking to a Jewish father who can't give up on his flesh and blood," he told her.

"An orthodox Jewish father would have written him off for dead a long time ago."

23

"I can't do that," he told her. "Stan's trying. I got to hope for the best."

"Hope is cheap," she said. "You want to rescue him from the dead? Let him stand on his own two feet."

"Oh, dear Mrs. Kaddish," he said, "the only thing orthodox about you is your name."

Kaddish—the Jewish service for the dead. Hilda Kaddish, rescuer of dead souls.

2

So much was coming up in her work with Kaddish, Gloria had told him. Memories of a self-indulgent mother, an indifferent father who had neglected her, a first husband who degraded her, a second husband who deceived her. It was the usual mess left by the past, and, with the present leaving him feeling more and more deprived, he had less and less sympathy for her efforts to deal with old ghosts.

"I need the time for myself, Nat," she had said that last meeting in the leafy shadow of her garden. A late summer afternoon was turning evening.

She had invited him over to discuss why, for now, she needed time off from their "relationship," a word that gave him a slight chill, making him feel the word had become almost the opposite of any warm connection it might have once suggested. She met him outside her front door, and the chill he felt grew icy. No, she didn't want to go upstairs and have a glass of the cold chardonnay he had brought, an expensive Robert Mondavi.

"I desperately need the time to come to terms with my past, these patterns I seem to be repeating," she was saying. "I'm always putting myself in the position of being a victim, a victim of other people's needs. I've got to stop doing this to myself."

"I see," he said indifferently, "and now I'm going to be your victim."

Now, thinking back, he wondered if he had really made the remark. *It was a mean thing to say even if I felt that way*, he thought. *How did I feel? Mean and selfish*, he had to admit. *Cold, mean and selfish.*

But Gloria ignored his remark. "This vacation from each other could do so much for both of us, Nat," she was saying. "You need time for your own work on yourself. You've got to learn to relax, for your health and peace of mind. This time off could be the best thing for you."

"Thanks, but I've got a therapist."

No, that wasn't exactly the way it went, he recalled, trying to remember the nuances of that last conversation in the garden.

The way he had first remembered it, her words sounded stagy. He himself seemed so bitchy. It was as if they were both made of cardboard. And yet, in his resentment, much as he tried to recall the exact words and feelings of that last meeting, he couldn't help himself.

But the Gloria he knew was warmer, gentle, natural, not condescending. And for all the weight of her own problems, she was generous with her money and time when it came to disturbed children and stray pets. And yet she was pleasantly wayward, although capricious, too.

25

She had stopped, even in the thick of that difficult last conversation, to call his attention to a bird that had suddenly alighted atop the fence, exclaiming *churr-dee churr-dee churr-dee-durr-chit churr-dee-durr-chit*, interspersing its song with clucking, whistling and mewing. "See, Nat, it's a thrush, the mockingbird kind, I think."

In his troubled memory, it was hard to recall the precise details. So much easier to come up with something lifeless.

Coming back from a story, under deadline, he remembered, there would be a similar difficulty at times, thinking back whether someone he had interviewed had actually said something or other. Had the mayor or the police chief said a dumb thing like that? Forget the nuances, had he gotten all the facts clear? He would sweat it out, as he sat down to write. But then he had his notebook to verify a quote, or he could always call back the mayor's press aide to check it out, or he could write around it, for the first edition at least, until the deadline pressure eased off.

Sometimes he wished he could bring a reporter's notebook along on his relationships so he could check back on what was said or not said or misheard, especially now that he was getting older and felt helpless at times, as if his hearing and memory were going.

"Nat, come here," he now recalled her saying. She held him and kissed him. "You're such a handsome man. You can be so strong and ballsy, so vigorous that sometimes I feel overpowered by you. It makes me feel helpless and scared . . . I need some of that vigor you have, Nat. I need my own strength."

They sat on the white iron mesh chairs she had finally bought for her front garden. The chairs were uncomfortable, as uncomfortable for Nathaniel as her words.

Along with coming to terms with the past, she said, her present life was a mess. Her mother and father's estate had been through probate, and her inheritance from her father's commercial art business was substantial, a windfall from parents who, until their deaths, had lacked generosity or even kindness.

"They left me all their worth, but I've never felt worthy," she said. "Maybe that's why I have to keep busy with what I'm doing . . . to keep proving my worth."

Her words glimmered with the insights of Hilda Kaddish, their Colma guru.

"Those things are worth doing," he said, forgetting his distaste for good causes. "You don't have to look for any dark reasons for doing them. You enjoy it, and you do a good job."

Now he could hear the insincerity in his voice, how he, Nathaniel Dorn, veteran tracer of dark reasons, who seemed to resent any good cause except himself, was just trying to manipulate her into a better opinion of herself so she would have a better opinion of him.

She had seen through his manipulative flattery, or had simply ignored it. "I've got to find the time, Nat, to take care of myself," she said. "I have to learn to be a little more selfish."

And all that money she had been left, it made her anxious, trying to handle so much after having to scrounge for a living most of her life. She was so fearful of money advisors who usually turned out to be scoundrels.

"I've tried to help," he said. On several occasions, he had used his *Standard* contacts to check out a few of the scoundrels.

"You have, Nat, you've been wonderfully helpful. And that may be part of the trouble. I have to learn to do these things myself. I have to be less naïve, less trustful."

More Kaddish again, he thought. "Less trustful of me?"

"Oh, Nat, not you . . . I have to get out from under all this paperwork before I can be in my right mind."

And, although there were signs of improvement, there was that mysterious virus, she reminded him. The strange nerve ailment might not be encephalitis and fatal. Still, it was like an overcast sky where there had been a clear blue outlook moments before. It was scary. Sudden appearances of objects, things that came into view but weren't really there, a clock or a car, ordinary things. And non-existent sounds, an upsurge of wind or a door opening or even words he hadn't said. Some specialists felt the virus had affected her temporal lobe, which would explain the misperceptions of sight. Several psychiatrists felt, of course, that it was all psychosomatic. Maybe so.

"Perhaps it's all these money anxieties," she said. "I used to worry when I had no money and was alone. Now I'm fearful over having too much money I didn't earn."

"Maybe it's me," he said. "Maybe I'm making you sick."

She nodded. Gloria wasn't one to shirk any possibility. He admired that willingness and, at the same time, was unnerved by it. "Maybe," she said. "Maybe the vacation from each other will be a test."

He remembered his clouded feelings, a mix of dismay and guilt over the possibility that he was responsible for her problem. The possibility made him think of Rachel and how his behavior might have contributed in some way to her cancer or to his son's problems with drugs. A psychiatrist he once interviewed had said there were toxic personalities, carriers whose provocative traits or weaknesses triggered addiction and illness in others. Was he one of them? A carrier, Typhoid Nathan?

This is crazy, he thought, *I'm thinking too much. Too much time for guilt and putting myself down. This retirement, maybe it's driving me crazy, after all... No, of course not, it couldn't be my fault. I've been seeing Gloria right along, going with her to the specialists, helping her with her money affairs. And her health has been improving. She looked so lovely that evening we said goodbye. Damn it, lovely...*

He saw Gloria again in her garden, holding him that last time. "Oh, Nat, I'm going to miss you," she was saying.

Much as he desired her, even feeling his cock getting hard as she held him, he had flinched from her embrace.

"Are you sure you don't want any wine?" he said. He still held the bottle, cold in its aluminum foil wrapping. No, no wine. "This is a hell of a thing you've decided," he said.

"Oh, Nat, don't you see? This is just the right time, now that you're retired, to find out how you really feel, about me but most of all about yourself..."

Oh, shit, he had thought, *she's trying to con me, manipulate me. Of all people, Gloria!*

"Don't try and manipulate me," he said. "Don't make it sound like it's for my own good."

Trying to recall the conversation exactly, not just from within the mist of his own dissatisfaction, he remembered how she had suddenly stopped talking, how she had looked into his eyes and said: "Your eyes are so green, Nat. Have you ever noticed how green your eyes can get? And it isn't from the reflection of the leaves above us. It's getting too dark for that." Thinking back, he felt, *she did care, she does care.*

At the time, though, all he noticed was that her dog, Clara, a stray from the SPCA who had greeted him with her usual enthusiasm when he first unlatched the gate, had stopped sniffing at his pockets for her usual treat. She had doubled back and was taking a shit near the yellow rose bush he had once brought Gloria. "Clara!" Gloria called out "Not there!"

Again, she had become a scolding object lesson. "You're the one, Nat, who used to complain how covering stories forced you to manipulate others," she was reminding him. "What you had to do, you said, turned you into an observer so you hardly had any feelings of your own. All those murders and fires you had to cover, those lying politicians you had to be civil toward, you used to say how it all gave you emotional calluses."

"I seem to recall the phrase, emotional calluses."

"Your words, Nat. That's one of the reasons I cared for you—"

"Cared?"

"Care, all right? Even in the midst of what your job forced you to pretend, you showed some honesty about yourself . . . Now you seem to be giving in to the dead part of you. I'm starting to feel it even in the way we make love. Maybe it's me, partly, but things used to be alive. There was a wild innocence about us."

Talk about phrases, he had thought. *I like that one. Wild innocence. I'll have to use it in a bad poem someday or, maybe, for the title of a cheap romance novel.*

"How long do you expect this 'vacation' will take?"

"I have no idea," she said. "Whatever time it takes. We both have a lot of work to do."

"Has Kaddish put you up to this? Next thing, you'll both be saying Kaddish for me?"

"You're far from dead."

"Don't count on it, Gloria . . . So what about Kaddish? It's her idea, isn't it?"

"We've discussed it, but it's my idea. I do have a mind . . ."

"I wish you wouldn't read those books," he said. "They're not doing you any good."

"What books?"

"Oh, never mind."

"Do you mean books on feminism?"

"Forget it."

"They're not your enemy, those books, Nat . . . You're your own enemy."

"What do you mean by that?"

"Oh, forget it."

He stared at her, intently, as if his intenseness could convert her and make her see the foolishness of what she had proposed.

"Look, Gloria," he finally said. "I never doubted you had a mind of your own. And I'm glad you read those books. I've read them myself, starting all the way back with Mary Wollstonecraft's *Vindication of the Rights of Women* . . ."

"*A Vindication of the Rights of Women.*"

Oh, she could be such a stickler for damn, piddling accuracy! "Yes, of course, A *Vindication* . . . I never doubted your intelligence. I wouldn't have asked you to marry me if I felt you were a dummy or a doormat." *I wonder*, he thought now. *Maybe, after all, I did want a doormat, an interesting and attractive doormat, but a doormat.*

"Look, Nat, I appreciated your offer to marry me. I did. It was sweet . . . You know I love you for overlooking the fact that I can be a crank, along with my other faults. But I haven't been much of a success at marriage. It's one of the things I'll be looking into. Meanwhile, maybe you can find out why marriage seems so important to you. There's no biological reason, is there? Not at our age. We've had our children."

31

"Look, people do get married at every age. We don't need babies to be a family . . . We could learn by doing, doing things together."

"Doing what?"

"Hanging out together. Having someone there. In sickness and in health, as they say. In old age." The words came back to him now stilted and plastic. He had not been ready for marriage, certainly not then, and Gloria had seen through him.

"Oh, Nat, being old and being alone, always alone, that fear, it's dreadful," she was saying. "Especially in sickness. I do understand. That's why it was so wonderful the way you cared. Thank you for going around with me to the specialists, with my brain virus, whatever the hell it is . . ."

"That's all right, you're welcome. So, in return, you're saying goodbye when I ask you to marry me. Thanks a lot."

"Nat, Nat, Nat . . . What am I going to do with you?"

"I had one suggestion."

"You don't understand, Nat. Look. I'd marry you in a flash, if you were sick, really sick."

"I've got a heart problem."

"I mean dying."

"Marry me if I were dying?" It was as if she had slapped him. "I have to die for you to marry me? That's crazy."

"Not at all. It's just that I care for you and want you to know I'd be there if anything happened. In a flash."

"But that's so crazy. I'm not asking you to be my widow. I want you to be my wife. In health as well as sickness."

"No, Nat, I want it this way, for now. A vacation, without the distraction of each other."

It's so crazy, he thought. *What am I doing with this crazy woman? What virus has gotten into me that I've let myself become hopelessly involved with her?*

She turned me down. It's inconceivable. She could have been the wife of Nathaniel Dorn, graying distinguished former newspaperman, worldly but romantic, confidante of lying politicians and conceited judges, cops and artists, visiting movie stars and North Beach flacks. Any other woman would be flattered by my offer of marriage, whether I'm ready for it or not. Imagine, in this day and age and in this city, a proposal of marriage by a bonafide heterosexual, a man without AIDS, of mature substance, if semi-crazy, and she says no or, at best, not yet.

I make her feel helpless, she said. She wants her own strength. But she'd marry me, in a flash she said, if I were dying. Dying and helpless. He winced at the thought.

No, he wouldn't give up on her. If nothing else, his pride wouldn't allow it.

And give her credit, he thought now. *Like it or not, she's a woman of extraordinary force of will. No wonder I consider her so special. She's special even though she's making me doubt myself. After all, who am I now? What's so special about me?* He wouldn't say it to anybody else, it was difficult enough to say it to himself. *Yesterday's newspaperman is like yesterday's newspaper. Out of date, out of mind. Formerly distinguished. A distinguished has-been.*

"Maybe I'm just not the woman for you, Nat," she was saying. "Taking this time off from each other may help you decide what you want from a woman and from yourself."

"What about sex?" he suddenly asked. "It's going to be a hardship for both of us. The sex was always good, in spite of what you said."

"It can be better, Nat, take my word for it . . . Once I work things through for myself, I'll be able to give more of myself, to you, to others."

"To others?"

"Well, Nat, you're not the only one in my world. That's one of my problems. I've depended on you too much."

"But being in bed with a warm body. So it may not be perfect . . . We're going to miss each other."

"Nat, you'll manage. You can be your own warm body . . . Learn to masturbate, if it comes to that."

She wasn't being mean but it sounded that way. Masturbation had never appealed to him, he had once confided to Gloria. He could never get off that way. He had often wondered why, and had meant to bring up the subject with Kaddish. But he had not. Maybe it was just that he didn't have the patience to masturbate. It seemed to take so much time.

"I don't understand this at all . . . I ask you to marry me, and you propose we separate. You say you'll marry me, but only if I'm dying. It's crazy."

"For the time it takes for us to find ourselves. Not forever."

"Oh, great. And when will we know it's time?"

"We'll know. For one thing, if it was meant that we should be closer, we'll miss each other. We'll miss each other terribly. And when we see one another again, when it's time, we won't take each other for granted. We won't have wrong conceptions of each other."

"I miss you already, Gloria."

"You're going to do all right, Nat. You'll survive your retirement from the paper, and you'll survive this. Just hang in there."

But hanging in there seemed like a death sentence. He felt a tremor of anger and bitterness. "If I ever do get married," he said, "I'll be sure to invite you."

She looked at him steadily. "What I have to do, Nat, is

important. Try not to give up on me, and I won't give up on you, no matter what happens. I really care for you."

No doubt, possibly, she loved him, he thought. "Yes," he said blankly. He stared at her hard, then his expression softened. "Why are you doing this, Gloria? Things were so lovely—"

"Things may turn out to be lovelier," she said.

"But why?"

"I've *told* you . . . And I'm afraid, Nat."

His uncomprehending eyes studied her.

"Afraid," she repeated, "afraid of Stan . . ."

"Oh, let's not bring Stan into this . . . He's trying to rebuild his life. Let him be."

"And you, I'm afraid of you . . . Afraid of your need to get married, of all your needs now that you're retired. I feel you starting to lean on me instead of making a new life for yourself. I'm afraid of being swallowed up by you . . . Oh, Nat, it's not only you. A lot of husbands don't seem to know what to do with themselves once they retire."

"Maybe I spoke too soon," he said. "Look, Gloria, we don't have to get married, not right away. I expect I'll get the hang of retirement . . . Don't do this, Gloria."

"We have to do what we have to do." She did him the favor of not smiling when she said it.

"I need you, Gloria," he said, knowing at once, too late, it was the wrong thing to say, never mind if it was true.

"See, Nat? . . . It's just too much for me, too much." She got up from her chair and turned toward the door. Her drawing away was as if, through her refusal of marriage, he might become himself again, familiar if not innocent, unscarred by the experience of desire or the experience of headlines.

35

"Take care of yourself," she said, and closed the door behind her.

Alone with his thoughts, he watched the door shut. *I'm cast adrift. She's my life raft. But she doesn't want to be my life raft. She's hipped on being her own life raft. Glorious Gloria, damn her.*

On his way to the front gate he removed the foil from the bottle he held, used it to cover the crap Clara had taken and dumped the mess in Gloria's garbage can. Then he placed the chardonnay under the yellow rose bush, and left.

3

After two weeks of separation, he thought Gloria might be seeing someone else. He began driving past her house at random, sometimes in the early evening or late at night, as if it were a job and he was on an investigation. He would look for her car or unfamiliar cars. He would scan her windows, noticing if her bedroom lights were on; that would mean, as usual, that she was reading late. If her lights went off too early, she might, conceivably, be taking someone to bed, or maybe not. But he couldn't tell the difference from what he knew of her usual routine.

One time, he parked his car up the hill, across the way from her house, determined to wait the night out, to see if any strange man came to visit, or left. There was one caller between 6:00 and 9:30 p.m., but it must have been a salesman or someone with a petition to stop the invasion of Nicaragua; in any case, the straggly stranger left in five minutes. So did he.

On several occasions, he followed her. One day, it was to the shelter for disturbed children, then to The Women's Building for aerobics. The next evening he followed her to her Spanish class and waited across the street until she came out. The next day she drove to her dentist and, afterward, to lunch at the Washington Square Bar and Grill where he followed her in after a half hour wait in his car. He was sitting at the bar when she left with Doris, an old friend. He shielded his face with the glass of wine he was drinking. They didn't see him, he thought, but soon after they had left a waiter brought him a full bottle of Kenwood Vintage Red, the table wine he and Gloria usually ordered when they dined at the Washbag.

"Compliments of a gracious lady," the waiter said. "You must be a special man in her life."

"What lady?" he said defensively.

"She just left."

"Was there any message?"

"No message."

The waiter had uncorked the bottle, set up a fresh glass and was poised to pour even though he had not finished the white wine he was drinking and had not asked for the red. He held up his hand. He noticed his hand was trembling.

"Whenever you're ready," the waiter said, smiling.

He rummaged in his pockets for a tip, some change, but could only find a dime, and said, embarrassed, "I'll catch you later." He stayed at the bar, getting drunk, until he had finished the bottle. He found his wallet after the last drop was gone. Then he searched the tables for the waiter. The tip he left him was large enough to cover the cost of the bottle.

Another time, he followed her car through the city, figuring, finally, he was on to something. She led him across the Golden Gate to Marin until he realized she was on her way to visit her daughter.

As he dogged her, the intensity of his interest in her kept dogging him. *Am I in love with her? I think I am. I am, perhaps.* He played with the thought, keeping her car in the corner of his eye. The thought gave him a more palpable sense of purpose now that any purpose in his existence seemed, at best, dormant. *I love, therefore I am. Who was it who said that? Not Descartes . . . Maybe I did.*

There were the obvious reasons for his interest in her. He had grown used to her. They had spent more than five years with one another. It was like a marriage. Usually, without the need of words, they understood each other. He had known her last husband and could understand why she had left him and felt disenchanted with the idea of marriage. And she had known Rachel. She had appreciated Rachel's qualities. He didn't have to explain why he had loved his wife.

He was different from distant Jonathan, her last husband, Jonathan with the roving eye, and she was so different from his dead wife. It was the reason, perhaps, he had fallen in love with Gloria, if he was in love, he thought. In her own gentle being and distinctiveness, Gloria had left room for him to mourn Rachel, to keep a shrine for her in his memory, now a fading shrine.

And Gloria was beautiful and had her own money. And there was something familiar, almost familial, about her.

The phone rang one evening. It was Gloria.

"You've been following me," she said.

"Following you? I haven't been following you. That's crazy."

"I saw your car behind me. You must have been following me across the city. It was your car. Dark blue, the same luggage rack, same car."

"Where was that?"

"Near the tollgate, at the bridge."

"The other day?"

"The other day. Yes, Nathaniel."

"Oh, yes," he said, with time to think of something. "I went to see Ruthie's new place." She knew his daughter had just rented another place, near Sausalito, the third apartment since leaving a teaching job in Boston. She had wanted to be closer to her father after his heart problem, she told school officials.

"In the morning? Isn't she teaching?"

"You know Ruthie. She's really valued at the university. She can make arrangements to skip a class without anyone saying boo to her." He admired how glibly he could still lie. Bending the truth had often been necessary in milking a source for a story. He still had the knack. Not that he was particularly proud of fudging the truth or manipulation; it was often necessary, that's all. Like now.

"That wasn't the first time you've followed me."

"It wasn't me, Gloria. I haven't been following you."

"Have you been paying your son to follow me?"

"Stan?"

"That's the only son you have."

"Stan hasn't been following you."

"And the time at Washington Square? You hadn't followed me there, I suppose?"

"I do have an occasional drink there, Gloria. Oh, by the way, thanks for the wine."

"Please don't follow me, Nathaniel. I need my privacy. That's our agreement."

"I won't follow you, Gloria," he assured her.

Instead, he followed her in his dreams. In one, he told Kaddish, he had crept up the path in Gloria's garden to her front door. The night was still except for the sound of Gloria at the piano. He had never heard her play better. The music was of an unearthly loveliness that stimulated images of the two of them holding each other like enfolding beams of light. He caught the glint of her smile as the music flashed in his ears, with a galaxy of arpeggios. He held his breath not wanting to make a sound until he could hold his breath no longer and the air suddenly burst from his lungs in an *uh-uh-uhhhh* sigh. And before he could escape, she had flung the door open and she was staring at him with a look of venomous hatred.

"What does it mean?" he asked Kaddish.

"What can it mean?" Kaddish said. "Overnight, am I a magician? What do you feel it means?"

"It means, I guess, that I don't know where I am or where she is," he said. "Anyway, I sure would like to know what she was playing. I wish I could have asked her. It was lovely."

It was Gloria who had recommended Kaddish to him. He was glad his appointment was a day later because it meant he could try and wheedle hints from Kaddish about just what the mysterious Gloria might be thinking. But Kaddish seemed on to his manipulative ways and kept their confidences to herself.

What Kaddish didn't know, although he figured she did, was that he had rented the dumpster to dump the past because he thought it would please her. She would be proud of him when he told her how he was ridding the attic, the attic of his psyche, of all those out-of-focus photos of his dead wife, the shots of himself that gave him a start (those pictures before he lost forty pounds), the peeling board games with missing pieces the kids had lost, old Christmas cards from people he never saw anymore, old vials of mottled vitamins, even a baby's leg cast from Stan's clubfoot operations. It was easy to get rid of the past. All he had to do was carry the junk to the open attic window and cast the past to the winds, hopefully hitting the dumpster. That's all.

But he had not gotten far unloading the past. He would stop to read a forgotten letter that he had never answered. Too late now, he decided, coming on a touching letter to his dead wife from a woman friend with whom he had slept and who obviously had been more in love with Rachel than with him. He turned to one of the games and hunted for a missing piece before giving up. Then there was Stan's baby cast, with all the messages the family had written on it, including his sister Ruth's scribble, "I don't like you." It was cute, he thought, and maybe, now that he was clean from drugs, five years now, finally, Stan would want it some day to show to his own children, if he ever settled down with someone. And when he came on something interesting like that, the tiny leg cast, he would call his daughter at Golden Gate University and share it with her until Ruth made it clear that he was being a nuisance, dear Daddy.

4

She was so efficient, his daughter, his lovely, shrewd lesbian, sometimes bisexual, daughter. In seconds, it seemed, she had gotten service at the crowded Italian lunch boutique in Levi Plaza, brought the tray of minestrone and half a sandwich for each to the table, served the food, disposed of the tray and was back at the table, sat down, reached out her hand for his and looked into the eyes of her old papa with a caring smile.

"How's it going between you and Gloria?"

"We don't have to talk about Gloria," he said.

"We're going to talk about anything you want to talk about. This lunch is for you, dear Daddy."

Oh, my dear, dear Ruthie, he thought. *This was a daughter's love, to be willing to endure still another talk about my woes with Gloria, trying to understand our extended vacation, our separation, our estrangement.*

He knew he had just about exhausted the patience of friends, his friends and even one of Gloria's, Doris, talking about what was going wrong between them.

Not that he had learned anything from Doris. She was almost as good as Kaddish in resisting his efforts to worm information from her. "Be patient, that's all I can tell you," Doris had told him. "I can't tell you what on Gloria's mind. All I know is that she has work to do on herself. Don't do anything drastic, Nat. Just be patient. Try and wait it out."

Thanks, Doris. Thanks a lot. Doris couldn't understand how impossible it was for him to be patient. It was like telling him to postpone an important deadline. Ever since Stan's stabbing, ever since Gloria's illness, his heart problem, his retirement, he had felt there was no time for patience. Things had to be settled now, or they might fall apart completely. And sometimes, as he had told Kaddish, a voice in him whispered: *I might die before it's all resolved.*

And here was Ruthie, Ruthie who had her own problems, what with academic backbiting and her shifting relationships with the women and men in her life. But she was willing once more to be bored and baffled by her papa's happy-go-unlucky, mad, sad, mysterious goings-on with Gloria.

Ruthie cared for Gloria, he knew. She saw something of what he saw in Gloria, her gentleness, her loveliness, her honesty, her independence. But she was troubled by how unhappy his love for Gloria was making him, at a time when papas, especially papas who have lost a wife like her mother, should be enjoying these late, hopefully serene and carefree years.

"It's not going well," he said, holding her extended hand for a moment before they dipped their spoons into the minestrone. He hesitated before telling his daughter about how he had been following Gloria.

"Oh, Daddy," she said. "But I understand. All of us are capable of that sort of thing."

"Tell me, Ruth. You're smart. What's wrong with me? Why have I let myself get so crazy with this woman?"

"I think you're in love, Daddy."

"I know. It must be. But what am I doing wrong?"

"Look, Daddy, it's all very understandable. You've been through a couple of major stress situations. It's thrown you off your stride. Your heart problem, retirement, it's made you feel very much alone . . ."

"Gloria's made me feel very much alone. I was counting on her. I didn't need this at the age of sixty-two."

"She has her own problems. Both your plates are full, and I'm afraid you're not helping matters, dear Daddy."

"What am I doing that's so wrong?"

Ruth smiled. "I don't think you want to know."

He thought he did. "Of course I want to know."

She studied him, her sad-eyed, clever, handsome, aging, tanned, pepper-and-salt bearded papa. "You're looking well," she said.

"A person can get a good tan, sitting in the hot tub in the sun while he's miserable... I want you to level with me, Ruth. I respect your opinion."

"Let's finish lunch first. I'll have to be going back to school for an important meeting. But we've got time."

"I want to know, Ruth."

But they finished lunch first, and she talked to him about her work as a public administration instructor at Golden Gate, about her lover, Roberta, sweet but sort of crazy, and a new man in her life, a university administrator, married, brilliant, but a baby, and how she was so tired of moving and how, with the money she was making, she needed to buy a house, the tax break would be so advantageous, but how houses in Marin and San Francisco were too expensive.

"I've got a house," he said. "The one next door. I could let you have it."

"You need the rental income."

"I need the cash flow... You were going to inherit it. You can buy it from me. For a song and easy, monthly payments."

She smiled. "It's not a bad idea, my papa. We'd be closer."

"We'd be even closer." It was one of the few real joys in his life now, their closeness, a closeness that had been tested through Rachel's cancer and death, Ruth returning from Boston on a leave to be with him, and his final acceptance of her bisexuality, her lesbianism, her worth as a person. There was nothing they couldn't talk about. "Now tell me what I'm doing wrong."

She didn't hesitate. "There's nothing wrong with what you want, dear Daddy. All you want is some contentment now, somebody you can count on. You're a lovely, sexual man who has years to live . . ."

"Don't bullshit me, Ruthie. I might die any minute," he said. "You know where my will is."

"I know, Daddy. But you're not going to die, and you shouldn't have to face death alone. That's not bullshit."

"I've got you. I've got Stan."

"Yes, Daddy, lucky you, two sort of crazy kids. You should have somebody else, Gloria or somebody. Grandchildren, like Gloria's. It doesn't look like I'm going to have them for you. Or Stan."

"Your happiness is more important than grandchildren, Ruthie, remember that. I'm not your standard grandpa, anyway."

"I know, you'll survive without having grandchildren. You've survived Mama's death, you've survived Stan's problems and the fact that I'm a lesbian, and you'll survive Gloria."

She hesitated, knowing the subject made her father anxious and fearful. "How is Stan?"

He gave her a pained look. "He's all right, Ruthie . . . I don't see that much of him."

"He's downstairs."

"I know, but he's busy studying. Look, Ruthie, phone him yourself . . . We used to be a family. Give him a call. I'm sure he'd like to hear from you."

"Is he clean?"

"I think so. Look, I don't watch him all the time. Call him yourself."

"He can call me . . . I've got my own life."

"Everybody's got their own life. Nobody cares anymore."

"Oh, Daddy, I care. I care about you. You know that."

He took her hand again. "Ruthie, tell me, you're smart, what am I doing that's so *wrong?* Why, all of a sudden, aren't I getting what I need, what I want?"

She gazed at him, not unfondly, as if she were the parent. "Oh, Daddy, it's no mystery. You're making it a mystery to keep from taking responsibility."

Oh, shit, that, he thought. *Old EST crap, human potential, here we come. Creative Management I.*

"It's what Mrs. Kaddish tells you," she continued. "It's what I keep telling you. It's your self-centeredness that gets in the way. You're like a big, angry baby. You carry your problems like a chip on your shoulder. You come on too strong. It keeps you from hearing what Gloria or anybody else might be telling you."

"Well, thanks, I needed that," he said, floundering. "I was beginning to think my bad hearing came from old age."

"I've made you unhappy."

"No, baby, it's all right. You're just speaking your mind, like your mother always did . . . Look, baby, you better get back to work."

"What will you do?"

"I'll be alone," he said, feeling embarrassed as he said it. Poor Nat.

"You need to be alone."

It's what Gloria and Kaddish often told him: "Learn to be alone, not lonely but alone. Find your own strength." Oh,

46

how all that psychobabble shit bored him. All such good advice. All so fucking easy and right when it's not your problem. Suddenly, he wished he was back in the City Room again, immersed in other people's problems, in the tangle of voices and ringing phones, in the clatter of typewriters, the roar of the press, as they used to say, before the silence of computers took over.

It was as if he was afraid of calmness and being alone, Kaddish had told him.

"I've got all the time in the world to be alone," he said.

"I love you, Daddy," she said, kissing him.

"I know, baby," he said as she turned to leave. "I got you."

5

Gloria knew she was going to miss him—for all his intrusiveness and efforts to overpower her—and she did.

As busy as she kept, Nat kept coming to mind, not infrequently, and the feeling that came over her, despite everything, was not uncaring.

The cloud of a fatal nerve disease had passed when the doctors finally decided she had had a ministroke, not uncommon at her age. There was no sign of scar damage to her brain, one specialist said.

"No reason you can't live another couple of decades," Dr. Heffmuller had said encouragingly. "Of course we don't want you to have a serious stroke, and that's always a possibility. Right now, though, nothing's going on there."

"Well," she said, somewhat relieved. "I guess living on the

edge of a dormant volcano is better than living on the edge of an active one."

She wanted to call Nathaniel right away despite the agreement, and she dialed his number, then thought better of it. It was too soon. Anyway, he would learn of it from their friends, or she would tell him another time. For now, missing him as she did, she wanted the peace of being alone in her garden on an unclouded day.

She looked up from *Farewell, My Lovely*, the mystery she was reading, and put the paperback aside along with her turquoise-rimmed reading glasses.

Reading a mystery was a Sunday afternoon routine for her, along with her gardening, once Nat would leave after Saturday night and Sunday breakfast together when he would make some exotic egg dish, maybe with mangoes, and serve it with bagels and cream cheese.

For the last few weekends she had slept alone, missing him, and now, in the garden on an unclouded day, she was alone with Clara, her dog, and Sara Teasetail, her cat, tail wavering under the yellow rose bush.

Gloria could see him in her mind again, walking toward the front gate. After she came inside, that evening their vacation from each other began, she had watched him from the curtains of her bedroom window upstairs.

Don't slouch, Nat... You're walking like an old man, as if the weight of the world is still on your shoulders. You're out of the news business, Nat. Let the world go for a while. Take care of yourself.

Life was so much simpler without Nat. Simpler, yes, and duller. *Oh, exotic handsome, sexy, hairy-assed Nat*, she thought. *Funny word man, closet poet, caring when you listen, intensely yourself, tempestuous to the point of being a pest. Dismissed for your sake and my sake, dismissed and missed. Oh, Nat...*

48

At first she felt pleased with herself for having taken control of the situation. Suggesting the vacation from each other, maybe temporary, maybe not, had given her a sense of power, a power with a man she had never achieved in all her sixty-plus years. It seemed right for her own peace of mind and for his. She hoped Nat would use the time as a chance to shake himself free, to relax, to enjoy retirement, find himself or find something relevant to do.

And maybe, she feared, *find somebody else, although I would hate that*.

"Why would you hate that?" Kaddish had asked her.

"It's simple," Gloria said. "I still love him."

"Nat? This impossible man you describe?"

"So?" she had said. "It's possible to love an impossible man."

She could live with indecision for a time, if need be, the indecision of whether she and Nat would ever get together again. She could live with it if it led to something better between them. Living with indecision, living on the edge of a dormant volcano, was easier than life with Nat, a Nat Dorn adrift, who needed her too much.

They had been on vacation in a beach cottage in the Yucatan when Nat suggested they get married.

They had gone there just after his retirement from *The Standard*. The Caribbean, near the Mayan ruins of Tulum, seemed the perfect place for the two of them to unwind, Nat from his heart scare and she from whatever was happening to her health.

She felt Nat was doing the wrong thing, letting his son stay in the apartment downstairs, even though Stan could take care of Golem and make it easier for them to get away.

Nat didn't want to talk about Stan, but she knew he was preoccupied with what his son might be up to. She was apprehensive.

Oh, she had tried to warm to Nat's son, but he seemed as distant a loner as Nat was intense and close. She had heard of Stan's past, his time in jail, the halfway house, his addiction, his apparent recovery and the stabbing. Maybe she didn't want to share Nat with his son. Maybe it was a throwback to her own difficulty with a distant father . . . But she was scared of Stan, dreaded that he might be back on drugs, and she was scared of the way Nat always defended him and clung to him.

She and Nat traveled to the Yucatan, and it all seemed forgotten there—Stan, her dread, Nat's anxieties over retirement, what to do with the rest of his life, and their troubled health.

All of it vanished as quickly as the flash rain that came and went in the Yucatan, leaving everything balmy and dry in the hot sun. And Nathaniel actually relaxed.

Sometimes they swam from the silky white beach near Punta Bete, snorkeled among the iridescent fish in the grottos, tried to climb the crumbling towers of Tulum or searched for ruins of their own.

But mostly they made love in the sunny afternoons and the cool nights.

Then, the morning light coming through the palms, before a breakfast of papaya halves and *huevos revueltos*—revolting eggs, he called it—they would stay in bed and play word games or games of musical trivia.

Anything about Vivaldi or Bach or Mozart was fair game, but sometimes they would stretch the parameters to include Monteverdi and Handel or Gluck. Once, after getting into his shorts and then returning to bed, he fell asleep in the middle of a challenge to name five operas by Gluck. She kissed him until he stirred. "Wake up, Morpheus in His Underclothes," she said.

But word games were preferred, especially Derivations, Definitions and Meanings.

"The difference between aviary, apiary and lapidary?" he had asked.

"Not that again—it's an old one and a penalty for repeating yourself and being an O.F.F.," she said.

"O.F.F.?"

"Old Forgetful Fart," she said. "Now for the penalty. Massage my back."

He massaged her back, and she turned on him and tickled his armpits when he tried to drop his hand and rub her ass.

"Now my turn," she said. "The meaning of oxter?"

"Oxter? Never heard of it, never in all my many years of journalism."

"It's a perfectly good word," she said, reaching to tickle his armpit again. "Take it from a Scottish lass, it's a word known to a fine poet such as Bobbie Burns."

"Well, I'm Jewish and I give up," he said, "and stop your tickling, Jock."

"You're so dumb," she said, poking him in the armpit. "Oxter. O-x-t-e-r. Another word for armpit."

He reached for her ass. "And you're such a wordy monster..."

"Not there," she said. "The penalty. My big toe. Kiss my big toe."

He had kissed more than her big toe. And, afterward, langorous from their lovemaking, he leaned over her and gazed into her eyes before he spoke.

51

"Marry me, Gloria," he said.

She held him and kissed him. "Oh, Nat, you know how I feel about marriage . . . It's so sweet of you, but don't ask me that. Not now. I'm too happy to marry you."

Remembering it all, she remembered his disappointment and how his body seemed to go numb. But she knew, knew then and knew now, in her garden on an unclouded day, that Nat's offer was some kind of gesture of sweetness and bravado, a sort of dare. He was no more ready for marriage again than she was.

If Nathaniel would only listen to his deepest feelings, she felt, he might realize that his offer of marriage was something of a substitute for his lost life at *The Standard*, an answer to loneliness and nothing better to do.

Too late in life, I'm finding my own strength. I'm not going to be like those wives with idle husbands who have retired and are underfoot all day. "Now I have to make him lunch as well," their wives would complain.

Gloria missed those lovely Sundays in bed with Nat, but she had no intention of becoming Nat's mother and Stan's mother as well. Teaching art at La Casa de los Niños, the shelter for disturbed children, was enough mothering for her.

Oh, find yourself, Nat. Find yourself, and you'll find me.

6

Lonely. Lone. Only. One. No. He thought of the feature or contest the papers used to run, the one where readers had to make as many words as they could from the letters of one word. *One as in lonely. Only one. No. No one. Yen. A yen for somebody. Noel. Holidays like Christmas were the worst time of all for the lonely. Yell.* Loneliness made him want to yell.

Now that he was gone from the City Room, from family, from Gloria, the thought of loneliness crowded his mind. Sure, Stan was downstairs, but he was in a world of his own. Studying, or whatever he was doing, then whizzing off on his motor scooter. Golem was company, perhaps more company than any dog could be, but he was a dog.

And there was Gamel, the ancient Norse word for old, his 14-year-old cat. She had abandoned the house ever since Stan's bruiser of a garage cat, Smudge, had come to live with him. Gamel would only come to the other side of the stone wall when she was sure Smudge was away and allow Nathaniel to pick her up by the neck scruff and feed her before she ran off again to her hiding place, a crawl space somewhere or an old, unused attic two houses down. First thing, in the morning, he would call out, "Gamel! Gamel!" and she would come, flashing her grayish white tail through the garden next door, wary and coy when she came to the stone wall, fearful that Smudge, the bruiser, would be lurking nearby to pounce on her.

Nathan had fears that one day she would be attacked by Smudge, or some other cat, and have to inch her way back to her hiding place, crippled and helpless and abandoned, to

53

die. Ah, Gamel, poor Gamel. "Old when she was young," he would say, thinking of her name, of his lonely cat, of himself too.

He had stopped going to the health club. He had taken a rest from keeping fit. He had taken a rest from getting rid of the memorabilia of the past. It was the past. It could wait. It could all wait.

Instead, he began to watch daytime TV. At first, he shook off the pall of guilt in wasting precious time at the tube by telling himself he was getting in touch again with America. This was what the heartland of the nation, housewives and children and shut-ins and the retired, people like him, millions of us, were doing, he told himself. Of course, for him, the crassness and deadness of the soap operas and the game shows, with purported adults making fools of themselves, was largely sociological. Gradually, as the eyestrain became a habit, he began rooting for the maniacal contestants, riding word games and spinning wheels to a fortune of schlock goods. He also hung on the snail-paced words of soap opera philanderers and their victimized wives, faithful husbands and faithless other women, eking out demi-semi-quaver revelations by the half-hour, their ceaseless tragedies continuously interrupted by headache and hemorrhoid commercials. Eventually, the guilt and eyestrain of it all made him click off the set. *Kiss your hemorrhoids goodbye!*

I'm alone. I'm really alone. I'm going to be alone like this for the rest of my life. I might die alone, a cripple, alone and old and helpless. At first, when he began to panic at the thought of being alone, he would snatch the leash and call out to Golem: "Come on! We don't have to stick around here. Let's do something, kid." But he was faced again with his loneliness when they got home.

He would focus in his loneliness on the telephone, waiting for it to ring. He had phone jacks put in each room, from the hot tub in the deck to the attic. He already had a message machine, and he got himself a cordless phone so he could answer if it rang while he was working in the garden.

He would count, 12345678...54-55-56..., up to 100, picking a number—69—when the phone would ring. But he gave up before 100. Then he would look for his address book and begin calling others. Most of them were never home, and there was a limit to how often he could bother old friends at the paper.

Or he would fixate on the mailbox, waiting for Golem's yelping to tell him when the mailman had arrived, usually with inquiries from real estate salesmen who wanted to sell his house for him, and junk mail, particularly from the Publisher's Clearing House, saying that he, NATHANIEL DORN, may have already won big SWEEPSTAKES CASH, UP TO $1 MILLION. And if the mailman didn't come at the time he expected him, he would call the post office. "Nobody's received any mail up here," he found himself shouting. "Don't we count? We pay taxes, too." Then he would hear Golem barking. "I think he's finally here," he would say sheepishly into the phone. Again, the mailman would have left him his share of junk mail.

He began to hate restaurants and movies. His favorite restaurants only reminded him that Gloria wasn't on the other side of the table. And movies. Movies were even more of an ordeal. Afterwards, he was so used to stopping in a coffeehouse with Gloria and discussing every shade of the movie's meaning. Seeing a movie alone left him bottled up with words afterward and he found it difficult to sleep. And he wasn't ready to go to a movie with anyone else, not yet. Gloria might relent any day, and he wanted to be sure he had not shared a particular movie with anyone else.

He tried to drink, smoke pot, read, or lull himself to sleep with TV, but the thought of his loneliness would soon distract his attention from whatever he was doing.

He bought a camper, like his old attorney friend, Fergus Nelson. He thought of taking it to Modoc, a county he had never been to, where the Indians had held out the longest against the California settlers, where the desolate caves where they hid were decorated with pictographs, as interesting in their own way, he had heard, as the cave drawings of Spain and France. He thought of just jumping in the camper with Golem and heading east to see his brothers and sisters, or leaving Golem and Gamel in a kennel and taking off alone for the Yucatan, where he had been with Gloria, or Tuscany, where they had once planned to go together. But the thought of traveling alone, far away, seemed so lonely. And what if he wasn't there when Gloria came to her senses?

He brought up the subject of his loneliness with Kaddish.

"Have you ever been lonely before?" she asked.

He thought. "I seem to have always been too busy to be lonely."

"Take your time, Nathan. We got time. What about when you were a boy?"

A boy? He *was* a boy, a sixty-two-year-old boy. But he let his mind roam over the streets of The Bronx when he was also a boy. He thought of Mosholu Parkway and De Witt Clinton High School, of his days as an editor of the school paper, of Raphael Philipson, the paper's peppery faculty advisor, of Poe Cottage where the poet of panic and obsession had lived with his child bride, and roamed again in memory the scenes of his childhood near Fordham Road. He remembered reading Melville for the first time and learning that the old sea wayfarer had finally come to rest, ignominiously it had seemed, in the stone haunts of Woodlawn Cemetery. It was only blocks from where they lived, and he remembered the adventure, fancying himself on a quest for the white whale, searching for Melville's grave and, hours later, finding the simple stone. Then he thought of Fordham Road again, of his father's store there, all the sports paraphernalia, and how he would visit in the basement, wielding the different tennis rackets and trying on the baseball mitts which always seemed so huge for his small boy hands. Then he began to sweat.

"Where are you, Nathan?"

"I'm thinking of my father..."

"You were a boy when he died. You must have felt lonely then."

"No, it's a time when I was smaller. They, he and Lonnie, my older brother, we had gone downtown. It may have been my first time. Maybe Daddy was taking us to Radio City Music Hall, maybe when it first opened. I remember we had taken the subway to 42nd Street and were going to walk. We were on Broadway, it was something with all those lights, the crowds, the traffic. Then, suddenly, I was alone in all that noise and confusion. I looked for my father and Lonnie. They were gone. I looked around. Where are they? All I saw were strangers. I began screaming. Then I saw them. They were coming toward me, laughing. They had ducked into a doorway and had been watching me, in all my panic, there on the corner of 42nd Street and Broadway. *It's all right, Nate, they were saying. No need to cry. It was just a joke.* A joke. I felt so lonely and abandoned, so helpless."

Tears filled his eyes.

"Where do you feel your loneliness?" she finally asked.

"Where? In my eyes, in my head, all through my body."

Kaddish reached over and held his hand. "How does it feel, your loneliness?" she asked.

"It makes me feel afraid," he said. "Afraid and helpless. Old and helpless."

"Take a deep breath, Nathan, but stay with your feelings . . . Breathe out now, deeply."

He let his breath out, a sighing breath.

"How do you feel now?"

"Empty," he said. "Alone and empty. I feel so goddamn empty."

"Where are you, Nathan?"

"I'm in my grave. I'm dead."

7

In his prime as a reporter, colleagues agreed, Nat Dorn was one of the best newsmen on a slow day for news.

Oh, he did his share when it came to hard news yarns. Board of Supervisors. The dull rounds of city commissions. Murders. Campus disorders. Bank robberies. Leapers from the bridge and jumpers from highrises. Campus disorders.

He had been there from the beginning of the new age: the coverage of the hippies, the coming of the gays, the gentrification of the city and the assassination of George Moscone, the freewheeling mayor, and Harvey Milk, the gay supervisor. Right up to the rise of AIDS. Most of the big local stories, in fact. And he had even gone to six countries in Europe for a series on young revolutionaries who might have been influenced by the Berkeley rabble, as one editor put it, looking for the local angle. It was almost unheard of, the chintzy *Standard* going for a trip like that although one of the airlines paid most of the freight.

But his natural bent lay in coming up with something when there was little in the city worth reporting, a not uncommon phenomenon. Editors could count on Nat Dorn to find a twist, a follow, something stimulating, sometimes outrageous to interlard with the ads. He had the touch. He could squeeze a quote from a rock, if necessary, a pet rock. Manipulate a source, yes, but he never had to fake a quote or attribute a bright remark of his own to some fictional, untraceable character, like some other newsmen.

Many newsmen were conscientious workaholics, drudging away and checking every source to verify a story up until deadline. Good, competent, often dull writers. Others might take shortcuts, take chances on attributed quotes and second-hand sources, work up the story, file it in a desk drawer, disappear for hours, sopping up local color at some bar and returning just before the story had to be turned in. Good, dubious, graphic reporters.

Then there were, a few, the rather unsavory news-at-any-cost types. Workaholic and graphic as well. They were known, by phone, to impersonate a cop, a fireman and others to flesh out a story. One newsman made a regular practice of trying a variety of code numbers to retrieve messages on a contact's telephone answering machine. Some were also adept at reading desk documents upside down or palming police photographs before a rival reporter came along. Invariably, the city editor would say, "Good work, just don't tell me how you got it."

Terry Forman, his old buddy at the paper, used to be a news-at-any-cost reporter. Then the whole thing got to him, nagging his better judgment, at the time he was covering a serial rapist. The rapist was a middle-aged, sickeningly polite type with an Irish accent, according to his victims who ended up beaten, stabbed, and dead. For a third day follow, the city desk had leaned on Forman to get a picture of the tenth victim, the last one. Up against a deadline and the competition, Forman had filched the only photograph the victim's mother had.

Forman was at Hanno's late that night, in his cups, hating himself.

"We're all fucking rapists," he was saying to anyone who would listen.

"I thought we were whores," someone said.

"Rapists and whores," Forman said. "Tell me the difference between us and rapists, huh, smartass? Nobody's privacy is safe with us around. Anything for a story. We're fucking rapists with the morals of a skunk."

"Speak for yourself," someone said.

"And whores, too," Forman said. "We sell ourselves cheap and let the papers screw us."

"You wouldn't feel so bad if you knew your story was going to make page one," someone said.

Forman tried to take a swing at the guy, maybe because the remark was true.

Nathaniel managed to get Forman out of the place and

drive him home before the city editor got there for his nightly martini. Forman was family, of a sort. In those days, before the picayune piranha took over the City Room, it was customary to help an old buddy in a jam, especially an old buddy like Terry. When Nat's wife Rachel was dying, Terry had pitched in to help him finish a series on drug peddlers, something Nat had no heart for, with all the heartache over Rachel and all that had happened to Stan. Terry had even refused to share the byline. Greater love hath no newsman.

News-at-any-cost wasn't Nat Dorn's shtick. Aside from conscientious and attentive and sometimes dull but necessary reporting, he got color into his stories in a more-or-less legitimate way.

On one occasion he had waited with eyes wide open until a highrise jumper crashed headfirst on a nearby sidewalk. He had not done that before, watched the body hit the pavement. It wasn't just for the shock value, he figured. A desperate soul had taken the trouble to jump and the least he could do was to watch to the last, final moment. The man's head, he reported, crashed with the squishing sound of a shattering cantaloupe.

Afterward, he tried to keep away from assignments like that or, at least, keep his eyes closed.

Instead, he would come up with a story on a slow Christmas Eve by spending the holiday in a burlesque house. He would find an articulate real estate man who was trying to peddle flooded property at the tag end of a disaster. He might track down an expert or two who would be willing to declare a week-old stolen Rembrandt to be a fake. Or a botanist with a theory that century plants that bloomed prematurely were an indication of an earthquake on the way. Earthquake rumblings were always good copy on a slow news day in San Francisco.

In his way, he had been one of *The Standard* cannons in its circulation war with the opposition. With Admiral Dred McNaughton at the helm as managing editor, they had won the war, almost sinking the other battleship daily by outgunning its old sensationalism. *The Standard* had triumphed with a new gunpowder mix of literate sensationalism and social concern that suited the city's self-image of caring sophistication.

Whenever something came along that needed a rhinestone setting, the city editor, dear gruff Ken Carleton, known as The Captain, or his first mate, Rick Mitchell, would decide, if he was free, to give it to Nat Dorn, "the poet," as they called him.

. He could still hear, though Carleton was dead nine years now, the boom of The Captain's voice: "Got a hot one, poet." Once it was a triple murder-suicide, with a wife doing everyone in, including husband and mistress. "She even nixed the family dog, a poodle named Valentine," The Captain, otherwise laconic, told him as he hurried off, with notepad and photographer. "Remember, a picture of the dog!"

"Aye, aye, Captain."

Oh, he knew it was something of a journalistic cliché, that image of a gruff dear editor and a raffish assignment, usually involving a dog, but the cliché was true, and, in part, the picturesque lure of the cliché was what had gotten him into newspapering in the first place and kept him there for more than twenty years instead of moving on to the lusher pastures of public relations or the bickering dullness of academia.

For a time, until his memories became frayed by a feeling

of déjà vu, he relished the remembrances of notables and un-
knowns who had provided him with some of his best stories.
If needed, a natural bent for friendly manipulation seemed to
do the trick. It worked with everyone from a topless dancer
to the Chief Justice of the Supreme Court.

Gigi Gander was the topless dancer, a Turkish topless
dancer, sweet-voiced and grotesquely endowed, who had
been threatened by Immigration on a charge of moral turpi-
tude. Admiral McNaughton took a fancy to Gigi. He called
her The Turkish Delight, saw the circulation possibilities in
her battle with Immigration and told Dorn he had a gilded
opportunity to rescue a maiden and a newspaper in distress.
"Let's do it up grand," he told the poet.

One morning in *The Standard* there was a full-spread picture as wide as the Golden Gate Bridge, with rhinestone
prose to match, that won the public's sympathy and helped
save the day for The Turkish Delight.

"You love your country, don't you, Gigi?" he had asked, in
his best friendly, manipulative way.

"For sure, you bet," she said.

"You would do anything to keep them from sending you
back to Turkey?"

"I would."

"You would even handcuff yourself to the Golden Gate,
wouldn't you?"

"I will."

And she did. The wires picked up the story and photo,
and Washington backed away.

Afterward he and Gigi celebrated. She bought dinner and
even all the drinks when Dorn told her he couldn't afford the
tab, not on a reporter's salary. "I'm going to do something for
you," she told him that night. Two weeks later, there was a

$20 raise in his pay envelope with a note from The Admiral, "Now you can buy a lady a drink."

As for the story about the Chief Justice, he had promised never to disclose why Earl Warren—known always as Governor to California reporters—gave him an exclusive interview soon after the Warren Commission report on the John Kennedy assassination. The Governor owed him a favor for not disclosing a remark about the case Nat had overheard while dining nearby. He had given Warren his word, the word of a gentleman journalist, then exerted a little friendly pressure to get the interview.

All that seemed ages ago. *The Standard* had won the circulation wars. Dred McNaughton was gone along with many of the deft old hands... *The Standard* was getting as gray as he was.

8

The last few weeks at the paper he felt he was disappointing his colleagues by not keeling over and dying in the City Room. At first Terry Forman and the others had been solicitous of his health after word got around about his heart. Word got around fast when his heart doctor at Cedars of Tabor suggested he get a blood pressure kit and monitor his beat at the desk, especially at deadline time.

"The pressure is bound to get to you, Nathaniel," Dr. Brett Z. Merman, cardiologist and collector of Mark Twainiana, told him. "Taking a reading on your pressure will take *crazy* your mind off the scandals, murders and all that newspaper mishegas."

He had chosen Merman out of the phone book because of his name. Brett Z. The name itself was worth at least ten bucks more a visit, and if Merman had spelled out what the Z stood for—Zachariah—he could have gotten twenty-five bucks more. Actually, the Guild health plan was paying the costs of his visits, so it didn't matter to him what Merman called himself as long as he could avoid Merman's bedside manner, heavily seasoned with quotes, misquotes, punning and paraphrasing of Twain.

"The news of your oncoming demise is greatly understated," he told Nathaniel before approving what turned out to be a brief return to the City Room.

He winced, and the cardiologist added smilingly, "All right, Nathaniel, on your way. No more Twain, I promise. I'll show you some Samuel Clemency."

Merman studied his notes on Nathaniel's condition. "Well, the pressure keeps going up and down, the beat's erratic, but the ticker is ticking, and I guess we can wait a while before we tinker with your errant valve," he said. "What else? Oh, your enlarged prostate . . . I don't want to poke up your ass to see how it's doing. At your age, one of these days, you're going to stop peeing, or worse. Frankly, Nathaniel, it's a race between your ticker and your pecker to see what goes first . . . You do need a good internist and urologist to check that prostate."

The cardiologist wrote out the name of an internist friend and handed him the slip. "He's no authority on literature, I'm afraid," said Merman, "but he has a sensitive finger and knows enough to wear a glove."

As he rose to leave Merman's office, the cardiologist with the bristling Twainiana mustache fixed him with a hard stare as if he, Nat Dorn of *The Standard*, was responsible for the low state of San Francisco journalism since Twain's days as a reporter there.

"That paper of yours is losing all the panache and flamboyance it once had," Merman said. "Your paper hasn't been the same since that old scalawag of an editor, Dred McNaughton, left. Your new managing editor and that poor excuse for a lady publisher seem to be trying to impress the eastern press. Where's that old daily yawp of the frontier?"

His bedside manner turned lugubrious. "I really despair more about your paper than I do about your health... *The Standard*, indeed! What standard? That's the question."

Merman finally noticed Nathaniel was ready to leave. "Oh, by the way, you don't smoke cigars, do you?"

He was expecting the parting dose of Twainiana. "No, doctor," he said.

"Well, remember, more than one cigar at a time is excessive smoking."

His colleagues waited a little more than a week before making evident their displeasure with his apparent unwillingness to keel over or retire, leaving the way open for someone else to enjoy his window desk, a better work schedule and the other perquisites of seniority.

Terry Forman led the pack with a good morning flash over the video display terminal: "Ah, I see you're still here."

"Still, but not still," he flashed back.

Then he got down to work on a waiting obit. Ever since his return, the new city editor kept him doing obits. If there weren't any fresh distinguished corpses to bury in print he was asked to update the on-file obits of California notables on the waiting-to-die list. Such politicos as Reagan and Nixon were prime candidates for updating along with elderly literati of the likes of Christopher Isherwood or such occasionally ailing musicians as Dave Brubeck or Turk Murphy.

"I sure miss those old Blackhawk days," he told Brubeck after tracking him down by phone to check an obit fact. "What were the years, Dave? Our clips are spotty, and I can't ask our late, great jazz critic. He's gone, of course...Oh, thanks, Dave."

It was ghoulish, updating obits, but professionals like Brubeck understood. It was as necessary a part of a reporter's job, they figured, as a saloon pianist having to play "Melancholy Baby."

The melancholy task came when he had to make a caller understand that a dead relative was not of sufficient caliber to merit an obit.

"I'm sorry," he would tell a widow, "your husband, I know, he must have been a wonderful man and father, but I'm afraid that's not enough. We can't print everybody's obituary, you understand. There'd be no room for the news."

So eighty-year-old plumbers who had held back the leaks of countless faucets, seventy-five-year-old teachers who had taught generations of kindergarten children, sixty-year-old mailmen whose daily round of burdens had sent them to an early grave, all usually went without editorial notice of their demise. (Important to kin but not important enough, sorry.)

On several occasions, despite the strictures against it, he and the others would let an undistinguished stiff into the illustrious fold of obits.

"Wasn't there something special she did?" he asked one man, obviously a black, whose wife, the mother of eight, had died suddenly.

"She was a good woman, that's all," the man said. "She took care of her children so none ever got in any trouble. She was a loving woman, that's all, ain't that enough?"

He agreed, and after eliciting the fact that Mildred Johnson, sixty-eight, came from a family dating back to colonial slave days, wrote an obituary in which he noted that the deceased was "a member of a pioneer family." Obits of members of pioneer families always made the paper.

The day before he left the paper he had put aside notes for the obit of a Marin county personage, a woman who was the author of several books on reincarnation. He had mused on authors he had known who had died, those whose obits he had written, Weldon Kees and Calvin Kentfield and Kenneth Rexroth and Jack Kerouac, too many. He leaned back at his desk, wondering about reincarnation and what embodiment his own familiar dead might take. He thought of his mother, and immediately had the sense that Esther Dorn would surely be a dog in another life, a playful, often lovable dog like Golem.

Then he thought of Junkets, named after John Keats, the dog he had when he was ten. Junkets and he were inseparable, but Junkets was impossible to his sisters. Their high-pitched voices drove the dog wild. Whenever they argued, as they often did, over who had taken whose lipstick, Junkets would tear after them in snappish ferocity.

One day he came home from school and found Junkets gone. His mother, maddeningly, unceasingly playful, told him that a butcher had come by, taken a liking to Junkets, promised the dog would have bones throughout the Depression if only he could take him. "What a wonderful, wonderful life Junkets will have!" she exclaimed. "You wouldn't want to keep Junkets from having good bones, would you?" He was furious, but his mother, a master at making funny sad faces, tried to cajole him. Instead, he got his wind-up phonograph and the saddest music he had, a Bach partita, and kept playing the record from early morning until his father came home. His sisters complained as much about the record as they had about Junkets. Then one day, after school, he found the record was also gone. "It must have blown out the window," his mother said, making a funny sad face. "I know what," she said. "I'll sing a song to take the place of that dusty old record." And he held his ears, in a rage, his heart pounding, as his mother sang an English music hall song.

> *I'm Billy Muggins,*
> *commonly known as The Juggins . . .*
> *Muggins, Juggins,*
> *that's what they all call me.*
>
> *I'm quite contented*
> *with my little lot.*
> *I'm going to save*
> *all the money I ain't got.*
>
> *I'm Muggins, I'm Juggins,*
> *Muggins I'll always be . . .*

He could feel his heart pounding even then, in the City Room, more than fifty years later. He took out his heart kit, put the cuff on his arm, squeezed the air pump and soon

69

heard the beat, just short of 170, and high at the bottom end. *So damn high. Oh, my funny mother, my too much funny mother, Esther Dorn, rest in peace but let me be.*

He looked up. The new city editor, Delmore Murk, was hovering by his desk. "Do you really have to keep taking your blood pressure?" he asked.

"Doctor's orders, Del."

"Jesus, it's grisly . . . You know, Nat, we don't want anything to happen to you at your desk, God forbid."

"I could write an advance obit."

Murk ignored the smart-ass remark. "When were you planning to retire, Nat?"

"Before I die."

"Suppose we make it possible, if it's only money? Of course, Nat, we'd hate to lose you."

That was bullshit, he knew. The front office would be tickled to get rid of an overscale veteran, high on seniority, now reduced to obits, and hire a young, cheap, eager wimp, to mold to their liking. "Del, all you have to do is make me an offer I can't refuse."

Later that day, Forman flashed him a mock VDT obit: "Nathaniel Dorn, veteran reporter for *The Standard*, died in his sleep at his desk yesterday."

By the end of his shift the front office made him an offer he couldn't refuse. It was time to retire.

9

In the hot tub he reached for the overturned silver bowl that covered the red phone. He put the bowl aside and started to lift the receiver. Then he put it back in the cradle. No, dear Daddy was not going to call Ruthie. And the last thing he wanted to do was to phone Gloria. They were not to talk to one another again for as long as it took to keep from taking each other for granted. In silence, there is the opportunity for growth, Gloria had said. They were supposed to be using the time "to find themselves." Their lack of contact was more than he could bear and he began to dial her number, then put the receiver down before she answered. He knew how the conversation would go.

"Why are you calling me?" she would say. "We're supposed to have an agreement."

"I wanted to find out how you're feeling."

"I'm feeling rotten because you're calling me."

"How can I make you feel better?"

"By hanging up, Nathaniel," she would say inevitably. "You're calling me because you don't know what to do with yourself. Concentrate on that, on you. Isn't that what Mrs. Kaddish tells you? You're too needy for me, Nat. Too needy, Nat."

Needy Nat, needy Nat, needy-Nat-needy-Nat-needy-Nat . . . Nat. Nat. Nat. The word buzzed in his ears like a gnat, like a mantra that was driving him crazy instead of serene. One of these days he would have to go to Zen Ranch above Muir

71

Beach, where he had scattered his wife's ashes eight years before, and meditate, as Kaddish had advised him. "Make yourself a mantra," she told him. "Maybe *Gloriagloriagloriagloriagloria*...I don't believe in that trendy nonsense, you know, but maybe a mantra will work in your case. Just repeat it until you're so bored with it you get some peace."

Instead, he decided to call Terry at the paper and find out how things were going. He didn't really want to call Terry. The call, he knew, would put him in the opposite of the serene place he wanted to be, that place of innocence, pure feelings, for which he now longed in his retirement.

Terry, he knew, would joke about all the dead piling up since he had left the paper. Terry would make punning allusions to how dead certain he was that Nat missed the obit beat. Frankly, he would rather talk to the dead than to Terry. But he called Terry. He had nothing better to do.

The phone kept ringing. Finally, the operator at the paper answered. "Good morning, San Francisco *Standard*."

"Terry Forman," he said.

"Oh, I know that voice," said the operator. "It's Nat Dorn. How are you, honey?"

"Just swell..." He couldn't remember who the operator was from her voice. She must hear so many voices each day, he marveled, and yet she remembered his voice. There must be only a half dozen operators at the old *Standard* but he couldn't remember any of their names. Oh, maybe Mary.

"Well, that's wonderful, honey," said the operator who was, indeed, Mary. "Old Mary's here and ready to take your calls any time you need me, retired or not. Now you just hold on, honey, and I'll get you Terry Forman...You just take care of yourself."

"Thank you, Mary. It's good hearing your voice again." He was relieved that she had mentioned her name. *The Standard* operators were at the heart of the paper. They were like family, and he never bitched about them; they had saved his ass too many times in tracking down stories.

As Terry's phone kept ringing he remembered the time he had to reach a whorehouse in a place in Nevada that didn't even have a name. It was outside some town's district. The county sheriff had been playing around with the madame, and the sheriff's wife had tossed a Molotov cocktail through the whorehouse window. He had been assigned to get a quote from somebody in the wrecked house to fatten up the wire story. Mary had tracked down the whorehouse maid, who said, "If Mrs. Muldoon and her little fuckers think I'm going to clean up all this shit, they got another fuck coming," end, comma, quote. Of course, he did have to clean it up a bit, but the quote helped.

Still no Terry. He was probably at the coffee machine, or home with a hangover, or looking at a posted clip from some prestigious journalism review, knocking the awfulness of the sometimes raffish and awfully successful rag. Well, he missed Terry but he didn't have anything particular to say. He started to hang up when there was that familiar bored voice.

"Terry Forman," the voice said.

"Nat here."

"Nat?"

"Dorn."

"Nat Dorn, yes, I do remember a Nat Dorn, owes me a

drink, I believe. Well, comes the Dorn . . . How are you, old fellow?"

He winced when people called him old, even in an affable tone. Sixty-two wasn't that old, not the way the life span was increasing. "I'm just super, Terry," he said.

"Oh, a regular Clark Kent. A portrait of Superman at sixty-two, eh?"

Should he hang up? Just say, "Some other time," and hang up? No, he had to guard against continually seeming peevish, as Gloria complained. Peevishness made him sound old. "Actually, I'm calling from my hot tub, Terry, looking over fair skies and standstill traffic," he said, trying to be light-hearted. "I thought I'd add to your weekend weather roundup."

"In your tub, old fellow? That's a hell of a place to be when people are dying. They've got to be given a decent burial in print, you know . . . In a hot tub at this early hour, you, a dedicated newsman, the voice of the dead?"

"Let them rot, dear souls."

"What's that, you say? I can't believe it. You, dedicated to the dead as you are, showing such utter disrespect. My, my . . . Now you get your ass down here. I won't hear of any foolish retirement, Dorn. You can't retire from the press of events. The news never stops."

Forman was caught up in the rhythm of newspaperman badinage, that relief from the press of disasters which seemed to make many newspaper people drink and make them emotionally punch-drunk.

And here he was, out of the business, carrying on the same way. "Fuck you, my friend," he said, reaching for the martini he had poured himself before getting into the tub. "I just

called to tell you the temperature in the tub. A lovely counterpoint to the chilled martini I happen to be drinking. A
blissful 104."

"Hot as hell, I'd say. Which brings to mind the dead and
gone. How's Gloria? Are you both still on the outs, old
Romeo? Are you sure that hot tub isn't a form of pussy com-
pensation?"

"No, I'm not sure." He wanted to end the banter. "Anyway, we're not on the outs. We're taking a vacation from one
another."

"Some vacation... Now don't frustrate yourself, Nat. It's
bad for the heart. I happen to have some old discards for you.
Nice wenches, slightly winded, but good teeth, good head.
Remember, in your own immortal words, better laid than
never."

"Well, Terry, so good to be reminded of all the stale wit
I'm missing."

"No offense, old boy... Oh, by the lay, a little gossip...
Two of your old colleagues, Kunawa and Bluestein, are having a baby. In wedlock, can you imagine?"

"When's the baby due?"

"In nine months... And some more gossip for you—Rod-
macher may be getting married."

"Oh?"

"To his typewriter."

"Well, tell them mazeltov for me," Nat said.

But Forman was off and punning. "If you're not coming, I
must be going, as the call girl said. Time for coffee. And,
remember, it's Memorial Day this month. Give my respects
to the dead..."

Then Terry was silent a moment.

75

"Terry?"

"Oh, I'm here . . . I was just thinking how much I miss you, Nat."

Terry, as cynical as any two newsmen and twice as sentimental, had been his best buddy at *The Standard*. He was the one who had arranged the send-off for him—twenty bucks a person for a farewell party at The Washbag—and he was surprised at how many of his colleagues, sentimentalists all, had been there.

"I could always count on you for help," Terry was saying. "You always had the right word when I was stuck . . . Always ready to help a buddy who's had too many. These new young guys, they're as insipid as wire copy."

"Hey, come on, Terry," Nat said. "You're doing fine, all of you."

Terry seemed to have had too much to drink, even that early. In his cups or not, Terry could still outwrite anybody there.

"You were the conscience of *The Standard*, Nat. The gold *Standard*. Now it's leaden. You were the conscience, Nat. The poet."

Nat laughed. "Come on, Terry. I could be just as much an asshole as anybody."

"See? That's what I mean, Nat. At least you were honest."

"Yes . . . an honest asshole."

"Well, bye, Nat. Take care, old boy. Come by Hanno's one of these days and buy me that drink. We'll trade subtle confidences amid the noise of the liar's dice."

And Terry was gone. He was alone again in the hot tub with his thoughts. He was thinking of the paper, the loss of that easy identity, Nat Dorn of *The Standard*, honest asshole. And now he was no longer the insider, no press card, no

76

press parking pass, the parade gone by. Now he was old boy, as Terry called him. Old Nat, civilian. Nat the has-been, like a million others.

He shook his wet hair after ducking beneath the water. Without thinking, he reached down and touched his pubic hair, stroked his cock, then held on to it for dear life. "Old? Hell, I'm not old," he said aloud.

TWO

Make light of age,
Illuminate the darkening day.
        —Nathaniel Dorn

10

He thought of growing old.

Being old, in a way, was an age of wonder. It made him think of the schoolboy joke about Wonder Bread, the bland packaged bread that once upon a time his mother used for baloney or peanut butter and jelly sandwiches. The bread was so tasteless it made you wonder what was in it.

And growing old made him wonder about what had led to this point, all that past, those years, old scenes and old arguments, old friends and old wallpaper, where all of it had gone and what it amounted to. Now that the future was closer, death became a wonderment as well, an awesome wonder that made him flinch from the thought of that certainty. But the greatest wonder was the presence of aging, of wondering what to do with the rest of his life. Some, he knew, were content with just that—the rest of their lives, resting easily. The thought filled him with a dismaying wonder.

He thought of the old, the aging, the elderly, the graying. Geezers and geezettes. The maturians, as the slick oldster magazines called them. He had met them on stories at the Jewish Home for the Aged, Laguna Honda, senior citizen centers in Chinatown and across town.

There would be the old standby, an interview with someone just turned 100. Even a big, sophisticated, metropolitan paper was still a sucker for that venerable feature.

To what do you attribute your many years? he would ask the centenarian, usually a woman, face and hair as pale as gefilte fish or a wonton. She would be drooling to get to the big iced cake the home had hustled for the occasion. Her friends would be gathered around, waiting for old Hannah to collect her thoughts for the beaming TV news team so they could get on to sinking their false teeth into the birthday cake.

"Friends," one of the more articulate birthday ancients would say. "Friends and clean living." But he liked best one peevish type who told him, "I'm damn tired of all these effing questions. We want to eat cake, so beat it."

He found himself going through the telephone book, like he would as a reporter, looking for all the references to services for the elderly. The listings outnumbered anything for the young.

There was the Downtown Senior Center, something called the Friendship Line for the Elderly, Medi Claim ("We Do The Work—You Get The Money"), senior services for the Japanese, for the Chinese, for blacks, the L'Chaim Senior Center for Elderly Soviet Emigres, Road Runners West Travel ("Charter Bus Tours for Senior Groups"), Legal Assistance to the Elderly, the Gray Panthers, even a Senior Foot Care Program.

He decided to call the Friendship Line for the Elderly.

"I'm sixty-two and retired," he said in what he thought of as an elderly cranky voice. "What can you do for me?"

"We can talk to you," said the sweet-voiced volunteer at the other end.

"What do you want to talk about?" he asked.

"What do *you* want to talk about?" the lady asked in turn. "How is your health? We could tell you where you could get your blood pressure taken, or where to get flu shots, all for free, or a free lunch, or free movies. What do you want to talk about?"

He wanted to say *sex*, but he didn't have the heart for off-color banter. "Dancing," he said. "I'd like to talk about dancing."

"Would you like to go to a dance?"

"I don't have a partner."

"There are many partners at the senior citizen centers. There's Central Latino, always a dance there."

"I like young women."

"Oh, there are young women who will dance with you. They like nice men of any age."

"I'm not a nice man," he said and felt badly after he hung up.

Then, to salve his conscience, he called the Gray Panthers, the activist group, concerned he thought with the interests of the elderly. "I want to join up," he said, giving a woman named Fanny his name and address. "What activities do you have these days?" he asked.

"We keep young by fighting for a lot of good causes. Peace, Nicaragua, the Farm Workers..."

"There are others who do that," he said testily. "What about the elderly? Their health, Social Security cuts, isn't that enough to keep you busy?"

He sent in his membership fee anyway.

Now that he was one of them, among the aging waiting at the Social Security office, the elderly did not appear so old. In his mind, it was still them and they, not us, but they were somehow more alive than he had once imagined. Aging himself had certainly made a difference in how he saw others, on in years. After all, the blood was still flowing in his veins, as hotly as ever. Look at his passion for Gloria. He was still capable of losing his senses, of being as lovesick as he had ever been as an adolescent. Chronology was not necessarily deadly.

No, there was a big change going on. It was not only that he was one of them, and therefore old did not mean old. No, the elderly were getting younger in America, so it seemed. Like it or not, Ronald Reagan was symbolic of the times. President Ronnie. The septuagenarian on horseback. Ronnie and Nancy and their counterparts on the left, those Gray Panther militants and white-haired activists who got arrested demonstrating against nuclear havoc and apartheid, were only the more obvious examples of old people shaking off the years or, at least, not giving up the ghost. They were the discount airline elderly, flying from city to city, all the cities they could visit in a year on a flat rate. They were the gray-ing middle-roaders, the Winnebago old, in campers and trailers all over the highways of America, their eye glasses and wine glasses glinting in the sun as they searched out un-familiar destinations that had eluded them all their lives. They were the stay-at-home elderly with enough money in their pockets to enjoy senior citizen rates at the art films, the symphony, adult classes. Of course, if they were old and poor, or old and sick and poor, then the stereotypes held and you were the feeble gray of old. But many of the old, poor or not, were changing. They were living longer than ever be-fore. They were the new young elderly.

He remembered the time Ruthie had taken him to a lesbian bar on Geary where grandmothers were dancing with grand-mothers and grandmothers with teenagers and he, with sud-den bravado, tapped a grandmother on her shoulder and cut in to dance with his daughter. Later, a black entertainer, who must have been seventy, sang:

> *Dear God must love gay women,*
> *Must love us all God can . . .*
> *God brought us Baby Jesus*
> *By the grace of Virgin Mary*
> *With no help from any man,*
> *No help from any man . . .*

And she finished her act with a song of defiance and celebration:

> *Do I look like a dried up old lady*
> *Set to cash in all my chips?*
> *Take another look, you sweet stuff,*
> *While I shimmy and shake my hips!*

Old gays, old transvestites. Old sex fiends and old dope fiends. Yuppies on in years. Old hackers. Old mountaineers. Old health nuts. Old break dancers. Old age didn't mean wisdom or serenity or senility, either. Not for certain. Age wasn't the deciding factor by any means, not the way the life span was increasing.

"Got a cigarette, old-timer?" a waiting stranger at Social Security had asked him.

The stranger was grayer than he was. His full head of hair was carved Mohawk-style. He was garbed in black leather pants, wearing a denim jacket, a crimson T-shirt and a chain around his neck with a dangling locket. He looked like an ancient bohemian turned beatnik turned hippie who was now punk.

"I don't smoke," Nathaniel said.

"Hell, good for you. I still got some old bad habits." And he got up and wandered around the office, finally cadging a cigarette, before returning. Through the smoke, he gazed at Nathaniel. "Why are you all dressed up?" he asked. "You're collecting, aren't you?"

"I hope so."

"Then it's time to get you some comfortable duds. No need for a suit, man. There's places you could go, like Goodwill, get some neat, crazy duds, cheap, twenty percent off if you got a few years on you. Hey, I myself ain't been in a suit for forty years. How do you like this punk haircut of mine? Toni give it to me, says it makes me look sexy. What do you think? I'm seventy-two, a new wave seventy-two. I share a space now with Toni, been going with her since three weeks ago. She's my age turned around—twenty-seven. How about that? She's downstairs, getting us ciggies. I got to tell these people about my moving in with her, so my checks come to the new address. Toni shares my checks, and I share Toni. Who says you can't teach an old dog new tricks? I got taught. And it beats an old people's home, don't you think, old-timer?"

The words came nonstop, between puffs, from one of the new young elderly who now paused, blinked his clear blue eyes and looked at him appraisingly. "What's your life all about, old-timer?" he asked.

"I'm in love," said Nathaniel, the suited one, sixty-two, another of the new elderly.

"You poor bastard," the old punk said. "You're getting laid, I hope."

"Not anymore. We're on vacation from each other, maybe a permanent vacation. We're trying to find ourselves." He didn't understand why he was being so open with the old punk. But why not? One had a mouth and a breaking heart. The other had ears and time to kill.

"You poor bastard," the set of ears said. "You fell in love, you can fall out of love. Do something else before you're dead. I had a wife and a long-time mistress and children. They kept dying on me—if not by sickness, by leaving me. I got damn tired of it. So I'm just being, bohemian, beatnik, punk, you name it. No big involvement. Day to day, check to check, cheek to cheek." He smiled broadly, satisfied with himself.

"I'm at what I call my blast-off age, riding high like one of them manned rockets, checking out the unknown," he went on. "Why not? I'm not stopping after I made it to this point. I've survived them all so far, my wife, most of my friends, one of my kids, and a rash of everything that can afflict the old and afflicted. I've had that Richard Nixon shit, phlebitis, hardening of the arteries, constipation, bleeding gums, arthritis, emphysema, piles, ulcers, assorted aches and pains, you name it. I got premature floaters, nothing to do about that, and a prostate that got fixed up at the Veterans so I could pee."

"Floaters?" the breaking heart said.

"Spots in front of your eyes that don't go away. Floating cobwebs, this stuff in back of your eyeballs, keeps them lubricated, then dries up and crumbles as you get old. Eyeball debris, like the space stuff they say is out there floating in the heavens. You'll get it one of these days and think you're going blind. That's why you got to get on with it."

The old punk slapped his thigh. "At our age, every day without an ache or a pain is a victory. Every day you got a song on your lips and can get it up is paradise."

Nathaniel remembered a poem he had once written when he was younger. Jingling and rather jejune, he thought now, but he said the lines aloud:

Make light of age! It doesn't pay
For old and gray to moan and curse
The passing day.

Kick up your heels! What's there to say?
Be thankful that for young and gray
There's time to play.

Make light of age,
Illuminate the darkening day!

The old punk slapped his thigh again. "That's the ticket," he said. "Kick up your heels. Sing a song. Raise a fuss. Raise your dong. Don't get stuck on a dolly that's beating your brains out. Try something else before you're dead."

Before you're dead, the phrase evoked his worst fear, a dread that cut across any demarcation between the young elderly and the old elderly, the old old who were poor and unwell and the new old in good health and well-off. It was the fear of helplessness. He could see himself in the future, through cobwebbed vision, his eyesight obstructed by floaters. He could see himself alone in an empty house. Too crippled to get to any of his phones. A mind gone with Alzheimer's disease. At the mercy of strangers. Dying alone, the fate he feared for Gamel, his cat.

11

At first they had been everybody's favorite gray-haired couple. *How nice they look together,* friends and family said. While other relationships, young couples, old couples, even long-standing marriages, were crumbling all around them in an epidemic of breakups, Gloria Dell and Nathaniel Dorn, Dorn and Dell, Nathan and Gloria (their names were inseparable) remained a symbol of durability. They seemed to balance one another: the grayness of their hair, keeping pace, hue for hue; the trimness of their figures, helped by aerobics and an active sex life; his intensity, her graciousness; the similar wayward-ness of their minds, delightful for her part, provocative for his; her bright fineness of features and wavy lightness of hair, his dark Middle European handsomeness, a distinguished handsomeness now that he had cultivated a beard; the Australian sheep dogs each owned; their eye for art and literature and thrift store bargains; their ear for music, for Bach, Vivaldi and Mozart; their taste in fine wines under five dollars, in inexpensive restaurants, and, above all, the touching resonance of their bodies.

From all that others could tell, from the sparks of energy they gave off, Gloria and Nathan enjoyed each other, belonged in each other's arms. The aura of their intimacy gave their friends, and even their children, a good feeling, a glow, that these two, these two attractive and gifted geezers, defying all the norms of convention, of settling down in contented habit, remained passionate toward each other. Given their advancing years, they might well die in each other's arms, everyone agreed. It was a lovely, romantic thought in a world becoming less and less romantic.

Before his world began to fall apart, he found himself, in contentedly dotty moments, his mind on Gloria, repeating a snatch of old Victorian gush: *Grow old along with me, the best is yet to be* . . .

It held a deep appeal for him, this image of the two of them, Nathan and Gloria, the ideal couple, enduring time's onslaughts; hand in hand, even without the compulsion of marriage, until death did them part. For Gloria to come into his life when she did, an older woman of quality, just as his dead wife had begun to fade from memory, was some sort of sign, a miracle, almost like a victory over death.

His therapist made a face when he talked like that, as he did at Thursday's session. But Kaddish caught herself, mid-grimace, and said, "Tell me what that's all about."

He had been using the time with Kaddish to go over, over and over, from the beginning, what had attracted him to Gloria in the first place, what was happening to their love, why it seemed to be falling apart and why he persisted in trying to hold it together.

He tried to explain but the words now sounded hollow. A sort of sign. *Empty*. A miracle. *Pompous*. A victory over death. *Dead*.

"Back off, Nathan," Kaddish cautioned him. "Give her room to breathe. You've been coming on too strong. You'll kill it, this lovely thing you've had with Gloria. She has so much on her mind without your worries. Your worries may be scaring her off. Back away, Nathan."

"Scaring her?" he repeated in disbelief. "I care for her. I expect her to care as well. That's not asking too much, is it?"

"Yes," said Kaddish. "For now, it may be asking too much."

He shook his head. He couldn't understand why Gloria had to go off on her own and he had to back off, this ideal couple in their hour of need. Their love couldn't be so shaky that it was unable to withstand what they were going through. Or could it?

"Yes, face it, Nathan," Kaddish said. "It could be that shaky."

In his need, he refused to believe it. Sooner than later, he would make Gloria see the light. It was as if his life depended on it.

The lively, lovely times they had kept returning, even more attractive in retrospect. Now that he was stumbling in a desert of isolation their good and often nonsensical times took on all the golden aura of a mirage, and he had to remind himself that the memories were real, not figments of senility.

She had the capacity, as though she were still a girl, to carry on in a freewheeling way that renewed in him a sense of childhood. Like the time they were in Golden Gate Park, at the Garden of the Blind, enjoying the verdant spread of smells and textures. She began gliding like a bee from flower to flower, and he got in the playful mood, cavorting like some giant awkward bear, in a fierce and stumbling search for honey. In his slapstick movements, he bumped into a tree. "You won't find my honey there," she called out. "I'm a blind bear," he shouted, closing his eyes, his arms flailing out in mock-blindness. "Here I am," she said from a distance. Eyes closed, he came toward her, the she-bee, and she began to buzz louder and louder. He reached out to embrace her. But she was standing behind a sullen gardener in whose grip he found himself. "You shouldn't make fun of the blind," the gardener said, releasing him. "No, he apologized, "I'm sorry." As he backed away, he gently pinched Gloria's bottom.

Oh, they could be serious in their closeness. They talked, and not only about themselves. They had heart-to-heart, bracing talks about art and music, about love, Judaism and Christianity, about being sacramental but not religious, about the past, her husbands, his wife, their children, the state of the neighborhood, the world, and about growing old. They talked about their experiences and whether one ever learned from experience. But now he remembered best the lovely innocence of their silliness. A certain innocence, no matter what age, was needed, it seemed, to be in love.

Ever since his boyhood, when his mother's way with Cockney rhyming nonsense would dazzle his ears, he had a love for eloquent banter. Gloria had the touch.

He remembered the time she told him how she used to fancy a woman being able to give birth to anything she might desire, not only children. "Imagine, going into labor and giving birth, say, to a fine bottle of wine—oh, a few minutes of labor for that," she said. "Or a woman could give birth to a typewriter or a whole new wardrobe."

"You'd have to eat certain foods to get certain things, wouldn't you?" said he, playing straight man.

"Oh, maybe a few grapes for a bottle of wine."

"The wardrobe?"

"Cotton candy, of course."

"And what would you have to eat for a typewriter?"

She kissed him smack on the lips. "Your words," she said.

* * *

One night they were at La Boheme, a coffee house they had frequented since their first date. It was a funky hangout for young artists, students and chess players, a refuge in the Mission district from the growing gentrification of the rest of the city.

They had gone there for the solace of cappucino and poppyseed cake after walking out on a pretentious, socially significant comedy at the Roxie, an unpretentious movie house that took chances on showing anything, usually for one night only.

The movie they had seen was nothing, if anything. It had a contrived plot that involved a juvenile delinquent whose rehabilitation had become the passion of a middle-aged social worker who was actually an heiress who had become bored with the jaded life of the self-indulgent rich, and soon, snug in the track-marked arms of the delinquent juve, became addicted herself to a life of lighthearted despair and derring-do, eventually joining her young lover in burglarizing the homes of the idle rich she had once known, including her own family mansion, only she never told him she was from the right side of the tracks and these were her friends and her mansion . . . "Full of meaning and full of delight," the blurb from *The Standard* said.

"How do you think it ended?" Gloria asked, her lips touched with a creamy dab of cappucino.

"Oh, it's obvious," he said after a snare of poppyseed cake. "She adopts him, they settle down and they use their ill-gotten gains so he can run for State assembly on a program calling for a balanced budget and firm law enforcement."

"My juvenile delinquent," she said, reaching for his hand.

"My heiress," he said, taking hers.

"Do you love me for my money?"

"What else?"

They smiled at each other over the remains of the cappucino and the poppyseed crumbs.

"Our dialogue is just as good as anything in that dumb movie," she said.

"Yes," he said.

"O, eloquent one, tell me you love me."

"You I love."

"A funny way for a writer of repute, a stylist of the print media, to say 'I love you.'"

"Not at all. A simple declarative statement, a declaration of love. It puts first things first."

"Tell me more."

"First, you. You come first. I follow with love. *You I love.* Sounds more humble, more sincere."

"Not *more.* Humble is enough. Just sincere sounds more sincere."

"You're a regular E.B. White," he said, "not to mention Ludwig Wittgenstein."

"Even better in the sincere and humble department would be putting 'I' last."

"Oh?"

"You love I," she explained.

"Yes," he said. "Yes, I do."

There was the time they had gone to Zellerbach Hall in Berkeley for the opening of an all-Vivaldi festival. They had gorged on the Baroque avant-gardism of the Red Priest. All those concerti, twinkling with gaiety, unafraid of sentimentality. Concerti for flute, for bassoon, violin, mandolin, harpsichord, guitar, solo and tutti. A radiance of boyishness and girlishness that defied the erosion of age.

Their ears humming, high on the richness, Gloria had dared him to be as inventive as Vivaldi. "Hum me a concerto. Antonio," she said.

He hummed the Blue Danube as he took her hand and swung her through the night, and then, crossing the street, went into a mock-limp to halt the cacophonous campus traffic, as he and Stan had done years ago when his young son was finally out of casts and he had taken him to the Great Highway for strolls along the beach.

"I have a better idea," she said when they reached her car.

She started up the car, and as the motor hummed she began to disrobe. First, her scarf. "Tonight it's my place, and the first one in bed, naked, bare-assed, wins," she said, removing the white stone necklace, once Rachel's, he had given her.

Without a word, Nathaniel felt for the key he had to her place. Then he began untying his shoelaces.

"Wait, Nat, you haven't heard it all," she said as she turned from the curb to the stream of traffic going toward the bridge.

"All?" He had removed a shoe.

"The prize." She matched him shoe for shoe. "Winner gets his or her dearest wish, non-monetary," she said, starting to unpeel a stocking with her left hand. "Agreed?" She was now holding on to the steering wheel with her left hand as she started on her right stocking, adding that because she was driving he had the advantage.

"I plan to take full advantage."

"Put on a cassette, Nat," she said. "I love to undress to Vivaldi."

All she had on was a blouse and her bra by the time they got to the toll booth. His clothes were off, and he reached in

95

a pocket of his discarded trousers for toll money and handed her the quarters.

The night breeze over the bridge was crisp, but in the warmth of his excitement, his hand caressing her thigh, he didn't feel the cold. All chillness has left the world, he thought.

They were at her place, clothes left in the car, running nude, these two naked sexuagenarians, along the moonlit garden path. Her dog, Clara, yelped at them as they ran. He was first through the door, clambering up the stairs. He was waiting for her in bed when she came from the bathroom and finally got under the covers. She had taken her time.

"Victory is mine," he said, holding the coolness of her body close to him.

"Hold on," she said, drawing away, sitting up in bed, turning on the lamp. "I'm the winner."

"You?"

She held up his right arm, not in victory. "Look," she said, "you're not nekkid, my dear. You still have on your wristwatch."

She turned off the lamp and returned to his arms. "My dearest wish, Nat," she said. "Love me. Love me all night. Love me forever."

Dear Gloria, age can't tarnish or dim your innocence. And I can't forget. I can't forget you, how your mind, your sensibility, your body, awakened mine. I was still buried in mourning when we got together. At first it was as if I was just one of your good causes. But my senses came alive again with you. Your artist's eye helped me see again. Your love of music helped me hear again.

One night, in the loneliness of his king-size bed, while a cold moon shone through his bedroom window, casting a pale mocking gleam on his once-erotic mirrored wall, he called out her name, bringing closeted Golem on a bound to the edge of his bed.

"Gloria, Gloria, Gloria."

He let Golem stay, cradling his massive head.

"Gloria, Gloria, Gloria."

The sound reminded him of the Vivaldi recording, *Gloria in D*, he had once given her on her birthday. In his mind, he heard again the thundering opening, the stamping octaves against the thrust of violins and winds while the choral voices mounted in ecstacy. *Gloria, Gloria, Gloria! Gloria in excelsis Deo . . .*

He was rambling . . . A heartsick juvenile sixty-two-year-old man. He gave in to the rambling, the rambling about Gloria that was turning off friends and family. He didn't care. So be it. *O glorious shiksa, Ruth among the alien corn, come to rescue me from mourning.*

12

That afternoon, before Nathaniel left for his session with Kaddish there had been some parting words with Stan, pleasant words for a change.

"If you leave the camper, Daddy," Stan said, "I'll give it a tune-up. I've been promising you that."

Nathaniel was appreciative. *Well, Stan was all right, after all, he was trying to be a help, a help to himself and to me.* "Stan, that's really nice of you. But you have your finals, don't you? Do your studying. It's more important. Besides, it's late."

Stan insisted. "I don't do enough for you, and you do everything for me. I've got my tools and you're going to get that tune-up, finally."

Nathaniel smiled and put his arm around his son. "A tune-up, huh? Well, let's make it a good tune—maybe something by Vivaldi." He reached in his pocket, took out his wallet and handed Stan a twenty and a ten. "For spark plugs and incidentals," he said. "Incidental music."

Stan took the bills. He kept the money in his hand as his father leaned over to hug him. "Maybe we can have some supper together tonight," Nathaniel said. "I'll make something special. How about chicken and mangoes? Or we can go out. Someplace nice."

Stan said he might not be back in time. He was going to test drive the camper after he was through.

"Take care of yourself, Stan," Nathaniel said before leaving. *I love you and love that you're trying.* He wished he could say it out loud.

Stan waved after his father, the money in hand. Sometimes, when he was sober, he hated himself for all the shit he had pulled and was pulling.

But he couldn't stop. He felt helpless when he thought of stopping. And what would he do if he didn't do this?

Well, he'd use a few bucks for spark plugs. The rest would go for what he needed. Anything to deaden the pain. The pain of not being able to try hard enough. The pain of not being able to stop.

He needed the camper that afternoon. He had to make his rounds. He needed things to sell at the flea market on Saturday. He'd find an excuse to borrow the camper again.

Shopping malls and parking lots, especially at the airport, were best. With every junkie scouring the streets, it was crazy the way people still left stuff in their cars. Briefcases, adding machines, typewriters, jewelry . . . One time he even found an expensive art book that he gave to his father as a present for Gloria. Another time he boosted a new burglar alarm that somebody didn't have a chance to install.

Stan kept his flea market stock in a closet with a false partition. Hiding it all wasn't really necessary, he knew. His father never came downstairs, not without an invitation, and would never invade his privacy.

"This is your place, Stan," Nathaniel had told him when he took him home after the stabbing. "I'm not going to treat you like a kid. You're a grown man. I just don't want to hear about any trouble."

Stan made sure of that. His father didn't need the pain of knowing.

It had been easier when he had the car repair shop. Some of his best customers were his drug connections. A tune-up for a couple of ounces of the best grass to be had. Speed and ludes, uppers and downers for a ring job or a rebuilt engine. Of course, on ludes and dozing over a job, he or Nick, his helper, might leave a few loose nuts and bolts in someone's engine. A connection, maddened by the damage, might come at him with a wrench or a knife.

After coming out of County Jail and the halfway house he had started the shop on a loan from his father and managed while he was clean to make a go of it and even pay back half the loan. Then he was back to his old habits. Try as he tried it was no way to run a business, and after the stabbing he had to give up the shop.

Stan admired his father and loved him for caring. *Never at a loss for words, for something funny to say, a joke he had heard, so knowing and able, the nicest father in the world, loving, eager to help. Even somebody like me.*

Sometimes at night, unable to sleep, not knowing what else to do, Stan would even call on God to forgive and help him.

Now, in the dark of the downstairs kitchen, by the table where his textbooks lay open alongside a mess of dishes, he poured himself some Stolichnaya.

That's one way I take after you, Daddy...A taste for good vodka. Well, any vodka...

How did the joke go—the difference between an alcoholic and an addict? Jonah, the best of his new connections, a friend who took almost everything he could boost, had told him that one. *The difference? Both of them, the alcoholic and the addict, they'll steal from you, but the addict, he'll help you look for what's missing.*

Stan was loaded when he heard that one. He didn't get the joke at first but laughed anyway. Now, alone, he laughed again. Yes, an addict was always ready to put up a good front and help look. He laughed until he started coughing from the sting of the vodka.

In the dimming light, he opened his calculus book and tried to focus on a page of equations. But the light was too dim. It was crazy, he thought, how many months he had managed to stay at school the way he was. He had wanted to please Nathaniel, and he had tried hard.

I tried, Daddy, but I'm not going to make it. Those finals, I'm not going to make it...I love you, Daddy, and I love mama, her memory, but I'm not going to make it...I can't keep making it.

He must have taken a nap, he thought when Smudge, his cat, jumped on his lap and woke him.

He had dreamt, he knew, but it was a dream of dread, and

he tried to give in to the pump of adrenalin, the excitement of what lay ahead in the darkening day, anything to make him forget the dream, as he drove the camper toward the airport.

Often, driving at night, he saw shadows of the time in County Jail, fearsome in his memory, like the time they held the point of a can-opener to the back of his neck while others held him down . . . But this time the shadows of his dream were different.

The camper radio was blaring but the images of the dream kept coming toward him, clearer and clearer. Gradually he saw himself at three or four or five—no, still a baby—crying, howling, his feet gnarls of clubfooted flesh . . . He was trying to stand up and kept falling. He was reaching for the top of his crib and kept crying and falling, falling and crying.

Oh, Daddy, I can't stand on my own feet. I'm a grown man but I can't . . .

Then the first images clicked off and he saw himself at his bar mitzvah at a small synagogue in the Mission. He was entering manhood, but he kept holding onto the stand and stumbling over the Hebrew and the words of his speech. "I want to thank my mother and father for . . . for . . . for their faith in me."

And, suddenly, the stand had given way. He was falling again, everything was falling, the stand and the Hebrew book, falling, crashing to the floor, and all around there were frightened, embarrassed faces . . .

He had no memory of the bar mitzvah incident, if it had even happened. He never even understood why his father and mother, unbelievers both, had gone along with the ceremony in the first place.

"Some things an atheist does anyway," his mother, an athe-

101

ist and a Jew, had told him. "Don't do it for us, Stan. Do it for my mother's sake and your father's mother...It's not really necessary to believe in any of this."

It made him feel hollow, talk like that.

"How do you feel about God?" his father had asked.

"I don't know," he said.

While trying to stay clean he had been to twelve-step meetings at A.A. and N.A. where some recovering junkies and alcoholics talked of asking for the help of a higher power. He had tried asking, but he got no answers.

Stan gunned the camper, bringing up the speed, as if he intended to finish his errands in time, after all, to have dinner out with his father. But he knew he wouldn't be back in time and that his father would never know where he had been. It was better that the old man he admired, who lived above him and expected so much, didn't know. His father didn't need the pain. He would never ask and he would never know.

Oh, God, help me . . .

13

At Kaddish's, Nathaniel talked about his childhood and what he had wanted to be when he grew up.

"A magician, a private eye or a reporter."

"Why those, Nathan? Most kids then wanted to be firemen, something like that. A steady job during the Depression. Now I guess they want to be astronauts."

"Even Jewish kids? I don't know...In those days, I used to look through my brother Lonnie's magazines. *Astounding Stories, Amazing Stories, Wonder Stories.* I think the Jewish kids like my brother wanted to become scientists and build rocket ships and go to places where there were no Depressions and wars."

"And you?"

"I read the ads in Lonnie's mags. Ads about throwing your voice, becoming a ventriloquist or a magician, pulling rabbits from top hats, escaping from handcuffs. I also ate up those ads about becoming a private investigator, learning to take fingerprints, fooling around with lie detectors."

"What is it about doing those things that attracted you?"

His smile had a tinge of embarrassed amusement. "The deception, I guess."

"Even a private eye?"

"Well, you know, disguises..."

"Anything else?"

"Maybe the fact that each of them—a magician, private eye or a reporter—are in the know. They're insiders, in control. All of them have secret information. That's powerful stuff for a kid."

"And how did that make you feel, the idea of being deceptive, in control, being an insider?"

"Powerful."

"And now?"

"Now that I'm older?"

"Now that you're retired."

"Weak, I guess. Out of it. Powerless...Retirement may not be hell but it's something of a no man's land, a vacuum—"

"For some people, Nathan. Not for everybody. Some people actually find it's a pretty good place, a time of discovery."

"Well, I'd like to get to that place before I go crazy."

"Maybe you will, Nathan. You're working at it."

He stood up to leave.

"Wait, Nathan," she said. "Sit a moment . . . Tell me about your son. Are you working on that?"

He continued to stand. Stan and what he might be up to was not his favorite topic. "He's all right, I guess. Still going to school."

"Still downstairs?"

"Oh, he'll be on his own soon. His finals are coming up. Then he'll be getting a job, I expect."

"You don't sound too sure, Nathan . . . Don't the two of you talk?"

"Sure, we talk," he said. "In fact, we had a very nice talk before I came here . . . He talked more than usual. The kid said he was going to give my camper a tune-up. It was really nice of the kid."

"The kid? Stan's over thirty . . . Nathan, you and he ought to talk more. Find out where he's really at."

"Oh, that's easy to say," Nathaniel said. "You know, it's so hard talking to young people these days. And do they listen?" Then, hesitating a moment, he added, "Well, we're a funny pair, Stan and me. He hardly talks, and I talk too much. Maybe so I don't have to listen?"

14

Nathaniel badly wanted to talk to Gloria, to find out how she was. He was willing to use any excuse.

Abandoning pride and discretion, like some addict, he telephoned one morning and waited four rings before a voice came on the line, Gloria's voice. But it was an answering machine. Something new for Gloria.

He called the number again to listen to her voice: "You've reached Gloria Dell, but I'm away right now. I'll call you back as soon as I can. Please leave a message at the sound of the beep."

He didn't leave a message but the discovery of this new acquisition, an answering machine, so untypical of Gloria's nature, made him toy with the idea of calling Joey Milano at the paper. Milano was the one who occasionally dabbled in random code numbers to gain access to a contact's answering machine messages.

Even if he never tried to tap Gloria's messages to learn what she was doing, who she was seeing, there was no harm in knowing how it was done. He called Milano but Milano was out and he decided not to leave a message.

She had said not to phone her, but nothing about writing. He went to Mary Price's florist shop on 18th Street and picked out a card with a Matisse drawing. Self-portrait with beard. A vague likeness to himself, he felt. Well, the beard, at least. He also bought a single yellow rose.

Dear Gloria, he wrote in a studied script that he felt would

appeal to the calligrapher in her, *I'm ready to start over again.*
Nat. And he added: *P.S. Matisse sends his love.*

He didn't want to sound ponderous. No, a lightness of
touch, like Matisse. He read it over again, over and over. He
hoped he had managed that lightness.

He attached the rose to the envelope. Then he drove
toward Gloria's house and parked two houses away. Her
Corolla was in sight but she wasn't, and he placed the rose
and message on her mailbox before she appeared and before
Clara could bark.

At home the next few days he waited for an answer. And
waited and waited. The mail carrier brought him his pension
check, a PG&E bill higher than usual because of all the hot
tubs he was taking, mailings from the health club, from good
causes of his own, from the museums, from adult education
courses he had inquired about after retiring, from the Free
Nicaragua people, from a dance group, from a computer
club, from the Gray Panthers, from the nuclear freeze people, from the Publisher's Clearing House. And more bills.
And he waited.

"I'm waiting for an important letter," he told the mail carrier.

"Maybe it's this."

The mail carrier handed him a stamped folder. More junk
mail: a funeral home proposal, prepaid burial at a discount.
We apologize if this comes to you at a time of stress, the folder said.

"Anything else?"

"This." It was his copy of The New York *Review of Books*,
its recondite reviews a distraction from stress. Seeing it, he
frowned. He didn't *want* distraction.

"Here's something else," the carrier said. "Oh, it's just a
postcard."

It was from her. It was a quiet Matisse, a serene line drawing from the Matisse chapel they had visited in southern
France years before. She had remembered. She had been
saving it for an important occasion, he decided. It had taken
her time to find the card, the perfect card for the occasion. So
that was why her answer was late.

The mail carrier had left. He put the card to his nose,
trying to sniff some trace of Gloria's fragrance. The smell was
the smell of a picture postcard. Then he turned the card over
and read: *Dear Nathaniel: I'm not. Best to Matisse. Gloria.*

His heart felt drained of blood. The card, with its cold
salutation to *Nathaniel*, was so terse. Not even a signoff of
love, a throwaway love. Friends wrote love these days, even
acquaintances. Simply love, that shouldn't have hurt. He
studied the card again. Well, she had written *Dear Nathaniel*.
That *dear* counted for something, he supposed. And *Best to
Matisse* did sound light-hearted. Yes, she was feeling lighter
toward him. It was progress. And the drawing, a keepsake of
lovelier times. She cared, that was undeniable. Then he noticed under the drawing, below the Matisse signature, three
additional words from Gloria: *Please don't write!*

From the kitchen, he heard the outside buzzer over
Golem's barking. It was the mail carrier again. "I forgot this,"
he said, handing him a letter.

It was also from Gloria. He tore the envelope open,
wounding the flower inside. Just a flower. All the envelope
held was a pressed scarlet flower. An impatiens. One of the
petals had been severed in his haste.

He found his Elmer's glue, dribbled a careful line of white
along the edge of the severed petal, sizing it to the rest of the
flower which lay on the surface of the purple tiled counter.
Within minutes the impatiens was whole again.

His heart surged. Gloria cared. The flower was proof she cared. She cared. Not that he was sure. Gloria always took pains in expressing herself. She was a stickler for the exact gesture. With her feeling for art, every nuance could mean something.

Was she telling him something by sending him an impatiens, a pressed, dried impatiens? She could be scolding him for his impatience, his restlessness, his lack of calm, his eager desire for relief or change. The definitions he found in the dictionary were relentless in admonishment.

And the flower itself. It was dried, finished, lifeless. Did she mean their "relationship" was dried, finished, lifeless? And red? Red was the color of anger. She was clearly angry at him for following her, for calling her, for writing her, for intruding on her privacy. He found his *Western Garden Book* and looked up the listing for impatiens: *The annual kinds grow best in sun; the perennials in partial shade in all but coastal areas.* Which kind was he? And did it matter? *Ripe seed capsules burst open when touched lightly and scatter seeds explosively.* That seemed significant. Perhaps that's what she's afraid of, he thought. He was like that: touchy, quick to scatter seeds explosively. Then his eye caught the other name for impatiens, *touch-me-not*, and he felt the blood drain out of his heart again.

"Tell me, Nathan," Kaddish was saying, "why do you persist? There are other women. Why her? And if you want her despite everything, why don't you keep to the agreement and keep away?"

"I don't know," he said. "It's one of the reasons I keep coming to you. Besides, it wasn't my idea, this vacation. And I never really agreed . . . How is she?"

"Who?"

"Gloria."

"She's working hard on herself. Now let's get back to you."

"I suppose I shouldn't have written that card of mine."

"Why not?"

"It didn't work."

"How didn't it work?"

"It didn't accomplish what I wanted. I wanted her back. This vacation from each other, it's gone on too long. It's no vacation for me. A vacation is supposed to make you feel calm and rested."

"How do you feel, Nathan?"

"Exhausted."

"Why are you particularly exhausted now?"

"Oh, her card, I suppose. Her answer was so curt."

"Pertinent," Kaddish said. "She took some pains to be pertinent in her reply, Nathan. She was showing some caring."

He hesitated. "Do you think so?" It wasn't the sort of caring he understood. "To me, she seems more distant than ever . . . I send her a yellow rose, and I get a dried, lifeless flower in return."

"An impatiens."

"Yes, I'm impatient, that's what she's saying, isn't she? Of course I'm impatient. I miss her, and I'm horny, and this has gone on too damn long."

"How do you feel now?"

"Angry."

"And exhausted?"

"More angry than exhausted."

"Your face has gotten red."

"Like the impatiens . . ." Suddenly, despite his anger, he smiled.

Kaddish waited.

"I'm thinking of my father," he said.

"Your father?"

"He was always so angry. His face used to get so red. So angry at my sisters for staying out late. At my mother, my happy-go-lucky, playful, silly mother . . ."

"I want to hear more about that, Nathan."

He looked down at his watch. "My time is up," he said.

Kaddish shook her head, as though admonishing a small boy. But she was smiling. "That's my job, Nathan, keeping track of the time . . . You have such a need to control things."

"It's one of my problems."

"We'll talk about it next time, Nathan."

At home, he plopped himself disconsolately on the couch. Golem sat haunched by the side of the glass coffee table.

"Don't look at me with those damn sad eyes," he told the dog. "I don't feel like going for a w-a-l-k." He spelled out the word. There was no sense getting Golem excited.

A walk, pulled by Golem, was the last thing he felt like doing. He was too exhausted by his hour of therapeutic probing. Therapists could talk of the satisfaction of emotional growth but the process was more like cutting through a jungle of undergrowth.

Golem had retreated into the bedroom closet, and Nathaniel reached abstractedly for his copy of The New York *Review of Books* on the coffee table. Momentarily he dipped into the longeurs of reviews of a history of the devil, a study of the obsessiveness of Flaubert and a work on the origins of Marxism before turning to the personals. The personals, he would admit only to Kaddish, was his main reason for subscribing, although he had never succumbed to answering that literate embarrassment of temptations, the like of:

Lovely, menschy woman wishes to dance to the music of the spheres, seeks tall, healthy, intellectual partner in mid-60s and mid-Manhattan. NYR Box 1001.

Perhaps Kaddish was right, he thought. Perhaps he should check his own obsessiveness with Gloria and check out other women, maybe place a personal himself and let other women check him out, an alternative that seemed much less exhausting.

The pad he used to jot down reminder notes was near the telephone. Looking for something with which to write, he hoped the phone would ring and it would be Gloria telling him that her notion of a vacation from each other was a whim, a mistake, foolish and cruel. But the phone was quiet, and the only messages on his answering machine seemed to be from investment counselors, with plans for zero bonds and other financial esoterica, or real estate agents wanting to help him cash in on his house.

Thinking of a likely personal ad, the right words came to him almost immediately: *Growing, graying, retired newspaperman, worldly but romantic*...Pushy but true, he thought, and continued ... *seeks caring, sharing Bay Area woman with mind of her own, eager to explore*...Explore what? The jungle motif again, he thought. The Yucatan where he had been with Gloria? No, nothing he had done with Gloria, all that was practically sacrosanct. It had to be something vague, in case Gloria ever came to her senses. ... *eager to explore life*...Life, of course, he thought. ... *life, each other, creativity, distant places, the future*...Perfectly vague, vague and persuasive, just the right mix, he decided. Or perhaps too vague, he thought,

111

and he added *Photo appreciated*. He counted the words, $1.65 per word, plus $10 for a box number and for forwarding replies. He wrote out the check. Then he found a stamp, an envelope, addressed it all to the *Review* and put it aside for another day. He would give the phone time to ring.

15

One proviso they made, all three of them, when he called to remind them, was that under no circumstance would he use the occasion to talk about Gloria. He had talked to them enough about his troubles with Gloria, they said. They had been called, at times, around the clock, and always about his obsession with Gloria. They were tired of Gloria.

"And most of all, Nat, you need a holiday yourself from thinking about her," Nelson told him.

Every time he mentioned her name, Pinelli proposed, Nat would pay them each five bucks. He wasn't happy about it, but he promised.

The four of them—one about-to-be-retired, one semi-retired, one retired and one long-retired—were "members in good walking," as Fergus Nelson, long-retired attorney had put it—of the Oofty Goofty Memorial Marching Society, named after the old San Francisco character who used to cadge drinks and money by allowing others to take a free swing at him.

"Oofty is representative of life itself," said Nelson, a despairing man despite his usual geniality. Although a lapsed

Catholic, he couldn't bring himself to end an unhappy, forty-year marriage. Instead he traveled alone. "Life is like that—a wallop in the stomach," he said.

"I thought that was what retirement was like," said Potter.

Sam Pinelli, a lapsed Marxist and semi-retired bookseller who claimed to know everything, said Oofty got his name by the sound—*Oof*—made when you get whammed in the solar plexus. "A couple of hundred whams like that and anybody would get goofty," he said.

Nelson said that one of these days he would research how the name came about but he never got around to it; he was usually too busy spending his retirement on camper trips across North America, including Newfoundland. "The Winnebago Kid," Nat called him before he got his own camper.

The membership was rounded out by the pure WASP among them, Dr. Gladwyn Potter, Presidio Heights psychiatrist and about-to-be-retired-but-ambivalent-about-it. Occasionally, Potter gave up spare hours spent in womanizing to be with them. He talked about retiring but, as Nat once told him, he would never give up his practice. "All those clients threatening to kill themselves, it makes a wonderful excuse for leaving one woman for the bed of another."

"What will I do when the clients are gone?" Potter would implore the experienced retirees. "I'll probably sit all day on the therapeutic couch wishing they were back... Maybe Nat will come and keep me company. I'll give him a discount like that therapist he has."

Nathaniel's involvement with Kaddish was a constant source of banter on Potter's part. "Imagine, he turns down a friend. It's like me buying my books from someone else than Pinelli, or giving my legal business to some other shyster than Nelson . . . What do you say, Nat? How about giving a friend a break so I can afford to retire? My hours after midnight are free. What do you say, Nat?"

"I say, let's walk."

And, with that, they began to bestir themselves from their conversational ease on his black leather couches for the afternoon stroll from Potrero Hill to North Beach, with nostalgic Nabuco's as their final boozing destination. The tour had been proposed a month before by Nathaniel, his turn, and it was obligatory that all members show up unless reduced to crutches with a note signed by a physician other than Potter.

Golem watched Nathaniel, obviously hoping that his master would go to the closet for a leash so he could join the society for their basic purpose, a long walk. But dogs were not allowed, according to the group's unwritten charter. "No, you stay, another time," he told Golem, making Potter wince at the chummy tone he used.

"Is that what it's like when someone retires?" the psychiatrist said. "They get goofy? They hold intimate conversations with dogs?"

"A dog is a man's best friend, doctor, haven't you heard?" said Pinelli. "I've got books to prove it."

The Oofty Goofty Memorial Marching Society, not including dogs, was dedicated, occasionally, to walking up and down the keepsake streets of the city, observing landmarks of a personal autobiographical nature and, as the cost of membership, buying a round each at favorite bars along the way. Except for Potter, who had a liver problem and drank mineral water, they ended up feeling little pain from the walk after it was over. Then the tour guide would call his wife or a woman friend to drive the four of them home—to the east, west, north and south of the city. With Gloria out of his life for now, Nat would have to pay for a cab.

They were nearing the crest of Rhode Island Street. Many of the streets on the hill were named after American battleships, not the states, Pinelli, a cigar-chewing, slow strider, informed them. He began to list them—the USS *Vermont*, the USS *Arkansas*, The USS *Mississippi*, the USS *Pennsylvania*, the *Wisconsin* . . . but the others had moved ahead, out of earshot, and were staring eastward over the rooftops toward the glide of Bay with Berkeley and Oakland spread out beyond, and to the north the downtown highrises glinting in the sun, casting shadows on the streets below.

Pinelli, catching up to the others, thought he could see the building in the Tenderloin that housed his bookstore. Potter pointed out what he thought was 450 Sutter Street where he had an office. Nelson was disgusted. "Shit," he said, "the two of you are walking advertisements . . . Let's have some autobiography, Mr. Dorn."

He was staring to the side of Rhode Island where Gloria lived, hoping to catch a glimpse of her in a window or the garden, but he saw no one. He said her name silently but said nothing aloud.

"Nat, are you with us?" said Nelson.

"We had Ruthie there," he said.

His attention had turned toward the corner of 20th and De Haro Streets, where Ruth had been born. The little house— an attic, kitchen gallery and two rooms, one on top of the other, approachable by rope ladders—was gone. It had been replaced, as the city's growth made the hill more fashionable, by a comfortable, colorless three-unit structure. It occupied the little backyard garden where Ruthie had slept in her carriage under the avocado tree. He remembered the stretch of casement window in the little house itself and saw again, with the eyes of a husband and younger father, the old familiar view when even with a storm raging outside everything seemed timelessly secure, lovely in its ordinariness.

The house was little, he had written in the poem for Rachel,

> *so I opened the door—*
> *the house was big*
> *with the wind's roar.*
>
> *You opened the window,*
> *the wind tore past—*
> *the house shivered,*
> *so fierce a blast*
>
> *we went to bed*
> *in that hullabaloo,*
> *and the bed was enough.*
> *We made it do.*

The rounds of drinks kept being poured in the hours before they reached Nabuco's.

At Hanno's, the other reporters' pub, he told them of the time he had gotten to be friends with George R. Moscone, before George became mayor and long before the assassination. He recalled the interview at campaign headquarters on Mint Street, a block away, when he asked what the "R" stood for (was it Raphael?). They had shared memories of their fathers. George's father was an alcoholic. They had talked of some of the sins they had committed, George's political and Catholic sins, his, mostly journalistic.

116

He looked down at his geranium, a substitute martini with straight gin and a twist of lemon, a drink invented by long gone photographer Ken McLaughlin, who had felt that vermouth was an interference with a drinking man's passion.

He thought of Ken and George Murphy, another veteran drinker and damn good reporter, dead now, who had every Tin Pan Alley song ever written at the edge of his lips. He used to tell Murphy, across the desks, to sing one for him. What would he sing now? And the words floated in to his mind: *I'd rather be blue, thinking of you, than be happy with somebody else*... With a shrug, he shook away the thought of Gloria.

For a moment the images of newspaper veterans, long dead gone—Carleton of *The Standard*, Mullivan of *The Courier*, Anspacher, Paterson, Waite, Wallace, Root, Murphy—appeared like faces in a mirror behind a bar. Murphy and the others may have found the biggest story of their lives, life after death, if it existed or not, but they would never get a typewriter to tell the news. Now their blue gray faces in the mirror of his memory were speaking to him, and he looked away.

He shook his head. *Poor Moscone, poor Ken, poor Murphy*. He shook his head as if trying to rejoin the reality of the day. The lines of his glass were blurring. It was early for him to be drinking like this, and he didn't feel drunk, not yet. He put a hand on his eyes, feeling the tanned pouches underneath.

"You miss the paper, don't you?" said Potter. "Retirement is the shits, isn't it?"

"Sure," he said. "Sure, I do. And I miss Rachel. I miss George. I miss Ken. I miss a lot of things." He also missed Gloria. "And, damn it, yes, I miss Gloria."

"Okay, Nat, that's a free one," Pinelli was quick to say. "We'll let that one pass. But next time it's five bucks each."

They also stopped by at the M&M, where Lennie the bartender poured them substantial martinis and they had greasy overdone hamburgers, a tasteless match for the omelettes with the unmelted cheese that Wilson had served them earlier at Hanno's.

"You newspaper guys don't care how you ruin your stomachs," said Potter, the psychiatrist, he of the ruined liver. "You'll put up with anything for a little praise and some bonhomie."

It was a little late for bonhomie at the M&M. His old friends at the *Standard* and the *Courier* were leaving: Milano, Snow, Ward, Lennon, Jeffries, Darrel, Lawry, Perlmutter, Mercury and the others. Who were the others? He pressed his mind for their names. His memory was going. Who were they? Oh, yes: Diamond, Olivet and Gugenheim . . .

A familiar figure, rounding the bar on the way out, tapped him on the shoulder. "I know you," the knowing face said. "Didn't you used to be Nat Dorn?"

It was Terry Forman. He reminded Nat that a drink was owed him, but another time. He had to heed the press of daily events, a logjam of obits if nothing else. "There goes the Dorn," he said, leaving.

On the way to Nabuco's they took in the sights of Hallidie Plaza, the itinerant preachers telling them they were all damned, the bongo players, the drifters with vacant eyes, the tourists with vacant eyes. They caught the cable car for a few blocks until Nat said the whirring faces of the passing shoppers and the damn cute cable car gonging was getting on his nerves. In Chinatown, after studying the live fat chickens and dead fish faces in the market windows, they stopped by

for crab claws and pork buns at one of the dim sum tea-
houses. Pinelli said it was time for more drinks at the Tao
Tao, where there were "all those simpatico photos of old
Chinatown," and he and Potter, who fancied himself an expert on Eastern philosophy, got into an unTaoist squabble
about the meaning of the tao.

By that time he was getting a little sick and a lot drunker,
but he was able to interrupt the contending experts and recall
the words of Chuang Tzu, the poet of Taoism, whose disci-
ples had remonstrated with him when they found him playing a silly tune on a flute after his wife died.

" 'People will feel it's most unseemly, most unseemly, that
you're not, not weeping,' they told old Chuang. But wise old
Chuang, he told them, 'Hey, fellows, believe me I've done
my mourning. But, look, she came out of nothingness and
went into nothingness, and between the two of them, nothingness and nothingness, she gave me the gift of herself.
That's what would be unseemly, carrying on, weeping,
weeping, as if I begrudged that gift.' That's the tao, you
guys, that's what the tao is."

"You miss her, don't you?" said Potter.

"Sure, sure, I miss Rachel," he said. "And, fuck, I miss
Gloria. Oh, fuck."

"Five bucks," said Pinelli. "Five bucks each."

He gave Pinelli a venomous stare.

"Five bucks, we agreed," said Pinelli. "I'm just keeping
tabs."

At the edge of North Beach, after browsing in Ferlin-
ghetti's City Lights bookstore, Nelson pointed out a cheap
hotel where he had "my first almost sexual experience." He
was sixteen and had accumulated $20 in singles by selling *The
Standard*. He went to a bar, now gone, and had picked up, or

she had picked him up, "a jazzy redhead of advanced years who said ten bucks would take care of the room and ten minutes of her time."

"Once we were in the room," he said, "she told me to take off my clothes, lay them on the bed, and go in the bathroom and wash myself down so I didn't give her the crabs. When I came out she was by the open door, still dressed, and stopped long enough to look at my diminutive member and say, 'I can see you're not ready for me, sonny,' and with that she flounced out, and the rest of my singles went with her... That's one person I miss, bless her black heart."

At Nabuco's, they sat in the back and ordered Irish coffees to start. Nat was feeling sick, woozy and starting to nod, but he stuck his thick tongue into the edge of the cup, tasting the cool cream. Then he put the cup down, spilling it and getting the warm stain on his pants. He ignored the wetness. "I want to know," he said, "who any of you would bring back to life if you had the chance. Anybody, ancient or otherwise, famous or not. And what would you ask them?"

"An interesting game," said Potter. "And it's possible, you know. I don't mean any mumbojumbo. But there's this shrink, a guy named Progoff..."

"He did a book on Jung," said Pinelli.

"Yes, that's the one. But I don't hold it against him, a good Freudian like me. Anyway, he's got other books on what he calls the intensive journal. It's a method for holding dialogues with people in your life with whom you've got unfinished business. Anybody, dead or alive... Look, Nat, you get Kaddish to tell you about it, or read the stuff yourself."

"Look around my store," said Pinelli. "I've got a copy or I'll get one. Ten percent discount to senior citizens, Nat."

"How do we play this game?" said Nelson.

"Well, you think of the somebody you want to talk to. Think of all you know about him or her, put yourself in their moccasins, as they say in Marin. Then get yourself in a meditative mood, and just let it happen... We'll each pick our own special dead specimen, okay? A moment's silence..."

All they heard was the blare of the Nabuco jukebox. An aria from the Puccini opera, sweet like the Irish coffee, melancholy like whiskey, hemmed their silence.

Nat felt on the edge of nausea, but he sat, stunned, drunk, sick and exhausted by the walk, the drink, the bad food, his thoughts.

Then Potter said, "All right, Pinelli, you have the floor. You start. Who did you talk with?"

Pinelli removed the cigar from his mouth. He was smiling. "I talked to the old guy, Karl Marx himself. I asked him if there was life after death."

"That's a dumb question to ask someone you're trying to bring back to life... What did Marx say? Is there life after death?"

"He said no."

"A comedian," said Potter disparagingly. "What about you, Nelson?"

"Jesus Christ."

"I thought as much," said Pinelli.

"I asked him about what he thought of Christianity, 2,000 years later, and what the world needed."

"I bet he said that Christianity sucks," said Pinelli.

"All he said was, 'Be kind.' "

"Aldous Huxley said the same thing," said Pinelli. "Those were his dying words... What about you, Doctor Gladwyn?"

"I brought Buddha back to life."

121

"Good for you," said Pinelli. "How did he, the Enlightened One, define the tao?"

"That was Lao Tze."

"Oh, I know that, asshole," said Pinelli, the drink making him more and more belligerent.

"Easy, easy," said Nelson. "Be kind."

"Anyway, guess what I asked Buddha."

"I give up," said Pinelli.

"I asked him what, after all, was the sound of one hand clapping. You know what that wise old bird said? He said, 'Which hand?' "

"Nat?"

He had started to get to his feet when Nelson and the others looked toward him. He had to get to the john.

"Nat?" Nelson asked again. "Tell us before you go."

He hesitated. "Rachel. I talked to Rachel."

They waited for the word from the dead.

"I asked her what to do about Gloria."

"Oh, oh," said Pinelli.

"She didn't say a thing. Nothing. Not a word. Not about anything. Not a damn thing. Not Gloria. Nothing."

"That's another," said Pinelli.

Suddenly he was shouting over the blare of the plaintive Puccini aria. "Fuck you, Pinelli! Fuck you!" He fumbled in his pockets, drew out his wallet, then began throwing the contents at Pinelli. "Gloria!" he shouted. "Gloria! Gloria! Gloria!"

Mario, the bartender, was at their table. "What's wrong with this guy? Come on, get him out of here."

But before they could get to him he had begun retching, and sobbing, doubled up like somebody hit in the solar plexus, holding onto a chair, falling, trying to stand to get to the john, throwing up remnants of undercooked omelette, overcooked hamburger, crab claws and pork buns. The outpouring fell on scattered credit cards, on the money from his wallet, on the floor of Nabuco's, already wet with Irish coffee.

16

At first, when they began seeing each other two years after his wife died, he had trouble reconciling himself to Gloria's age. She was four years older than he was. At fifty-seven he was still a young man. She was sixty-one. When he was sixty-seven she would be in her seventies already. It was ridiculous for him to be going with someone so old, he thought, and he would study her face for any new wrinkles only to be disconcerted by her bright, knowing smile. "You're looking for wrinkles, aren't you?" she once asked.

"I like the look of your face," he said, feigning innocence.

She sighed. "Then kiss me, you dirty old man," she said quietly.

He had started going out with women even while Rachel was dying. She wanted it that way, she told him. "I want to know someone's taking care of you, Nat," she said. "You're a beautiful man, I should know. You're strong. You're caring. And you're crazy. You shouldn't be left out at dark without somebody."

Before her cancer, after the children left home, she had gone back to college and gotten her master's so she could work as a rehabilitation counselor for disturbed women. She had a knack, strengthened by her own feelings of being different, even an eccentric, for talking the language of certifiable crazies. To one client, who claimed to hear voices, she counseled, "You get your voices to wake you up in the morning so you can get a job and be independent." Two years later she got a note from the woman who said she was now a legal assistant and studying to be a lawyer. "You and my voices showed me the way," the woman wrote.

Then, dying, Rachel was still at it, helping Nat to survive her death.

In her hospital bed she made a list of women she thought would make him a good mate. Gloria's name was not on the list although she had been an acquaintance, a neighbor, for whom their daughter Ruthie had babysat, and was recently divorced. He wondered now why Gloria's name was not on the list but others, some more attractive, were. If Rachel were only alive, he would ask her.

"Pick one of them," Rachel said, handing him the list with four names. "Go to a movie. Go to bed. I can't help you there, Nat. Just don't tell me about it."

Rachel, who had been his wife for thirty years, was extraordinary. An atheist but as close to a saint as anyone he had ever known, a notion that would have made her angry.

She drove away a hospital rabbi who tried to console her.

"I'm sure your intentions are good but you're annoying me," she told him. "Maybe when you're dying you'll understand."

The young rabbi met him as he was coming into her semi-private room. "What's wrong with your wife?" the rabbi asked.

"She's dying of cancer."

"I know, but she won't let me comfort her."

124

"She wants to die without illusions."

"God is an illusion?"

"I don't know. Maybe one day I will." Rachel was an atheist, and he was a maybe-ist, as he called himself, something more of a believer than an agnostic. He thought of the dying words attributed to Rabelais: "I am going to the great *peut-etre.*"

"Talk to your wife. She should make her peace."

He felt sorry for the perfectly well-intentioned rabbi. "She's made her peace. It's her own peace. Maybe you can find someone else to comfort."

He was certainly not going to talk to Rachel about helping the rabbi find peace for her, not with the cancer riddling her with holes, and she avoiding painkillers so she could die with her mind clear to talk to him and her children and friends until the last moment. Not Rachel whose radicalism and sense of social duty had been nurtured by the unionism of the 30's and what she had read of Emma Goldman, the indomitable anarchist of old.

"I just can't bullshit and not say what's on my mind," she said, two months away from dying of bone cancer. "Not now . . . Pick a name, Nat. Just pick."

To calm her, to satisfy his curiosity, he looked over the list. They were all desirable choices. "I don't see your name," he said.

"Please, Nat, cut out the crap. Just pick."

He made a mental note of one of the names, crumpled up the note to throw it away, then slipped it into his pocket.

"Good," she said. "Now I don't want to see you here tomorrow. I want you to take a holiday from this place. It's bad enough I have to be here."

The next night he followed Rachel's orders. There was a

new restaurant opening near the Embarcadero, *The Desert Mirage*, and the owners had invited the media to a pond of alcohol and an oasis of paté. He brought Danielle, an old family friend, told her that whatever they did had dying Rachel's blessing ("You know Rachel," was all he had to say), and they got so drunk that it was all he could do to drive to a nearby motel instead of taking her home to San Rafael, and they ended up in bed, laughing at each other's nakedness but too drunk and embarrassed to do anything but fall asleep.

He called in sick the next day, took Danielle home and visited Rachel at the hospital by noon. "I don't want to hear about it," she said.

She lasted until a week after Passover. It was enough time for her to learn to use a walker and leave the hospital against the orders of her doctors, who wanted to put her through another hopeless operation. She came home to say good-by to her children, Ruthie and Stan, in her own home.

"I love you, Ruth," she told her daughter. "I hope you find someone you're happy with, man or woman."

Then she asked for Stan. "I've always loved you, Stan, even when you were a dope fiend. You've been off the stuff a whole year, so now I can tell you that I respect you as well."

Finally, that last night, she wanted him. "I want you to make love to me one last time, Nat," she said. "Remember, you once told me, that's what your mother did before the morning your father died."

When he got into the hospital bed he had rented for her, she turned to him in the dark and whispered in his ear, a smile in her voice, "Easy on the bones."

Afterward she said, "You must be tired, Nat. Go in your bed, have a good night's sleep. I'll watch a little TV, even if it's only Johnny Carson."

In the morning, when he brought her a tray of coffee and a sweet roll, her face was turned toward the wall. "Rachel," he called out. But she was dead. There was a smile on her lips. She seemed glad to be dead.

Later, he found a penciled note under her pillow. "I love you!!! Don't grieve. Peace," the note said.

During her childhood days in the tenements of Brooklyn, one of Rachel's dreams was to have a gazebo of her own, like one she had seen in a city park. Together, they had fulfilled that fantasy, copying a gazebo in the Japanese Tea Garden in Golden Gate Park and building a small version in their backyard. After her death he put the note and the urn with her ashes in a space he dug under the foundation of the gazebo until he was ready to scatter her ashes off the rocks at Muir Beach.

17

While waiting for Gloria to come to her senses and come to him, he tried to evoke the other women in his life after Rachel's death. The memory that there had been others made him feel, in retrospect, stronger, more virile, needed.

But it was not easy to remember. The pain of Rachel's death and the frustration of Gloria's rejection kept coming between him and his memories of—what were their names? —well, there was Mara, a sales promotion assistant at a downtown department store near work, Mara O'Hara, the movie name they had hit on for her, and there was Kim, spectacular Kim, the demonic one, a model he had met at a party given by someone at the "Women's Department," now in these times the "Trend Department," and last, yes, Natalie, dark and intense Natalie, the only one of the faith after Rachel, more a sister than a lover, a lightning rod for his grief and rage, dear Natalie. And the first? Oh, the first . . . First, yes, there was Cassandra, Cass, who got loopy on pot the day of the garden wake for Rachel.

Their features, their bodies, the panache of their being seemed to elude the focus of his memory. They were like tropical fish in murky water tanks, dimly seen, only occasionally discerned when one would come close to the glass of his mind, usually with a disapproving look, a sort of piscine pout.

Mara, Kim, Natalie, Cass . . .

Rachel would have loved the Yiddish wake. There was a spread of all her favorite foods—herring with sour cream, eggplant parmigiana, mounds of matzah brie, a tangy pot roast, a roast duck. The smells floated back as he remembered the bright and sad day, women friends in garden hats, the men in their not-so-funereal best, jeans and cords, except for Fergus Nelson and Dr. Gladwyn Potter. *Don't come in mourning,* the invitations had said. *Don't grieve,* she had implored. They ate and drank and Cass smoked pot and tried to console him by feeling him up while nobody was looking and then, later, with abandon.

Only he and Ruth and Stan were allowed a few solemn moments of farewell.

"I'll always remember Rachel," said Ruth. "Her strength and honesty were wonderful, in her life and her death. Goodbye, Mama."

He remembered how touched he was by that simple mama. Ruth had always called her Rachel. It was a mark of their own individuality and independence. Now, in death, Rachel had also become *Mama*.

Stan took her place at the entrance of the gazebo. "I've not always been a good son," he said. "I hope I can do better. I wish you were here to see me try."

In memory, everyone seemed to freeze at the words, like a movie still, glasses of wine and champagne in hand held in stillness, tears in eyes, glistening in the speckled sunlight, never dropping.

The poem he had written after he found her was sentimental and idealized, perhaps, but real enough. He read it at the wake, and it helped make the pain of saying goodbye real again:

> *Thank you, Rachel,*
> *for the gift of yourself,*
> *for the time we shared,*
> *even the bad moments*
> *that shook us and warmed our blood*
> *and led to some truths—and didn't.*
> *Thank you, Rachel,*
> *for allowing me to prove*
> *I was capable*
> *of being a good person,*
> *and sometimes strong.*
> *I wanted so much*
> *for you to live, for us to love.*
> *You wanted it*
> *on your own terms,*
> *the Rachel of spirit and strength.*
> *Thank you for Ruth and Stan,*
> *for their strength and spirit*

in this time of your loss.
I shake, I feel the chill, I cry
for you, for myself, for all of us.
O, pure spirit, our loss,
you gave us your blessing.
It fills our being, it lies on the gazebo floor:
"I love you! Don't grieve. Peace."

Cassandra, in the throes of pot and champagne, began weeping while he was reading his farewell poem.

"I'll take care of Nat for you, Rachel," she cried. "Rest in peace, Rachel. Don't worry!" She now flung herself at Nat, clinging to him in frenzy, kissing his eyes and nose and mouth, kneeling down, trying to unzip his pants.

To keep the wake going the happy mourners put Cass to bed. That's where he found her, in his king-size bed, when the mourners left.

He had just gotten undressed when there was a knock on the door. It was Ruth.

"You can use my room," she said. "You need a good night's sleep. I'll see about Cassandra."

"It's all right, Ruthie," he said, his voice muffled by drunkenness. "We'll be all right. I'll be all right. Your father's a grown man."

The memory of that night kept fading on him. All he knew, dimly, was that Ruthie persisted, and he had the tangled remembrance of the two of them, he and Cass, trying to fight off his daughter's efforts to separate them and maintain the dignity of the day.

But, at best, the women in his life until Gloria were mostly diversions, sometimes helpful, half-remembered interludes between Rachel and Gloria: from Crazy Cass to bright-eyed

Natalie, needed and necessary, bless her, but too intense, too intense for his own intensity. The others were more fleeting: Mara O'Hara, only twenty-two but a slapstick polymath on every screen comedian from Buster Keaton to Woody Allen . . . and demonic Kim, the statuesque witch in the night, even younger than Mara, who kept a snake and a salacious parrot as pets and slept with a butcher knife under her pillow.

The months with them, before he settled on Gloria, a woman closer to his time of life, were like an amorous nervous breakdown in which he was observing the order of Rachel not to grieve, to live for the both of them and, as Kaddish would put it later, "masking your hurt by hiding your feelings." And with guile, he thought, the never-ending guile of the reporter, who could roll his own feelings into a ball, a tennis ball, give it a special cut, and swat it, with the smile of a knifer, into the opposite court.

When his colleagues at the paper learned about his liaisons with Mara and Kim, they sent him a greeting card signed by the cards among his colleagues. "Nothing could be finer than to shack up with a minor," the card read.

In one of her more serious moments, movie buff Mara asked him how old he was. "How old do you think Paul Newman is?" he asked guilefully.

Once he had asked Ruth how she felt about his being with women younger than she was. "Oh, Daddy, I understand," she said. "You're just trying to bring back those days when you were courting mama."

Now he remembered how, at first, it was so comfortable being with Gloria, being able to act his own age. Once upon a time it was actually comfortable, he thought.

18

That Monday, on Memorial Day, the dead and Gloria kept intruding into his thoughts. He tried to meditate them away, to give his mind a rest. But Gloria, Rachel, Ben, Esther, Doree—his woman, his wife, his father, his mother, his dead sister—held out their arms in his mind. Welcoming him, pleading with him, pushing him away...

He decided to take Golem to Muir Beach where he had scattered Rachel's ashes years ago.

He reached the rock ledge just in time to keep Golem from lifting his leg against it. It was the same ledge from which he had cast her ashes, molten fragments larger than he had first imagined human ashes would be. The moment the ashes descended into the water, with Ruthie and Stan looking on along with a family friend from Marin who played a tape of a Buddhist chant, it was as if the ashes suddenly coalesced again into Rachel's form and ascended with the wind into the sky, a figure dancing toward the horizon.

He had been startled. "Did you see that?" It was Rachel, floating in the sky, dancing away. His eyes strained to see the last glimpse of her. He felt a chill in his bones and he shuddered as she vanished.

But it wasn't just a beautiful imagining. He had the distinct feeling then and he felt again, as sure as Golem had lifted his leg to pee, that the spirit of Rachel, militant atheist Rachel, had taken tangible form that day in the expanse of blue in the rim of his teary eyes.

Now by the rock ledge, after shooing Golem away, he

132

studied the horizon as if thinking that Rachel was still there, waiting to open a door in the sky if only he could think of the right words to summon her. Not that he believed in an afterlife. No, he might not be as fervent an unbeliever as Rachel, but anything like that, especially to a hard-nosed newspaperman, even a retired one, seemed like so much mumbo jumbo. Still, if the dead lived, even if only in our thoughts, what harm?

Standing on the rock ledge at the edge of the immense Pacific, he felt more lonely than ever. Rachel would never have the sad opportunity to be where he was. He was the survivor, the damn survivor. He remembered how she had said, when he left her at the hospital one night, how glad she was she wouldn't have to mourn him. One of these days, it might be years or any minute, he would die and she wouldn't be there to mourn him. She had done her dying. Unlike him, she would never have to mourn again or get any older.

He spoke her name out loud: "Rachel...Rachel." He scanned the horizon, as if searching for that door in the sky.

Golem was sniffing at a beached starfish.

"Rachel, I need you. I feel lost." If he were writing a novel, at that moment he might have let his prose pick up the sound of wind in which the hero would discern the sound of her voice. But there was no wind, no voice, just the sound of Golem sniffing, the interval between waves crashing and spuming, and the water lapping at the rock ledge.

There was no answer from the sky, and he couldn't blame her for any reticence if, indeed, she could speak. He wanted to ask her about Gloria. Why wasn't Gloria on her deathbed list? Had she just forgotten Gloria? Or did she know that Gloria would only eventually cause him heartache?

He heard again in his memory her deathbed words: "Just

133

pick." What he did was up to him. She was free now of any concern over his interest in other women, Gloria or whoever.

"Just *pick*."

19

Stan was sitting on a deck chair, spooning ice cream from the container, when he came home from Muir Beach.

"I've just been out to Muir Beach where we scattered your mother's ashes, you remember?" he told his son.

His son, with a tinge of a smile, shook his head. "I don't remember." Then he added: "I took some of your ice cream, some coffee. I hope it's all right."

"Sure, it's all right." He had enough ice cream in the freezer for a children's birthday party. "It felt like your mother was there."

Stan didn't want to hear about Muir Beach. "I drained the tub. There's fresh water now."

"Oh, good. I was going to take one."

"I'll start the heat going... Look, I'd like to borrow the camper tomorrow morning."

"Where are you going?"

"Can I borrow it?"

"Sure, I'm not going anywhere. Anyway, I have the car."

"I'm making a flea market run."

That's what he had expected and feared. Flea markets were thieves' dens. As a reporter he knew that's where the dope fiends went to sell stuff they had stolen and get the money to buy drugs. But Nathaniel buried his dread. He tried to be light and even helpful. Stan was off the stuff, he needed to hope.

"I've got some things in the attic. An old bicycle of yours, your flippers and snorkel, maybe you can sell them."

"I'll take a look."

"You know, I found your cast when I was cleaning up. That little cast we all wrote on, remember?"

His son smiled. "No, I don't remember." And he was gone, leaving behind the ice cream container. For some reason the discarded container irked him more than what seemed like Stan's smart-ass attitude. Shit, he said, realizing that Stan hadn't turned on the heat in the tub or turned off the hose. The water was dripping below the deck and running off into the crevices of the brick walk.

He sat in lukewarm water, trying to exorcise his son from his mind. He was weary of Stan and his junkie-minded evasiveness, a holdover from those years when his son was on the hard stuff. Stan could have easily said something sympathetic about the visit to Muir Beach and his mother's memory. He didn't have to be such a smart-ass . . . Well, Stan was going to school now, at least. He had been out of trouble for five years. He would still be in business if not for the stabbing—some asshole junkie robber holding a knife to him late at night, his son had said. Give Stan credit for trying.

Gloria had found it hard to take Stan, he knew. Well, he couldn't really blame her. "He should be on his own, Nat," she had said when they were still talking. "He's over thirty. He'll never get on his own feet. You're spoiling him. You're spoiling it for us."

She was probably right, and he might have listened if she were his wife. But she had her problems with marriage. Her divorce had left her wary of marriage, unlike his own experience of being married more than thirty years, mostly happy years, until Rachel's death.

He couldn't write Stan off. Go your own way, kid. He *had* to take his son in after the stabbing. Stan had been clean for five years. That counted for something... He had to be mother and father now that Rachel was gone. Keeping the family together was up to him.

Gloria, with her dismaying experience of family life, couldn't appreciate that, he supposed. But he could still appreciate Gloria.

Five years before, after they had been to bed the first few times, he had written her a poem. He recognized how derivative it was, with its Yeatsian echoes, and he had taken liberties with a rhyme word—her nose wasn't "askew," but he needed the rhyme, and she had liked the poem, one of the few he had written in years:

> *They were young, as lovely,*
> *and maybe, one, even more.*
> *Their noses weren't as askew.*
> *Their lips were just as red.*
> *Our touch was close enough.*
> *They cared, I think, as much.*
> *They kissed as deeply as you do.*
> *And yet, and yet, and yet.*
>
> *They fitted in my arms.*
> *Our words were close to love.*
> *We laughed and thought no more*
> *of past lovers in our time.*
> *We explored each other's differences.*

We quickened to our joy.
It made such timeless sense.
And yet, and yet, and yet.

After reading it in bed she had asked: "And yet?" And yet, he told her, he didn't know. There was something profoundly familiar and intimate about her that transcended the brief time they had been with one another. She had laughed. "Oh, Nat, you can sound so damn lovely and pompous in one fell swoop," she said, pulling at a curl of his body hair, making him cry out in not-so-mock pain. And yet, the difference between Gloria and all the others, since Rachel's death, was that he might be in love with her, already, even then.

For all his concern with family, Gloria remained at the center of his thoughts. Nothing seemed to help dispel her from his mind. He thought how good it would feel if he could do something for her that would bring her closer and make her more, well, appreciative of him.

20

There was no sign of Gloria or Clara, her Australian shepherd. The garden was quiet with a Mendocino lushness. He looked for a spot where he could leave the diosma, the spicy shrub he had discovered at the nursery down the hill just before the place closed.

Taking it from the hatchback, the white breath of heaven had needled the air with its peppery fragrance as he bruised a twig. He could imagine Gloria brushing against the unexpected bush as she turned the path to her door. The memory of her smell—warm, quietly erotic, not at all the smell of an older woman he expected in younger days—drifted toward him.

Every time she came to his mind he felt the need to be physically close to her in some way. The photo he found of her posing in Paris along the Rue Jacob, the drawing he had made of her as she napped at the Hacienda Uxmal during their trip to the Yucatan, nothing seemed to help quiet his mind. The photo and drawing only gave a sharpness to the past, like stab wounds, a jaggedness of longing. He badly wanted some present closeness in her absence. And, finally, he remembered it was Memorial Day, and she wouldn't be home.

Just before their enforced vacation from one another she had taken back her house key. "You won't need this," she had said. It was as if she had slapped him. *Well, that's it, it's all over with Gloria. I've lost her, she's dead to me.* Then she had added, "At least, you won't need it for a while." He felt a little better, but he decided, after a twinge of pique, to let her keep his own house key. He occasionally mislaid his, and it would be good if she had a spare. Besides, the key, his if not hers, was a token of closeness, a hint of intimacy. And, he thought, he could always use the key as an excuse for seeing her.

He wished now that he had made a duplicate of her key. If he was unable to see her until this separation ended, he could have the satisfaction of enjoying the familiar scene of so much of their intimacy, in her absence at a time like this. Her house, with her drawings, her piano, worn but elegant furniture going back through so many years of her life, her bed, all spoke her presence, the quiet, erotic aroma of her. And he wondered, too, if the pictures she kept of him, the two of them together, were still on the kitchen mantelpiece. Seeing them there, still in place, would be a sign of how she felt.

Then he remembered that the downstairs side window was weathered and shaky, the frame was rotting and it would be no trouble to slip the catch and gain entry. Breaking and entry, yes. But he would only be taking a look. Testing the security, actually. He had always felt uneasy about her relaxed attitude toward protecting herself. Sometimes, after writing up a burglary for the paper he had called to remind her of the need for taking better precautions, especially about those downstairs windows. But she had laughed that beautiful innocent laugh of hers. "Nobody wants my junk," she would say. "And there are more desirable women around."

When it came to slipping his foot over the ledge, he hesitated for a moment. It was, he knew, an invasion of her privacy; his neediness again, his overbearing intensity, the busybodiness of the complete neurotic newspaperman, the would-be insider, never content to let be, always ready to meddle, always with a well-intentioned excuse. Well, he thought, at least he was honest in his own convoluted way. And he stepped inside her house. It would be a short visit, she and Kaddish need never know.

He closed the window behind him. The catch had given easily. He glanced momentarily at the piano, near the closet where she kept her wine supply, noting that a Bach piece was open against the panel of her upright. He remembered the dream, saw again the image of her venomous stare, and decided to move quickly through the house.

At the top of the stairs Sara Teasetail was mewling. "Sara, how are you, girl?" Sara's tail, the color of smoke, wavered against his leg. He took the time to get Sara a few crumbs of

Monterey Jack from the refrigerator, then looked for the photograph of the two of them that usually stood on the kitchen mantelpiece. He grimaced. It wasn't there.

Sara was following him about the kitchen, nudging him with her silky gray ears and head. He looked down at her, and her eyes stared back at him. *"Damn,"* he said quietly, trying to control how miffed he felt that Gloria had removed the picture. "Don't keep following me. Go eat your damn cheese. Go catch a damn mouse."

Well, he didn't much like the way he looked in the photograph anyway; it was one of those coin machine pictures that made his face look scrunched up, old and vaguely Hungarian, although Gloria, he remembered, was radiant beside him. Oh, they were happy then, and his lips tightened as he shook his head, wondering at the mystery of their estrangement.

He breathed deeper to settle his nervousness. Instead, the remembrance of her presence settled over him. It was tangible in the few drawings of hers that she kept on the bookshelves in her dining room, along with special rocks she had scrounged from the seashore, a plaster head of her in younger days, innocent and radiant, done by a sculptor who had been her lover, a few books of poetry—among them Yeats and Blake—and, strange counterpoint, a two-volume set of *Gargantua and Pantagruel.*

He remembered, when they were first getting to know one another, her revelation, chiming with his own early enthusiasm, that Rabelais was one of her favorite authors as a girl. "He taught me to love laughter and the things of the flesh," she had said and then, suddenly, had reached out and tickled him in his groin, just above his cock. It was one of the astonishments about Gloria that enchanted him, that lovely, dis-

140

concerting mix of graciousness and bawdiness. "You even fart gently," he had once whispered in her ear as they were making love. Oh, Gloria.

Her calendar pad was near the phone. He glanced over the boxes for the six weeks they had been separated. The entries were sparse—visits to the dentist, to an oculist, to her daughter, to Kaddish, lunches with old friends like Doris. There were notations about his calls, his unwanted calls. She had been keeping score, it seemed. The last few notations were in red pencil with an angry scrawl: "Stop!" But at least there were no unfamiliar male names in the appointment boxes. She was not seeing anyone else.

He examined her answering machine. It was one of the beeperless sets, with a remote accessible code. Well, he wasn't remote, he was there, but he decided not to listen to her messages. Oh, leave her some privacy, he thought with a twinge of conscience. But he looked at the sticker under the cassette lid and found her code. It was what Joey Milano did at the paper. Just call the number on a touch tone phone, wait for the beep tone, then press the code number for three seconds. It was diabolical the way any decent privacy was vanishing from the world. And one of these days, he knew, driven by desperation, he might try, he might. But he hoped not.

Across the dark dining room table, showing the marks of many shared glasses of wine and candlestick dribbles of intimate dinners gone by, the expanse of window was starred with the downtown freeway lights of motorists trying to make their evening way to the Bay Bridge. The homeward-bound cars were forced to move so slowly that they hardly seemed to be moving at all, and he had a sense of time standing still, as though nothing had changed, as though he and

Gloria were still at her table, holding hands in a brief silent meditation before sharing the night.

The cassette tape he put on, the richly plaintive melody of a Vivaldi concerto for lute and mandolin, filled the darkening room. The tape was one of many he had given Gloria after surprising her while she was away from home by installing new speakers for her system. He shook his head, remembering the tinny speakers she previously had; she, a music lover, an amateur pianist in the best sense. For someone who was wealthy enough through inheritance to treat herself lavishly, if she wanted, she could be so begrudging as far as her own well-being went.

Maybe that's why she's going to Kaddish these days, to find out why she dislikes herself, he thought. *Maybe that's why she's breaking off from me. Maybe she doesn't think she deserves me? Oh, sure, you bet.*

As the melancholy music rose, he remembered how he had told Gloria, in an embarrassing but irresistible burst of self-pity that anticipated her refusal to marry him, that he wanted her to play the slow Vivaldi movement, now in exact time to the slowness of the freeway cars, at a memorial service after his death. "If I'm still alive," she had said with a laugh. "But I don't think I'll go to your memorial service. It would make me too sad. Besides, Nat, you're not going to die, not ever. Your ego wouldn't permit it." Despite his misery he couldn't help smiling, remembering her remark. *The bitch, the gentle lovely bitch.*

He went into the bathroom and took a leak, taking care that he flushed carefully and that no telltale drops had fallen to the floor. He noticed that one of his old gifts lay on her bathroom scales, the unabridged Webster's International Dictionary, weighing in at eleven pounds, and his glance then turned to the top of the toilet tank and a copy of another translation of Rabelais, also a gift, alongside a pair of Gloria's turquoise-rimmed reading glasses. He was pleased. Whatever she now thought of him, at least he was there in the form of his gifts, present in her most intimate moments.

Before zipping up, he held his cock, as if weighing his manhood. *Oh, boy, sixty-two, and still in the throes of adolescence*, he thought, marveling at the audacious mystery and misery of coming to Gloria's place in his smitten neediness.

The slow movement of Vivaldi continued to unfold as he moved into the bedroom with the cat following behind him still mewling. "Come on, Sara, you teaser, you Teasetail, let's try the bed," he said in a whisper.

He lay back, his mind lush with Vivaldi nostalgia and the remembered smell of Gloria's body. Their closeness in bed, their bodies in easeful sensuality, was one of the glories of their being together, when they were together.

His mind drifted back to those occasions, remembering the silkiness of her flesh and how he would let his hands glide for minutes and minutes millimeters above her forehead and nose and tits and vagina as if the surfaces were too fine to touch, before he touched her and touched her, while her hands, the hands that made those lovely drawings and spun Vivaldi on her piano, went over his body, through the curls of his body hair, in all the places, and then they would ease into each other's flesh, slowly, above and below, from hair to toes, in a fugue of hands and lips and belly and ass and cock and clitoris, the pace slowly hastening until they joined, closer and closer, her legs finally up over his shoulders in deepest closeness, and he would bend toward her, trying to penetrate even her lidded eyes and smile, until she would groan and begin to pulsate and his own body would start to throb so strongly it felt as if the next big earthquake had finally come, and they would lay back in each other's arms, the most delicious time of all, peaceful and content, their turmoil, care and age forgotten, as if all the slights of experience had vanished and a profound and lasting innocence was theirs.

He felt the purring of Sara under his hand. The music had stopped and in the quietness he heard a car draw up. He went to the window, and through the tangle of branches beyond the glass he saw it was Gloria's car. Her dog was jumping against the gate, eager to be let in.

21

He made it to the downstairs room, stumbling down the stairs, his blood pressure rising, feeling as if his heart would burst before he heard her key in the lock. He didn't dare open the window to let himself out, not yet. She might hear the noise, and Clara, her dog, would come yipping after him, always glad to see him, expecting the inevitable liver treat that he always brought on visits past. He had time just to slip in the wine closet before Gloria opened the front door.

He was flushed with panic, trying to ease his breathing, as he crouched against the racks of Robert Mondavi liters and Fetzer Premium White. He even remembered the complimentary bottle of Kenwood Red Gloria had sent to the bar after he followed her that day to Washington Square, and wondered in his wayward anxiety if there was any stored in the closet.

He heard the door close and Gloria bolting it shut. Then

there was the faint mewling of the cat, and for a minute, a dreadful minute, he thought Sara had followed him into the closet. No, the mewling was coming from the stairs, and he breathed easier until he thought of Clara and whether the wine smell in the closet would mask his own smell and keep her from sniffing him out.

Please, Clara, dear Clara, go to your water bowl. You're thirsty. Be a good dog, be my best friend. And you, Gloria, don't you have to go to the john? Go to the john, please. We senior citizens have to be careful of our bladders, and don't forget to flush. Please, a good, noisy flush.

He felt himself actually smiling, catching his breath. He felt exhilarated with his panic. What a time for exhilaration, he thought, and then, for no reason he could think of, the image of his dead mother, Esther Dorn, floated into his mind.

His mother's image seemed superimposed over Gloria's face, and he suddenly realized how much alike they looked— the broad face, the Slavic nose, the widely spaced eyes, the softness and silver of the hair, that same look of graciousness and dignity that masked their bawdiness, even more rambunctious in his mother's case. She was like his mother in so many ways, and come to think of it, his wife had been so much like his father. He wondered what Kaddish would make of it all.

His mother had died while he was in Europe in 1964 for the paper, covering the young revolutionaries, Tariq Ali and Bendit-Cohn and the like, seven countries in thirteen days, looking for a Berkeley and a Moscow connection, while AP and Reuters colleagues tried to line up some female comrades to get him laid, all else failing. Then he realized, yes, his mother would have loved the situation, the ridiculousness of it all, her son or not, and would have laughed uproariously. Laughter was always her way of dealing with disaster, that was one difference with Gloria. How he wished he could speak to her, laugh with her over this, once this was over, if it ever was.

He heard Gloria going up the stairs, the sound of Clara chomping on kibble, the beaded bathroom curtain being drawn back.

All was silent above. She was still in the bathroom. She must be reading, he decided. But he didn't dare risk leaving the closet until he heard the flush.

What could she be reading? Maybe The Standard? *No, she was taking too long. Maybe one of my gifts . . . that unexpurgated translation of Rabelais? At this rate it might be the eleven-pound unabridged dictionary. Gloria and her love of words! Idling on the seat, she could have flipped it open to the O's. O, Gloria, don't start with the P's,* he prayed. *Just a few more O's, please . . . Oxter, n. Scot. the armpit . . . Oy, interj. used to express dismay . . . Ozostomia, n. Med. bad breath . . .*

Finally he heard the metallic sound of the lever, the gurgling release of the flush. Before Gloria got to washing her hands, with the faucets going *whushhhh!*, he was out of the closet, and out the front door.

The phone was ringing when he got home. He could imagine who it was. He was right.

"Nathaniel, listen to me. Don't talk, just listen. I have half a mind to call the police and file charges against you. That would look nice in tomorrow's *Standard*, wouldn't it? I won't, but get this through your swollen, crazed head: I don't love you. If I ever loved you I don't love you anymore. I'm absolutely averse to you. You make my flesh crawl. I can't stand you, your ego, your meddling, your creepy ways. Stay away from me. Do you understand? Stay away." And she hung up.

Of course, he decided. *That was it. Of course, the tape in the machine. The machine was still on. And Vivaldi. And the unlocked front door. And my car. She could have seen my car across the street. Oh, dumb-ass that I am.* He wondered if she had noticed the diosma, at least. He could explain the visit. *It was innocent, after all. It came from love.*

He called her back. As soon as he said her name, she hung up. He called again. It was busy. She was calling the police or else she had taken the phone off the cradle.

He had ruined everything between them. But that wasn't the worst thing. Things got worse. And except for Kaddish, who got paid for the bother, there was nobody to talk to about his troubles except the dead. His father was first.

THREE

*I will consider the outnumbering dead: For they are
the husks of what was rich seed . . .*
                              —Geoffrey Hill *Merlin*

22

He kept trying to summon the dead but it was only after his son's arrest that the dead spoke to him.

The gazebo was the right setting for talking to the dead if the dead were ever going to talk to him, he had decided. The hexagonal marble slab turned face down in the middle of the gazebo was inscribed with Rachel's parting words, words that evoked what he considered a necessary devotional note for summoning the dead: *I love you! Don't grieve. Peace.*

But Golem had made a habit of using Rachel's gazebo as a crapper, especially on a misty day of this sort. Before he could begin he had to find a garden spade and scatter Golem's turds under the ivy leaves. Then he hosed down the gazebo floor while Golem got in the way, barking excitedly, trying to play with the spray. After he put the hose away he shut Golem in the house. Then he was ready to begin.

It was days before his mind was clear enough to try to talk to the dead in earnest. Gloria had dominated his thoughts more than ever. He tried everything he could think of to exorcise her from his mind after the debacle of the visit to her house.

He went to movies but kept thinking of her whenever his attention lagged, as it often did. He drank and got sick, he drank and got sicker, and it didn't help anyway. He drove through the night to the gambling tables of the Tahoe casinos, went without sleep playing poker, hoping the abstract

151

blur of the cards, round after round, would distract him from thinking of Gloria, but although a good player, he lost, lost heavily. His attention was not on the cards.

He wrote Gloria apologetic letters and tore them up after reading them to Kaddish. "Don't be so self-demeaning," Kaddish said. "Let her go. Maybe she'll come back, maybe she won't. But try and let her go or you'll go crazy."

"What can I do?" he had asked.

"Go back to the health club. Take a drawing class like you talked about. You'll meet other women there. Go out with other women. Maybe you'll finally forget Gloria."

Well, he had thought of going out with other women. After all those years he had thought of calling Cassandra, loopy, accessible Cass. He had even thought of a personal ad: *Growing, graying retired newspaperman seeks caring, sharing Bay Area woman* . . . But he had brushed the notion aside. With his luck, he thought, he'd probably get AIDS the first time he bedded another woman. *Forget other women.* His son's troubles had begun to make him forget.

His son had been arrested in San Mateo for shoplifting, he told Kaddish over the phone. Stan was in the Redwood City jail and had called to get bailed out. His son was crying, he told Kaddish. "I don't know what to do," he said. "They'll keep him there over the weekend if I don't make bail for him. I know he deserves to stay in jail, the bastard, after all my help. I don't know what to do."

"What's the bail?" Kaddish asked. "Can't your son raise it himself?"

"It's $500. He doesn't have that kind of money, and he doesn't have any friends. Ruthie says to let him rot in jail. All he has is me."

"What do you feel like doing, Nathan?"

152

"I don't know. It's just the weekend, then he can get out on his own recognizance. But I can't stand the thought of Stan being behind bars. It didn't help the last time he was in County Jail, years ago, and it didn't help me. My mind was behind bars with him every day for eight months."

"Oh, Nathan, what am I going to do with you?" said Kaddish. "You can be such an emotional addict."

"Well, maybe the dead can help," he said. He had tried everyone else.

In attempting to wake the dead he had followed, in his own way, the steps in the book Potter had mentioned. He took to heart the words of Ira Progoff, whose method it was, not to fall back on old patterns of exchange in talking to the dead or the living with whom a deeper understanding is being sought.

It was necessary to avoid the superficial and repetitious patterns of past conversations, the words that usually led only to frustration and anger. To get to what was in a person's heart it was imperative to heed "the words of the Prophet," as Progoff put it. *When depth speaks to depth between persons, that is dialogue.*

But Progoff had recommended writing the dialogues in a journal at a fast clip like automatic writing in a workshop setting with others who wanted to talk to "persons from the past, living and not living, who hold the potentials of an inner relationship with us."

He told Kaddish it was too much like being back in the City Room, that workshop, and he was bored with the written word, especially when journal writing of that kind was likely to be sloppy, helter-skelter, unprofessional.

"The next time you're here," Kaddish, ever the gestaltian, told him over the phone, "there's my chair. You'll sit and be your father. He'll talk through your mouth, only you'll be him."

"It's not enough," he said. Although he wasn't religious, a therapist's office, like a workshop, felt out of place for summoning the dead. Even a synagogue or a cemetery wouldn't do, he felt. The setting had to be right, familiar, natural for the living and the dead. "I'll find a way, my way."

"Good," said Kaddish. "I'm glad. Follow your own way. Use your own powers. That's what your son needs to do . . . Good luck with the dead."

It was the day before Rachel's birthday—sixty-two, if she had lived—that his father spoke to him.

At first he had wanted to talk to his dead wife about Stan. Sitting in her gazebo he had tried to bring her back to life but she remained invisible and silent despite his entreaties. She had enough with Stan in her life, he thought. Enough concern. Enough anxiety. Enough. With him it was different; he was still alive. The anxiety over Stan would probably persist until he or Stan was dead. Then his father came to mind— Ben Dorn, fifty, balding, lying under a red blanket in the back room of an apartment on Davidson Avenue in The Bronx, his hazel eyes closed, seemingly asleep forever.

Talking to himself aloud seemed silly at first. He was embarrassed, a man of sixty-two, Dorn of *The Standard*, obit expert, reporter emeritus, carrying on this way. Oh, if people like Terry Forman could see him! But nobody could see him. The lush angel trumpet bush and the fig tree by the side of the gazebo shielded him from view. His ancient cat, Gamel, now sitting on the stone fence underneath the angel trumpets, was his only audience. He relaxed as twilight came on and the dead came closer, out of the mist that lay beyond the

154

freeway, where the San Bruno mountains loomed. There, in that distance, Stan was waiting for him to come and bail him out.

"I can remember the room where you died, Daddy," he said. "I remember the color of the wallpaper, with yellow flowers, and the yellowness of your skin. There was a soft dead smell. It was the smell of cancer, I think. It filled the house."

He remembered the last day they had gone for a walk in the neighborhood before his father went to the hospital and then came home to die. His father was a fastidious dresser, befitting his apprenticeship to a fine London tailor long before emigrating to New York, and he had on, even for that walk in the middle of the Depression, a felt hat, an elegant heavy coat, pure woolen suit and highly polished cordovan shoes. Nathaniel—Nathan or Nate then—was wearing his best windbreaker and knickers as they moved slowly through the late afternoon of his memory. Every so often his father would start coughing, a hacking cough, and would stop under a tree by the curb, shaking like the leaves above, and spit into the gutter. He noticed that day that his father's spit was red.

In the gazebo he remembered what he knew of his father's early life: born outside Warsaw; emigrating to London with his widowed mother, his three sisters and his brother, Marvin; marrying Esther, the lovely Yiddish British flirt; having a son, Alfred, who died at eight of rheumatic fever and the seven other children who followed, Nathan the middle one; moving to America, to a farm in upstate New York that Esther's brother, Ed, now a real estate tycoon, owned; becoming manager of a sporting goods store on Fordham Road; then coughing out his life from cancerous lungs . . .

155

His mind roamed over the years that separated him from his father. It all passed before him: the trouble with Stan, Rachel, Reagan, Nixon, Watergate, Vietnam, his mother's death, the birth of his children, leaving New York, the Holocaust, Hiroshima, World War II, meeting Rachel, FDR, the Depression . . .

"I'm leaning over you . . ." he was saying. "Can you hear me? It's the same time as now, a late afternoon, a day in 1936. The light is dim in your room. Open your eyes and talk to me, Daddy."

Out of the mist beyond the freeway, across the miles and years that separated them, he saw his father as clearly as he saw his dusty white cat spring off the stone fence and return to her hiding place.

For a moment the figure before him, stretched out in bed, a sleeping face on a ghost-white pillow, was like someone seen in an old snapshot pasted in a tattered picture album. The face was vaguely familiar, the same family features of his own face, the faces of his children and the faces of his brothers and sisters, their children.

The figure, uncanny and ordinary, was still.

"Please, Daddy, speak to me," he said, knowing that moment he had touched a nerve of memory, a memory that had always been alive inside of him. "I need you, I need you."

Ben Dorn, fifty, dead almost fifty years, stirred. His hazel eyes trembled and opened. His sixty-two-year-old son had summoned him back to life, following the exact, proper, modern procedures of the psyche, ordained indirectly by ancient spiritual law.

"Speak to me, Daddy."

His father's voice had a slight British timbre to it, but it was shot through with the rough resonance of New York. He

156

leaned closer to make out the words. *Where is everyone?* his father was saying. *Who are you?*

He tried to answer but, at first, the words died in his throat. He tried to swallow. He was hoarse with astonishment. He took a deep breath and tried to answer again. Finally, the words came. "We're here alone," he said. "Just the two of us."

It's hard for me to see you.

He broke off some branches of the angel trumpet. He would have to prune the bush one of these days, he thought. Then he took another breath. "I'm Nathaniel, your son."

Nathaniel? I don't remember a son named Nathaniel. I have a son, Nathan.

"I'm Nathan. You know, or Nate, Nat, Nathaniel. Nathaniel Dorn. I'm a writer, it's a writing name. I'm your son, Daddy."

You? You're an old man.

"Just sixty-two."

Sixty-two? I'm fifty, and sinking fast. Where's Esther?

His father was asking about his mother, dead thirty years after he had died. And here he was, telling his dead father what had happened since that December day, almost fifty years ago. Future, past and present had merged in the dimming light.

Where's my Esther?

"She's dead, Daddy. Mama's dead. She died of—well, so many things, heart, diabetes..."

Why didn't somebody tell me?

"She died after you, Daddy. She was eighty-two."

He saw them again, in a faded film of memory, he as a boy and his father and mother, with the rest of the family, in their old apartment, sitting down to dinner, his mother hovering over the stove, bringing steaming mounds of potatoes and gravy, whatever she could buy those Depression days, more than many families because his father had a good job although sales of sporting goods were down, and all the kids boisterous, eager to get their plates filled, and his father irate at their greediness, suddenly shouting, "Keep this up, and nobody's going to have supper!" and his mother, looking over Daddy's turned head, making a face at them, with exaggerated, funny caution, as if saying, "Let's humor him."

I'm so glad she saw all of you grow. I never had a chance . . . What year is it, Nathan?

"It's 1985."

And Roosevelt? Is FDR still president?

"No, Daddy, Roosevelt is dead, so is Eleanor," he said, unable to withhold a smile. "There was another World War. The Nazis were defeated. Hitler is gone."

The Depression?

"It's over, the Depression is over . . . But it may come again."

So much has happened . . .

"That's why I'm calling you back, to tell you all this and to find out about you, my father, to ask your help with my own son."

So you're Nathan. Come close. Hold my hand. I'm cold.

He held his father's hand. "I'm glad you asked me," he said. "It makes me feel good to do this, holding your hand. I don't ever remember our being close like this."

You've got a bad memory, Nathan. I took you with me all the time. We used to take a tour boat to Rye Beach. We'd go to Radio City. I'd take you golfing with me in Van Courtlandt Park.

He thought of the time his father and Lonnie had left him abandoned at 42nd Street and Broadway, but he didn't men-

158

tion it, afraid that his father might take offense and fade from life. "I was your caddy when we went golfing," he said.

You were thinking of that time Lonnie and I left you on 42nd Street, weren't you, Nathan? It was a joke, a foolish joke. We meant no harm, but it was cruel. You were terrified. I'm sorry, my son.

He pressed his father's cold hand.

I was proud of you. I used to show you off at my sister's place on Riverside Drive.

"I mean our touching. That's what I missed, holding your hand like this."

His father sat up in bed. He adjusted the pillows for him. *I feel warmer*, his father said, taking his hand. *Oh, we used to hug and touch all the time. You were a cute boy. Are you trying to tell me I didn't love you?*

"I just don't remember. I remember mostly your anger. You had such a temper. You used to get so red in the face."

Well, it wasn't easy, with your mother and your sisters. A big houseful of children in the Depression, and Esther wasn't the best person to handle money and take care of a house. She'd rather draw and play with you kids. Do you remember how she loved to take bread crumbs and arrange them on the table in the figure of a doll or a duck?

"I remember . . ."

My Esther. She was a lovely woman, but she'd never have a hot supper ready when I came home from twelve hours in the store. And the trouble I had with your sisters and their staying out late with boys, hoodlums and nobodies. Look what happened to Helen, pregnant at sixteen from that hoodlum, what's his name?

"Dave."

That's the one.

"They're married. For forty-six years now."

That's hard to believe.

159

"Things turned out all right, Daddy. We managed. It was hard without you, but Mama and Lonnie kept things going."

She was such a lively one, that mother of yours, my Esther. And now she's gone. Oh, I loved her so much.

"She loved you, Daddy. She never remarried all those years."

That's also hard to believe. She enjoyed making love so much. She was so pretty and warm. You know, you're a man of sixty-two so I can tell you, when I was dying she came into my bed. We were together when everybody was asleep.

"Yes, she told me."

She told you that? Oh, that Esther of mine. Nothing was sacred to her.

"No, it was sacred. She just wanted me to know in no uncertain terms how much she loved you, how terrible it was when you died so early in your life."

And Rita and Janie?

"Janie calls herself Jill."

Jill? What kind of name is that? It's a nursery rhyme, not a name.

"She's all right, in wonderful health for seventy-one. She and Helen have great-grandchildren already."

So I'm a great-great-grandfather.

"Yes, Daddy."

And Rita?

He hesitated before answering. Then it dawned on him clearly, as if the dusk had passed into morning and the mist itself was clearing, that his father could read his thoughts. Nobody lies to the dead, he realized. They're beyond all dissembling. It had been one of the reasons he wanted to talk to the dead, to begin the move beyond self-deception. "I don't talk to her anymore. She was the first to enter Mama's room when she died. Rita stole all of Mama's jewelry. The rest of us got nothing." He trembled with the pain of the remembrance.

Oh, that Rita. She was so spoiled after our first son, your brother Alfie, died. Forgive her, Nathan. It's not worth your pain. Be kind to her.

He remembered Nelson's report of what Jesus Christ had said that drunken day at Nabuco's. Jesus Christ and Aldous Huxley and his father, Ben Dorn. The ultimate wisdom of the dead: Be kind.

And the babies, Dora and Paul? his father asked.

"Paul is fine. He's got kids, too . . . But Dora is dead. She died at thirty-three in an automobile accident, with her baby daughter."

He remembered his beautiful sister, her Hedy Lamarr looks at the time she was developing a line of her own cosmetics. She had been with Revlon as a product developer before starting her firm. Shrewd as well as beautiful, she had pretended at twenty-eight that she was middle-aged and her lipsticks and creams and eye shadows had made her look that young. Her success was phenomenal as well as notorious. Then, on her way home, after her doctor had told her she was pregnant again with an unwanted child, she was so upset on that icy road in New Jersey that she didn't see what was ahead . . . Poor Dora Doree. She had changed her name also.

My poor baby, Dora, his father was saying. *I used to love to have her sit on my lap when she was small. I'd run my fingers through her golden hair. She was beautiful, my Dora . . .* He made a dismissing motion with his hand, as if trying to dismiss death itself . . . *And, tell me, Lonnie and you?*

"Lonnie became very successful, an engineer with his own company. He's retired now."

And you, Nathan?

"I'm all right, Daddy. I'm retired, too."

I never got a chance to retire. All the time in the basement of that store. You're lucky, Nathan ... You're married, of course.

"She died, Daddy. Her name was Rachel. We were married thirty-five years. She was an extraordinary woman. You would have loved her. She was like you in many ways—the same honesty, direct like you, no fear ..."

Oh, I had fear. I had such a fear of death, leaving you all, leaving my Esther to take care of it all. He smiled, an ironic smile. *My child bride ...* His father reached for his hand. *You'll marry again. I wish your mother had. Get married, Nathan, it's no life alone.*

He was thinking of Gloria, and he knew his father knew he was thinking of someone named Gloria, *a shiksa*, as his father would say. "I've never been alone, Daddy. I'm trying it out now."

She's a shiksa, this Gloria. Why bother with her when there are so many good Jewish girls like your mother?

"Gloria's like Mama," he said.

Well, you've got plenty of time, and plenty of time to be alone when you're dead like me ... Nathan, how did you take it, my death? You didn't even cry for me.

He tried to remember. He was twelve, stunned, frightened and, maybe, underneath it all, relieved that this angry man, this angry man then, his father, was leaving them. Everybody around him was sad and weeping over Daddy, and his eyes were dry, then.

"I'm crying now, Daddy."

His father touched his arm. *Oh, Nathan, Nathan ...*

There were tears in Nathaniel's eyes. "And now I have a son, too, Daddy."

162

His father was silent for a moment. Then he spoke out of the depths of his dead innocence. *You've got a son, Nathan, who wants to be dead.*

23

The words were numbing. He felt dead himself. It was as if the words had turned his heart into a cemetery.

"Stan," he started to say, and took a deep breath. "He wants me to bail him out of jail."

He didn't want to mention to his father the shame of having a son behind bars, the first time it had happened in the family. But he didn't hesitate; his father could read his mind anyway. "It's not the first time he's been in jail."

It's not the first time for the rest of us Dorns or more than a few on your mother's side, his father said without elaborating. *And some of us were lucky. We should have gone to jail.*

He was curious to know what his father meant. But that was history. It could wait.

When you were children, we didn't talk about such things. We'll talk again, Nathan. I'll tell you then. Now you've got other things on your mind.

"I don't know what to do with Stan. Should I bail him out?"

Tuh vuss du moost toon biz du darsst es mehr nisht toon.

"I don't understand."

Do what you have to do until you don't have to do it no more.

It sounded more like what his playful mother might say, he thought, and then he thought again: How strange . . . how very strange . . . Yiddish was unknown to him, and yet the sounds of Yiddish and the meaning of the words were with him now, through time and distance, through the mouth of his dead father, who never spoke Yiddish as far as he could remember. Oh, maybe a word or two, a word like *shiksa*. But perhaps he had forgotten, or perhaps his mother and father, Yiddish and British, twice chosen, had spoken Yiddish behind closed doors. And perhaps all this was not a game, a serious game, his mind was playing. Perhaps he actually was talking to his dead father.

He could hear the telephone under the overturned silver bowl near the hot tub. The mist had turned to rain. As soon as he was conscious of the ringing and the rain, his father was gone. His eyes searched the expanse of watery twilight which now completely obscured the darkening mountains. There was no sign of his father.

He immediately felt the absence, the loss. His blood pressure was up, his heart pounding, but he breathed a little easier. The loss was not the old feeling of abandonment. The open moment with his dead father was enough for now. He felt sure his father would return.

The phone was still ringing when he got to the kitchen, shooing Golem away to get to the phone. It was his son. "They let me call again," Stan said, close to tears. "Please, come and get me. I can't stand it here."

He remained silent.

"Please," his son begged. "I'm afraid." He began to cry.

"What are you afraid of, Stan? You'll be out Monday, on your own hook."

Then his son broke off his weeping. He was shouting. "I

can't stand it, don't you hear? Don't you ever hear anyone else? You bastard, you bastard, I need you, I need you!"

He felt numbed by the outburst.

"Please, Daddy," his son was saying, now quietly.

He felt the numbness going, and he remembered his own words in the gazebo. *Please, Daddy, speak to me*...

"Help me, Daddy," Stan said. "It will be the last time. I never told you what happened when I was in jail before."

"Don't tell me, Stan. I don't want to know." He had his suspicions, it was the nightmare fantasy of gang rape that had weighed on his mind the last time Stan was in jail.

"This time it's worse," his son was saying. "I'm so afraid..."

"What is it, Stan?" He felt as if his breathing was about to stop. The apprehension weighed on his lungs. "Stan?"

"I'm afraid of what I'll do to myself."

He knew that what he was going to do was wrong. Kaddish would tell him that. So would Ruthie. So would his father. So would Gloria if they were still speaking to each other. It was easy for them to be right. But Stan was his son, not theirs. "Don't do anything, Stan," he said. "I'm on my way."

His eyes were on the freeway, staring through the swish of the windshield wipers, wary of disaster, intent on avoiding a sudden stop in the blur of cars ahead. He realized he should not have brought Golem with him. The dog's massiveness added to the danger. As if sensing Nathaniel's nervousness and despair, Golem had positioned himself in the passenger seat, nestled sympathetically against his thigh, massive head just avoiding the thrust of the gear shift. *I'm losing control of my life, first Gloria and then Stan,* he thought, *and now one wrong move and I can lose my life.*

Somehow the thought brought with it a sense of relief, that all the pain and worry could be over so quickly. But he tightened his hold on the wheel and lightened his foot on the gas. *Oh, Daddy,* he said aloud, *I'm not ready to die. I haven't finished, not yet.* He brushed the tip of his elbow against Golem's head, reassuring both of them of his desire to live. "My good dog, my friend," he said. Then he thought angrily of Potter's jibe about how the retired get goofy, holding intimate conversations with their dogs. *Fucking psychiatrists should have their heads examined. They just don't know the solace a dog can bring. Well, maybe Kaddish knows. She was against neutering Golem from the time Gloria suggested it.*

Watching the wet miles go by, he realized how hazy Gloria had started to become in his mind, now concerned with driving and Stan. *That's what it must take to forget Gloria, disaster.*

After telling Stan he was on his way, he had thought of calling Gloria or Ruthie. But he thought better of it. Ruthie wouldn't approve of what he was doing. He had no energy to argue. And Gloria did not want to speak to him, certainly not about Stan. She wouldn't be surprised that he had been arrested for shoplifting. The son, after all, of a man who had broken into her house . . .

Instead, he had called a bail bondsman to meet him, Nat Dorn, formerly of *The Standard*, at the Redwood City Jail. A little problem with his son . . . It would take not only the bail money but the deed of trust on his house as well, he was told. The deed was needed as added collateral that Stan would show up in court. The county merchants had pressured the authorities to make it as tough as possible on weekend shoplifters, the bail bondsman told him apologetically. "That's how it is, Nat," he said. "Your son, my son, it doesn't matter. But we'll get him out pronto, don't you worry. Just bring along the deed."

Damn, he had thought, *the fucking kid. The self-destructive bastard. He's destroying himself and trying to destroy me. It's crazy. I'm helping him and I can't help myself.*

In his anger he had stepped up the speed. The rain was pounding harder against the wipers. He slowed down. He was breathing heavily. "Get over on your side of the car," he snapped at Golem. "You're going to the pound if you don't watch out. The SPCA will fix you good."

Damn that Stan, he thought. *He's made me lose control of my life, my car, my house, and now he's got me shouting at my dog. Some damn fucking retirement this is.* Golem had remained where he was, his head nestled on Nathaniel's thigh. "It's all right, Golem," he said. "It's not your fault."

He put a cassette in the player slot. It was Glenn Gould and *The Goldberg Variations.* As the intricacies of Bach eased his mind, he wondered who Goldberg was and if he was Jewish and if Bach knew Yiddish. His father's words came to mind again. *Tuh vuss du moost toon biz du darsst es mehr nisht toon.* He heard his father's voice over the stereo hum of Gould accompanying himself. *Do what you have to do until you don't have to do it no more . . .*

He thought of the Dorns and his mother's side of the family and what his father had said about how some of them deserved to be in jail. And there was his own example, his craziness, breaking into Gloria's place, his newspaper invasions of privacy, the little embellishments to make a story more interesting . . . Maybe Stan was acting out the outlaw genes of the family past, like the genes that had stamped him at birth with clubfeet.

The image of Stan as a baby came toward him like a bright headlight of a car in the opposite lane. He remembered the photograph in the tattered family album he had found in the attic. That lovely baby, perfect despite the clubfeet, his face nuzzling toward Rachel's breast as she held her hand to shield the spray of mother's milk from his eyes, the moment he snapped the picture. There were casts on those tiny feet, casts that persisted through two operations. He could hear again, in the pounding of the rain and the whir of engines, Stan's cries in the night, cries alleviated only by the morphine of the hospital visits until, finally, the operations stopped, and their son's feet twisted into a shape like the clench of a fist, were as normal as they would ever be.

Oh, Stan, Stan. Once you were as innocent as the rain. Your poor feet made that innocence shine. Now you want to die, my father says.
Only rarely did he think of Stan's poor feet. Actually, Stan's feet were normal enough by now. Stan had to learn to stand on them. His feet were strong enough now to hurry off to flea markets with shoplifted goods. There was no sense making excuses for him anymore, Nathaniel had learned, or thought he had learned. *I'm not going to live forever to help him out of every jam that comes along. I want some peace, finally, to live my own life. I'm sixty-two. When is it going to stop? Oh, damn that Stan.*

The bondsman was waiting for him by the booking desk. "Hello, Nat," he said, smiling. "We'll have him out in a jiff." Nathaniel wrote out a check for $500, handed over the deed of trust, signed some papers, and waited. Then he saw Stan, huddled in a windbreaker as if trying to hide. "Thanks," Stan said, but he didn't answer. "I left the camper at the shopping center," Stan said. "Drive me there and I'll take it home." Nathaniel didn't answer until they were outside the jail in the rain. Then he said, finally, "You bastard, you bastard."

A week later, after he had fallen asleep and was dreaming of Gloria, there was a call.

In the dream, he was in the hot tub, looking through the vapor steaming over the rim, looking for a sign of his father. Then, drifting off to sleep in the tub, he found himself sinking under water and not concerned, as if he would find his father at the bottom of the tub. A poem began to form in his mind. The lines were in Yiddish.

Alles vuss ich hub ibbergehluzen . . .

Words from his father? It was unbelievable. But there were the words.

Ven ich hub mayne oigen far macht . . .

The lines were written in white on the darkness of his dreaming mind as he glided downward.

Iz varten farr dir
Ven du vacst oif . . .

And the translation, if not the meaning, came to him immediately.

All that I left behind
When I closed my eyes

Is waiting for you
When you awake . . .

There was a smile on his lips, the same smile he had seen on Rachel's face the morning he found her dead. He saw his body glimmering under the water, turning over and over, when he heard the phone above, near the rim, under the silver bowl, and he knew it was Gloria. "Nathan, we haven't talked in so long," she was saying. "I miss you. I miss your body near me in bed. Speak to me, dear Nathan."

But the call that woke him from the dream wasn't from Gloria. It was Stan. He was in jail again.

24

For seven days they mourned together. He sat *shiveh*, the ancient ritual of mourning, for his father. And together he and his dead father sat shiveh for a son and a grandson. They mourned his loss to them and to himself as if he had died the death he seemed to want.

Stan, charged again with shoplifting, this time in San Francisco had called a halfway house to help him leave jail on his own recognizance. The house couldn't take him in, not in that condition, two days into withdrawal from heroin. Maybe in seven days, he was told, if he was still alive.

The liaison man from the halfway house offered to drop him off at a hospital. Later, Nathaniel learned, his usually gentle son had told the man they could keep the fucking hos-

170

pitals. Hospitals had fucked him up enough since he was a kid. He would make it home himself. He took a few milligrams of methadone that another inmate gave him before he started out that evening.

He had walked, stumbling, carrying a brown bagged bottle of vodka like some Sixth Street bum, stopping in doorways for a swallow and to dispel the chill of cold sweat that beaded his face, nodding but unable to sleep, shaking all the way from City Jail, stumbling all the way home, his windbreaker zippered against the wind, stopping to piss the vodka away, his eyes burning from lack of sleep.

His only rest was for an hour on a discarded cot he found in back of the Galleria at the bottom of the hill. Someone punier was occupying the cot, and Stan summoned all his energy and anger to chase him away. An hour later, he had to take a piss and, in that instant, the earlier occupant of the cot materialized and hobbled off, dragging the cot with him. Stan chased the cot man, then gave up and turned toward the hill, stumbling and shaking, for the steep ascent home.

Nathaniel had heard Golem baying in the early morning hours. But he was tired from his own sleepless night, worried over Stan, determined not to bail him out again. He let the dog continue to moan until the sounds faded and he slept fitfully.

Golem was at the front door, baleful eyes staring up at him, when he went to get the morning paper. There, by the fold of the paper, slumped against the rail of the stairway landing, was his son, sweating, shivering, dazed.

"Stan," he said quietly, in a daze himself, not thinking of what he was saying, "you should have rang."

He managed to drag Stan into the house and, shooing

171

Golem away, get him into the book-lined den. He fussed with the windbreaker zipper, shirt buttons, belt, shoelaces. He removed the clothes and dropped them in a black plastic bag.

His son lay sprawled out on the red comforter he had thrown over the couch. He was struck by the moonlight paleness of Stan's body. Half dead, in a cold sweat, still shivering, Stan was like a being from another world, a world of his own. Nat found a pillow, a blanket, then another blanket and covered Stan. He sat on the edge of the couch, listening to Stan's troubled breathing.

His eyes strayed from his son to the bookshelves along the walls, holding the wisdom of the ages and the detritus of the times. *The Bible in Modern English*, Homer, Shakespeare, Rabelais, Pascal, Proust, Wilder, Michener, Mailer, Bellow, some of the volumes he had planned to read in his retirement, lay within reach. He reached out and pulled down a paperback called *Tolstoy's Bicycle*, which purported to be a compendium of human history, grouping "all moral achievement... by age from birth to death." At sixty-seven, the cover blurb told him, Tolstoy had his first bicycle lesson. Another volume, *100 American Things*, contained a poem by Whitman, *Give Me The Splendid Silent Sun*, a jejune effort he couldn't recall reading.

> *Give me for marriage a sweet-breathed woman of whom I should never tire,*
> *Give me a perfect child, give me, away aside from the noise of the world, a rural domestic life,*
> *Give me to warble spontaneous songs recluse by myself, for my own ears only,*

172

Give me solitude, give me Nature, give me again, O Nature,
your primal sanities!

Jejune or not, the lines had a calming effect. *A sweet-breathed woman and a perfect child. Primal sanities. Amen.*

He closed the book, put it back on the shelf and then closed the door of the den after him.

Nathaniel called Potter, his psychiatrist friend, who said he would hurry over, then put the kettle on for some herbal tea, the only tea he could find in the storage closet, Joy in the Morning. Spooning Joy into a tea strainer and thinking of the brand name's inappropriateness, he smiled a glum smile despite his racing heart. His own inappropriate remark came back to him: *Stan, you should have rang.* Inane or, more aptly, ordinary, he thought as, cup of Joy in hand, he stared out the kitchen window at the grayness of the morning.

The remark reminded him of the time at work he had phoned the family of a Golden Gate leaper, the 300th or 400th off the bridge. A feature suicide.

He had gotten the mother of the leaper. "Are you sure it's my son?" she had asked. "Did he really jump?" Nathaniel assured her that the police report said so. He politely offered his condolences and asked about her son. What was he like, the 300th or 400th leaper, the feature suicide? But the leaper's mother couldn't believe her son had actually jumped. "He was never the athletic type," she said.

Stan, you should have rang . . . the ordinary, heart-breaking hilarity of it all.

Then he thought: *What craziness. Here my son may be dying. His own fault, but dying. And I go on smiling and reminiscing . . .*

173

Potter had come and gone. He had given Stan Darvon for pain and chloral hydrate to help him sleep. "He's in withdrawal," he told Nathaniel, who half-listened, knowing Stan was back on hard stuff but not wanting to believe it, not even now.

"He's been taking methadone and heroin and vodka," Potter was saying. "He hasn't eaten for days. The booze helped and probably kept him from dehydrating. I've given him some vitamins . . . We should move him to Cedars, if he can be moved, but he wants to stay. He mumbles about wanting to die and wanting to be here or downstairs."

"He can stay here, not downstairs," Nathaniel said. "I took away his keys the first time he got arrested. That was last week. I looked down there. I found a spoon, a needle. I didn't want to believe it. Oh, damn him."

"I'm worried about you, Nat. You're all worked up. You need some pills for sleep. And you shouldn't be alone, not with him. Withdrawal can be terrible. He'll start shouting and worse."

"So he'll shout. Shouting goes with being a Jew. But I don't want any damn pills in the house, not even for me. And I'm not alone." He was thinking of his father. He wanted to tell Potter that it was working, all that talk about bringing back the dead. But he decided against it. He had the feeling that talking to the dead should have put him into a more serene and spiritual mood. If it had, any serenity had fled with the real-life appearance of his son. No, if anything the dead had left him with anger and dread, his father's old anger and a dread of Stan. It wasn't the time to tell Potter. "I'll be all right," he said.

"I'm worried about your heart."

"Don't worry about my heart. That's the trouble, I may

174

have too much heart." He siged, then clenched his teeth against his lower lip. "Tell me, has anyone seen Gloria?" *A five buck question.* His grim expression edged into a smile.

"She's fine. Looks great," Potter said. "I saw her at a little party Doris had."

Well, Doris didn't invite me, he thought. *Couples divide, and old friends divide up, too. Not that I could have gone to the damn party, not with Gloria going and all the trouble with Stan . . . damn Stan . . . and damn Gloria. Damn her great looks. And damn my heart.*

"I'll be back," said Potter.

He called Ruthie at Golden Gate but her phone was busy. He waited a few moments and called again. Still busy. *And damn telephones.* He called Gloria. Her voice sounded hesitant. "Hello . . . hello . . . ," she said. He hung up. He called Ruthie again. Before he could say a word about Stan she was into a monologue about the house next door, how they could finance it with good cash flow for him, how it would make retirement even more enjoyable from the money end, and how they would be close and would share occasional dinners and taking care of each other's animals when they were away . . .

"Stan's home," he said when she ran out of breath.

"Oh?"

"He looks like he's dying."

"Oh, Daddy."

"I don't know what to do."

"Get him to a hospital."

"He can't be moved. I called Potter. He did what he could. Stan's sleeping, I think. Or maybe he's faking just to stay here. I don't know."

175

"Just let him sleep . . . You can't do anything if he wants to kill himself. I can't come there today. I have a conference. I'm flying to Los Angeles in an hour. I'll be home tomorrow. Tomorrow . . . Daddy?"

"I'm here."

"Daddy, take care of yourself. Remember your heart. I love you."

"Yes, Ruthie, I know," he said. "It will be good to have you living close to me."

While his son remained in the den, lost to him if not dying, Nathaniel's father came unbidden. He was sitting in the pale shadow of the gazebo when he heard his father's voice.

Give him up for dead, Nathan. He's not worth your worry, and concern.

He shut his eyes. He tried not to hear.

If you were a devout Jew, his name would be a curse. He would be forgotten. Give him up for dead.

The night and his heart were chilled enough. His father's words made him feel colder.

Give him up for dead, Nathan.

"No," he said.

Forget him, Nathan.

"He's my son."

A son, yes . . . There was a sadness in his father's voice.

"Daddy?"

I was thinking of my sons. You and Lonnie, the oldest. I was thinking of the day I died.

"I was in your room, Daddy."

The two of you, the oldest, you never sat shiveh for me.

"Shiveh?"

Some Jew you are. The seven days of mourning for the dead. The mourners, sons especially, mourning and remembering. You've even forgotten the word. You didn't cry, and you forgot.

"I'm sorry we didn't sit shiveh for you. Forgive me, I was not even twelve, not even bar mitzvahed."

I forgive you, Nathan. I didn't mean to speak so harsh. Of course, I forgive you.

"And I never forgot you. You're here. I remembered. I brought you back."

Don't make yourself such a big shot. I came back.

"I don't need your anger. Let's not argue. It was your anger when I was a boy that made me afraid of you. It made me want to forget you... Now I just want to sit here with my thoughts of Stan."

So we'll sit, Nathan. I'm not angry. All the anger's gone out of me. For the dead, there's no anger... Come, boychik, we'll sit together. You'll sit shiveh for me. It's never too late. And we'll sit shiveh for your son. You'll tell me about him, my grandson. You'll tell me about all I missed, his childhood, his innocence, the good things...

"There are good things. He's not just drugs and stealing. That's why I can't write him off."

We won't argue, Nathan. We'll sit here and talk about him if it will make you feel better.

"I'd like that."

Good. We'll even talk to him, my grandson.

"Talk to him?"

To his soul, like you're talking to me. It's possible, even while he's sleeping.

"Dying, maybe."

Dying, yes, of course.

177

"Don't talk angry to him."

No, of course not. I tell you I'm not angry, Nathan. I'm not angry no matter what a gonif he may be. Besides, nobody talks angry to a soul, not a lost soul. But first, boychik, tell me about your son, my grandson, all the good things . . .

So they talked. They talked until he fell asleep. There were many good things they talked about, things as innocent as another dawn. Then a sudden wind woke him up. His father was gone. And, still sleepy, he went to bed.

Stan began shouting after the second day.

Nathaniel opened the den door and glanced at the screaming addict who was his son, this figure on the red comforter with straggly beard, puffy eyes from lack of sleep and forehead beaded with cold sweat. The look on his son's face was the same agonized expression he remembered when Stan was a baby with casts on both legs, trapped then by clubfeet, trapped now by drugs. His face was like a scream. The chilling pierce of his agony, joined by Golem's baying until Nathaniel put the dog in the backyard, seemed to muffle the freeway noises outside along the bend near County Hospital. Usually to accustomed ears the freeway traffic made a sound like the motion of the sea, a comforting sound that bathed the air. Nathaniel was grateful for the isolation of the cul-de-sac where he lived, looking across the Mission toward Twin Peaks. Stan had to scream, he knew. Stan might even get violent in his withdrawal from heroin, Potter had told him.

"I need something," Stan was shouting. "Get me some vodka or some pills. Call that damn doctor friend of yours. He should be here. I need something, something . . ."

Potter finally came with Darvon and chloral hydrate, and

Stan's shouts were replaced by crying. "Daddy, I'm sorry. I'm sorry...I've hurt you so much. I didn't keep my word..." And eventually he slept.

"Has he eaten?" Potter asked.

"Not a thing."

"Maybe tonight or tomorrow. Some ice cream or juice, even a Coke. They seem to need the sugar... He's in bad pain, Nat. Kicking heroin is not easy. Things will get worse."

"It's all right. I'll be here."

"Believe me, Nat, he should go to a hospital. He may get violent. It's for your sake, too."

"I'll stick it out."

Before leaving, Potter told him that he had spoken to Gloria on the phone. "She asked about you."

"Did you tell her about Stan?"

"Yes, I did."

"I wish you hadn't." He drew the blue robe he was wearing tighter, as if trying to shield himself from embarrassment. "I don't need her sympathy."

"She still cares for you, Nat."

He stared at Potter, wonderd if Gloria had told Potter about the break-in. Was he now the subject of jokes among his friends? Black Nat, the Lovesick Burglar?

"I have more important things to worry about," he said. But he resolved to call her as soon as Potter left and he was sure Stan was asleep. She did care for him in spite of everything. Her words in the garden, said so long ago, it seemed, came back to him: *Try not to give up on me, and I won't give up on you, no matter what happens.* And he thought: *She meant it, she must have meant it.*

Potter turned to leave.

"I'm grateful to you," Nathaniel said. "You don't have to do this. I could call some other doctor... I'm just so damn embarrassed."

Potter embraced his old friend. "Look, we're Oofty Goofties. This is what friends are for."

As soon as Potter left he went to the cordless phone in the kitchen to call Gloria, but he hesitated when he saw streaks of grime on the white phone. He wondered if Stan had gone to the kitchen while he was sleeping or mourning in the gazebo with his dead father. Perhaps his son had tried to call one of his damn drug contacts. He felt his breathing come in gasps as he wiped off the phone grime with a wet paper towel. *Damn. Maybe my father is right. Maybe I should write my son off for dead. Kick him out of the house. Let him sink or swim. Let go, as Kaddish wants me to do. Let go of them both. Stan. Gloria. If she's so interested in how I am, let her call me. The phone works both ways...*

He picked up the phone again. He held it tightly, his fingers feeling the trace of wet. He was not ready to let go, he thought. Then as he started to dial he heard a cry from the den. He put the phone down. Gloria could wait. She could call him. He went to the den door. He heard Stan whimpering. After a while the moaning faded. He opened the door enough to see that Stan seemed to be asleep. Then he remembered he had locked Golem outside in the backyard. He went to let the faithful beast back in.

That night, while he lay asleep, Nathaniel talked to the soul of his son. It was as if he was dreaming. A dialogue with a lost soul is possible, his father had said. It was as possible as a dream and as filled with impossibilities.

180

In the apparent dream, Nathaniel was sitting in the den on the edge of the couch where Stan had been trying to sleep. Books lay in piles around him as he thumbed through the pages of one volume after another. He was reading aloud from *Tolstoy's Bicycle*, a passage about Thomas Jefferson at the age of thirty-three, Stan's age, being chosen to help write the *Declaration of Independence*. "And listen to this, Stan," he was saying, "at the same time he is busy drafting the state constitution of Virginia."

But Stan wasn't listening. Instead, as his father read, Stan was shooting up. He was holding a lit candle under a spoon which contained a small glasslike rock. Then there was a syringe in his grip and he was searching for a vein. Nathaniel looked at him briefly, then looked away as Stan plunged the needle into his arm. He continued to read aloud. "Elizabeth Taylor is only eleven when she plays in *Lassie Come Home*, only twelve in *National Velvet*," he was saying.

Big deal! Stan shouted, the needle no longer visible. He was standing up, then jumping as if trying to rock his father off the edge of the couch. Nathaniel remained unmoved, his back to all the commotion. "Mozart's first compositions are written when he is five," he was saying.

Then Stan was crouching behind him, reading over his shoulder: *Charles Bronson loses his virginity in 1926 at five to a girl of six*.

Nathaniel put the book down. "Let's talk, Stan."

Suddenly Stan was under the covers, seemingly asleep.

"Talk to me, Stan," Nathaniel said. "You're hurting. I want to help. I don't know how."

I'm so tired.

"Try, boychik. I don't know what to do. My father says to

give up on you. He says to think of you as dead. I can't." A tear formed in his eye, a tear the size of the glasslike rock in Stan's teaspoon.

I can't help you. I can't help myself. I want to sleep. I want to die. Give up on me. It's such a weight, your worry.

"I love you, Stan."

Your love. It's a weight. Let me be. Let me go.

"I can't."

Do what you have to do.

"I have to talk."

Oh, Daddy, you and your talk. All that talk. All my life I hear your talk. I can't get away from it. Only when I'm stoned. Only when I sleep. Oh, damn your talk. He pulled the covers over his head to keep out his father's talk.

Nathaniel recoiled in his sleep as if his son had struck him.

Then Stan looked out from the fold of the cover. *There, I've hurt you again, Daddy. See? How many times do I have to go on hurting people who love me? It's useless. All your talk is useless. Let me be. Let me die. I don't know what to do with myself except to die.* He was sitting up in bed now, staring blankly at his father.

"You could stop all this craziness, Stan, the drugs, the stealing. You're a smart fellow, a handsome man, a good man, even now. Look at the way you talk to me. Sure, it hurts, but you're honest."

Stan laughed but there was no sound to the laugh. *Oh, Daddy. You're always ready to think the best, to hope for the best. You don't care how much misery you set yourself up for. Give up. Live your own life. Let me die.*

"That's stupid talk. I'm not going to let you die if I can help it. I care for you, and I don't care if you don't care. I care."

Stan laughed again, again a soundless laugh. *You're nuts,*

182

Daddy. You're the one who's talking stupid and crazy. At least I know myself. I wanted to be a dope fiend. I enjoyed it — the high, the running around, the excitement, looking for who's got the good stuff, the stealing, that was exciting, too, like a crazy dream, carrying a cassette player or a camera out of a store, nobody seeing me, like I was invisible, and me just hearing the silence, a droning, until I was in the camper, the terror gone like magic . . . I can't stop. Only getting caught and getting sick stopped me. But I can't stop. I can't.

"Stan, you did once. You were clean for five years. You had a business. Five years.

I did it for you, for Mama. And what did she do?

"Please, Stan . . ."

She saved up her pills, her painkillers, and killed herself. She left you and Ruthie and me. I'm not blaming her. She was in terrible pain. She knew it was pointless, those operations. She just wanted to end the pain. I respect her, don't you?

"Of course—"

Then respect me when I say I want to die.

"Your mother was old. She lived a life. You're young. You can stop what you're doing and build a good life for yourself."

It's not that simple. I thought I could stop. I keep trying to stop all the time. I know the harm. I've seen guys die from it. It's like the song says: Every junkie is like a setting sun . . . I've seen the needle and the damage done.

"Stop, Stan."

I can't. It's the only way to escape the pain. Hey, it's nothing for you to be ashamed of. You didn't wish me my clubfeet, that pain. You didn't wish that I couldn't make friends because I couldn't play when I was a kid. I gave my hand but it was spit on. I have all this bitterness inside of me. I once wrote a poem about it. Sure I write poems, too, Daddy.

183

A hand extended,
it falls limp with time.
A voice cries out in darkness
but no one answers
for no one cares to listen.
At last a tear comes and falls.
It breaks upon hitting the ground
for when the air is very cold
things freeze and become brittle . . .

"It's a good poem, Stan."

There was another needle in Stan's grip. He was shooting up again. *Ahhh*, he said. Then the needle was gone. *The poem? Oh, Daddy, it's crap. Self-pity. No connection with anybody or anything. The only thing I'm good for is being a junkie, a nice quiet Jewish junkie even a father might be proud of. A dope fiend with insight, stealing just from stores, not from people. Not one of your hooked, hope-to-die, needle in arm, blood running down, head sunk low, accident-prone junkies. No, if I was going to o.d. it would be because I wanted to. A thinking man's junkie.*

"Please, Stan, stop it. I don't want to hear it."

Then let me be, Daddy. No more of your worry, your hope. No more, damn it, no more. No more!

Stan had stood up again on the couch and was jumping with all his might. Nathaniel could feel the coils of the couch exploding under him as the couch shook with the pounding of his son's feet. *Whomp, whomp*, went the springs. He caught a look of glee in his son's eyes, a cruel ecstasy. *Whomp, whomp*, he was out of control. His own world was out of control. His world was exploding.

* * *

The crash shook the house. It was like an explosion. Golem was pawing him, his body cringing. He could hear Stan in the den. He was cursing and laughing. "All these fucking books," he was shouting. "I was looking for the light. All the books came down on me. Your damn books! All the bookcases. They could have killed me. Daddy, they could have killed me." And he was laughing, a high-pitched, deadly laugh.

That morning Nathaniel called Potter who arranged to have an ambulance take Stan to a psychiatric facility in Martinez. Stan had wanted to linger in the warmth of the hot tub. "I'll be all right," he was saying. "Let me stay here, I feel better in this heat. Let me sweat out the drugs. Then I can go to the halfway house. Let me stay."

The ambulance attendants had to wrestle with Stan in the tub. "Damn you, Daddy!" he shouted as he was carried, slithering and kicking, out of the house, then tied to a gurney in the ambulance and driven away.

Golem had run off while the front door was open, and Nathaniel wandered along the cliff of the cul-de-sac, shouting after him, watching the ambulance turn the corner. His heart was pounding. Finally he caught sight of Golem trying to hump a growling cockapoo half way up the block. "Damn it, Golem," he said, "this isn't the time for that sort of shit. Come on, back in the house!"

When they got back to the house, Golem trudging tardily behind, he found his father in the kitchen at the table, as if waiting for his morning tea, like in the old days, a good English breakfast tea with cream, glowing orange through the wavering steam of the cup.

"You saw?" Nathaniel asked.

I saw. I was there all the time. Give him up. It's for the best. Let go. It's the one bit of advice your dead father can give you. Let go, boychik.

Later, when she finally phoned, back from Los Angeles, Ruthie said the same thing.

But he was not ready to agree or disagree. He felt queasy, like he wanted to throw up. The dream, the talk with Stan's soul had left the bad taste in his mouth. His face was burning. He felt he could not talk to anybody about how he felt, not Kaddish, not Ruthie, not even the dead. "Here, Golem," he said, crouching low so the dog could lick his hot face. "I have only you and you have only me, a crazy master of sixty-two, gone in the head, who talks to the dead." Then he pushed Golem's massive head away. "Oh, Golem, I've got to wash you. You smell of shit." Then he hugged Golem, stroking his rump. "But it's good lively honest shit, and that's not nothing."

Talking to Golem, hugging him, even the whiff of honest shit, made him feel better. No, he thought, he might be ready to let go but he was not about to give up, not on his son, not on Gloria, not on himself. But it was so hard, this holding on and letting go.

Through the kitchen window a few evenings later he saw the image of his father. As he watched, the image receded toward the gazebo. The back door was open and he followed with Golem behind him. His father was in the gazebo, his figure crouching, his head covered with a black shawl, and he was swaying in the soft breeze that had come up. As Nathaniel came closer he saw that Gamel had come out of her hiding place and was sitting calmly on the stone fence beside the

186

gazebo, her tail moving like a charmed cobra while his father prayed that seventh evening of their mourning.

> *My God, his father was chanting,*
> *the soul You gave me*
> *is pure . . .*
>
> *You caused my soul*
> *to come into being,*
> *You breathed its spirit into me,*
> *and it is You*
> *who keeps it alive . . .*
>
> *I thank You,*
> *O God my Lord,*
> *God of my fathers,*
> *Lord of all good,*
>
> *Sovereign of souls.*
>
> *O God,*
> *blessed are you*
> *who restores souls*
> *to the dead . . .*

When his father's words faded, Nathaniel spoke. "Teach me, Daddy, to let go," he said. But his father was gone. His words hung in the air like an unanswered prayer.

25

Or, perhaps, a prayer was being answered.

After a week, he visited Stan in the Kaiser psychiatric facility at Martinez. Stan was watching the big screen TV in
the recreation room along with a score of other patients,
equally divided in gender and mostly out-of-control alcoholics. They all seemed pleasantly sedate and sedated as they
watched the 49ers playing the Los Angeles Rams. The only
thing strange about the knot of casually dressed football fans
was that they seemed singularly calm.

Stan, finally detoxified of drugs, looked well. He even
gave his father a hug. "I'm so glad to see you, but I wouldn't
blame you if you'd stayed away. I know how I've been—"

"Oh, come off of it, Stan," Nathaniel said. "Just take care
of yourself, that's enough."

"I behaved like a shit."

"It's okay, Stan."

"No, it's not okay."

"All right, blame yourself if you feel like it."

Stan looked at him. "Well, I don't want to argue, I'm just
glad you're here..."

They went to the ward's kitchen and Stan made his father
coffee and talked about when he first got there. "I was hoping
it would be a tall building," he said. "I would have jumped
off."

"Please, Stan..."

"It's all right, I'm not going to kill myself."

"That's good, Stan. I need you. You know, when you

188

talked about suicide the last time I thought how the Nazis killed six million Jews and here you were thinking of killing yourself. It was like you were going to do the Nazi's work for them."

"It's not so simple. The Jews who were killed, they had *their* pain. My pain was my pain. I was only thinking of freeing myself from pain, and you, too. I thought you wouldn't have me as a problem anymore if I killed myself—"

"And now?"

"The hospital here wasn't high enough ... I don't know why I don't think that way lately. Oh, I thought if I did jump off a building, somebody might call you and tell you to come and pick my body up. I actually thought of you having to scrape my body off the sidewalk."

They were both silent, then Stan spoke. "Forgive me."

"I forgive you," said Nathaniel. "Of course I forgive you." He hesitated. "And, Stan, if I've somehow failed you, forgive me."

Tears were in Stan's eyes. "There's nothing to forgive you for, you're a damn good father." And to himself, I love you, Daddy.

So he had forgiven Stan, or so he said, but he knew that unquestioned forgiveness, forgiveness without hesitation, without glibness, without an "of course," would take time.

"Think about it," Stan said as if reading his thoughts. "Real forgiveness may take time."

Later that week Stan phoned to say he was leaving the hospital. Now that he was free of drugs, he had been accepted by Emerson House, the halfway house named after the Sage of Self-Reliance.

"You've been to a halfway house before," Nathaniel said.

"What makes you think it will work this time?" As soon as he said it he regretted it. *Why be so negative? Stan was trying, wasn't he?*

"Maybe it won't work," Stan said. "I don't know. It's just that I'm getting older and tired. I'm tired of what I've been doing and I don't have any more chances left. I know that."

Outside Emerson House, formerly a Catholic home for wayward young ladies, was a sign that told addicts, "Today is the first day of the rest of your life."

The possible start of a new life for Stan, however tentative and shaky those first steps might be, was the only good news in the weeks that followed.

Otherwise, disasters small and large continued. They seemed to come in series, like newspaper accounts of mass murderers.

The pilot light to the water heater kept going off, and his tenant, the pastry chef, threatened to leave unless it was fixed immediately. Nathaniel burned his right hand trying to light the pilot and had to go to Cedars of Tabor to have the second-degree burns treated. No sooner was his hand out of a bandage when a drunk driver barreled down the cul-de-sac one night, hit his camper that was parked near the iron fence, ricocheted off the bumper and crashed into his car parked in the driveway. Then he lost his wallet or someone picked his pocket. His license was gone, and now he had to get a temporary permit. But most irksome of all was that credit card charges he hadn't made started showing up, and he had to wait for cards with new numbers to replace the missing plastic. He began to wonder what disaster would strike next. Maybe an IRS audit. Maybe Golem would run away.

* * *

The downest time of the months without Gloria, the week from Christmas through New Year's, came and went.

Previous Christmases had been spent with Gloria's daughter, Maria, in Mill Valley. She had a three-year-old son, Ron who enjoyed the paper gliders he made that sometimes lasted five minutes. Ron called him Oom-pah-pah. It seemed to be the closest he would ever get to being a grandpa.

There was a New Year's Eve party given by one of *The Standard's* veteran single women that he was invited to. He thought of taking Cassandra, lusty, loopy Cass who had almost bedded him the night of Rachel's garden-wake. But just the thought of coping with Cass was a turn-off. *No, for better or worse, I'm saving myself for Gloria,* he thought, and didn't even smile as he thought it. Where Gloria was concerned he was dead serious, which, he did sometimes realize, was part of the trouble. Instead, after calling Gloria to wish her a happy year and finding her not at home, he went to a horror movie, something about a man whose fingers were knives and killed everyone he touched. Back home, he looked for Golem in his closet, found him, drank too much brandy and fell asleep before midnight.

For a short while, life returned to normal.

26

"I'd feel happy if I didn't feel so awful," he told Kaddish.

"Why would you feel happy?"

"Oh, Stan, I guess. He's safe for now. I can relax a little."

"Good . . . And why do you feel awful?"

He allowed a sigh.

"That's a deep sigh, Nathan. Let me hear you sigh some more. A good sigh . . . Let the air out."

He did.

"Tell me about your sigh, Nathan."

"Tell you?" He laughed.

"A sad laugh," she said.

He shrugged. "Gloria," he said. "That's what the sigh's all about."

"Why Gloria? There are other women, Nathan. How long has it been since you went to bed with a woman?"

"Too long," he said, and the inferred pun brought a hint of a smile to his lips. "I mean too long a time."

"I know what you mean, Nathan," she said. "It does get long, doesn't it?"

Dear Kaddish, she doesn't miss a thing . . .

"And yet you hold on so tight," she continued. "Why her? Why Gloria?"

Yes, why? Gloria made him think of his mother. Sort of. Rachel had made him think of his father. Sort of. Was that it, some family resemblance? But they were also so different, and the differences seemed even more alluring than the similarities. So who had the answer, and what was the question?

"You know Gloria," he said. "She's your client, too. You see her. She's lovely. She's lovable. She's also impossible. But can't I want her?"

"Let go, Nathan, you know how crazy it's making you."

"*My* addiction."

"Yes, and you know what you have to do with a habit like that."

"That's what my father says," he said without thinking.

192

"What does your father say?"

Oh, Kaddish, she's a cool one. Talk to the dead? Fine. She's not one to make fun of my mishegas. Whatever works. Dear Kaddish, rescuer of dead souls.

"Like what you say . . . Let go." He smiled. "It's easy for the dead to say let go. It's easy for you . . . Only he doesn't charge."

Kaddish smiled back. "Good, Nathan. Now that's a good smile. And it's good advice, your father's advice . . . Tell me, does it embarrass you? I mean, talking about talking with your dead father . . . It shouldn't. We all carry our dead fathers in us. And our dead mothers. The dead who mean something to us . . ."

"No, I'm not embarrassed, not talking with you about it." He heard himself sigh again.

"Let go, Nathan."

"I can't, even now, even after all that's happened. I can't believe it's over with Gloria." *Letting go, it was giving up*, he thought. *I can't give up.*

"It's over, Nathan."

"Does she say so?"

Kaddish, therapist and Dutch Aunt, hesitated, made a risky decision. "She says so. I'm only telling you this to save you grief. I don't want to see you go crazy."

"No," he said. "She may say so, and you may believe it. I don't."

"Why don't you?"

"Her hostility against me. It's so intense. I can't believe that with all that feeling, so averse, *her* word, that she still doesn't love me. I can't believe it."

"So don't, Nathan. Call her yourself and find out. Do what you have to do."

"She doesn't want me to call."

"So? You're one to take 'no' for an answer? That doesn't sound like you . . . All I can say is do what you have to do."

"You sound more and more like my father." *Do what you have to do until you don't have to do it no more*, his father had said.

"Listen to your father," she said.

But he had to listen to himself, he knew.

He called Gloria as soon as he got home. Of course he felt apprehensive, it was so difficult to know how to talk to Gloria these days, and as the rings continued he hoped she wouldn't answer. Then, on the fourth ring, he heard her voice. "You've reached Gloria Dell," her voice said, "but I'm away now, and I'll call you back as soon as I can. Please leave a message at the sound of the beep."

He called again, first to listen to the sound of her voice, then, at the sound of the beep, he thought of her code and pressed the number for three full seconds. There was a message from Doris, asking her to dinner. Kaddish had called. There was a message from a man. "It's me, Gloria," the voice said. "I'm returning your call." The voice sounded vaguely familiar.

Who? He couldn't recognize the voice. And he couldn't listen to the voice again; his call had erased the messages, he realized. It could be anybody. She knew others. It didn't necessarily mean she was seeing somebody else. The voice bothered him, but what he had done, invading her privacy, like a rapist, a subtle rapist, bothered him, too. He tried not to think about it.

27

What happened between us? Where has our love
gone? My needs drove you away.
I want to talk to you, speak my love, but your ears
remain deaf to me.

In the days that followed, Nathaniel found he was neglecting
a daily routine that had long been an essential part of his
existence.

For weeks now, he realized, the morning newspaper had
gone unread. With his concern for Gloria, for Stan, with his
talks with his dead father, with sitting shiveh for his father
and for Stan, with arranging for Ruthie to buy his house next
door and helping her move, he had had no time for the news.
He had taken in the rubberbanded *Standard* each morning
when he took Golem for a walk to the park, and the papers
had piled up, unread, in a corner of the living room where he
had tossed them. That morning, when Mrs. Finney was due
for the biweekly housecleaning, he began tidying up so as not
to look like a slob. He came on the accumulated news and
started to reassemble what had always passed for reality, the
news of the day.

New probe of Oakland Police. Ten Die in South Africa. Plan
Offered for Candlestick Park Renewal. 11 Arrested in East Bay
Cocaine Bust. The sameness was remarkable. It was monoto-
nous and at the same time reassuring. He felt at home with
the daily disasters spread out before him in the familiar con-

text of department store offerings and savings-and-loan promises of safety and personal prosperity. The blur of other people's disasters, gazed at in the comfort of his kitchen, was a mindless distraction from his own *tsouris*, at least for the time it took him to go from the top of the news to the bottom of the classified. The way the headlines softened the blows of personal existence when he was a reporter, an insider caught up in the treadmill of news, had its counterpart, insidious and satisfying, in lightening the burdens of personal anxiety for the daily reader, the outsider.

It was while going through the accumulated disasters that he came on the entertainment pages and news of a tour by two East German defectors, Hans Perfiger and Erica Muntz, who were giving an all-Bach concert that afternoon at Davies Symphony Hall. The occasion was to mark their own artistic freedom as well as the 300th anniversary of the prolific master. With the bass line of foreboding over Stan and the counterpoint of desire for Gloria, he was not in a mood for just any occasion. But among the Bach pieces Muntz, a violinist, was playing the *D Minor Partita*, with its wonderful majesty and gravity, using the curved bow of Bach's time to gather up, as only that bow could do, a cluster of notes that allowed them to be played together as chords, the way Bach intended. And Perfiger, a pianist, was performing the Goldberg Variations on the cembalo clavichord. *The Goldberg Variations!* The thought of their elemental intricacy, bringing order out of giddy complexity, brought him an anticipation of at least musical peace and contentment. He would go to Davies and again, for the time being, forget himself, forget Stan, forget Gloria. It would also give Mrs. Finney free rein to clean house without his presence, and he would lose himself in the sounds of Bach, that lovely cosmic order of Bach,

196

instead of having to listen to the cacophony of Mrs. Finney on the Electrolux.

Our love has gone. What's there to understand? My need happened to *drive you away.*
Talk to you? Speak my love? Your ears are deaf. I want you. That remains.

With his wallet and credit cards gone, he would have to go to the bank and get enough extra cash for the ticket. But first he had to make a reservation. Before reaching for the phone he thought of calling Gloria. She had cultivated his appreciation of Bach. Her feeling for the Goldberg variations was almost like a self-conversion from *shiksa* to Jew, a mingling of intensity and gaiety that was religious and sexual in her devotion to the music. Call her, Kaddish had said. But at the last moment he decided against inviting her to the concert. The probability of her refusal would be more humiliating than the remote chance of her acceptance. Stan and Gloria had humiliated him enough. *No, let her call me,* he thought, without really believing she would.

Everyone seemed gray at the concert. It was like an assemblage of the 18th-century wigs, a carryover from Bach's time. More and more, he thought, the halls of culture—the symphony, the opera, the galleries and museums, the theater, the art film houses—depended for their support on the *uppies,* those in the upper-age categories who could afford the increasingly heavy cost of a ticket or take advantage of the senior discounts. And few people aside from the retired had the time to attend a matinee performance in the middle of the business week.

197

Sitting there, leafing through the program, he had the further realization that he was now a member of a new class, the privileged elderly, a recipient of the new homage paid to those of the genteel gerontocracy. *Medical science is giving us dividends of longevity. Just by continuing to exist, our property values are providing us with small fortunes. And our free time enables us to be a vocal pressure group for the rights and needs of the retired. Politicians don't dare mess with us. We're practically invincible. Great. Now, if only my personal life would stop falling apart . . .*

The sound of voices behind him, voices with a British intonation, made him turn around. A couple, both with gray hair and salmon-pink complexions, were discussing the program notes. For all the complex structure of the variations, its sense of order within all that intricacy, the man was saying, Bach had time for a musical joke and some homely wisdom "if you look what he does in the Quodlibet, the 30th variation, where he combines the melodies of two folk songs, *'Ich bin so lang nicht beir dir gwest,'* and *'Kraut und Ruben haben micht vertrieben.'*"

The German was close enough to Yiddish, or his father's presence was still at hand, or Gloria had once explained the words to him, for him to understand. "I have not been with you for such a long time," the first song went. The other song offered the humorous reason: "Cabbage and turnips have driven me away."

He wanted to ask the man if he knew anything about Goldberg and whether Goldberg and Bach spoke Yiddish, but he thought better of it and turned away. The talk about the meaning of the variations reminded him of his father's last words, the ultimate wisdom of the dead: *Let go, boychik.* Easier said than . . . but he knew he had to make the effort, work through to that point in his sessions with Kaddish or else go nuts in his obsession with Stan and Gloria. He felt he was in danger of losing his senses the more he lost control of his world, he, Nathaniel Dorn, privileged member of the American gerontocracy.

I want to speak about what happened, where our love has gone.
Your ears remain deaf to my talk, to my need. What has driven you away? Where are you?

He remembered the time he had brought Gloria the Caedmon cassette of Joao Carlos Martins playing the Variations. It was after he had installed the new speakers, the weekend she had returned from visiting her daughter, then living in Tacoma.

They were like teen-agers those days, he remembered. The heaviness of his mourning for Rachel had lifted. He and Gloria had their differences, and he would still feel a wave of anger, anger over his loss or wherever it came from, threaten to overflow the boundaries of their intimacy. But he had managed to hold the anger in check, and somehow the anger became the thrust of his passion for her.

The basic theme of the variations, the aria Bach had written for Anna Magdalena, his wife, arose and sounded in the air, filling the living room with its delicate fragrance. Gloria was dancing to the sarabande as he sat on her living room floor, fiddling with the dials of her JVC system. He had found the right balance of treble and bass and had looked up at her, at her swirling skirt. He had reached out, held her while she continued to dance with shorter and shorter steps, slower and slower movements, his hands reaching into her panties until she was just swaying, enjoying the dance of his fingers on the rim of her bottom, his hands skirting the cleft of her behind, holding the moons of her swaying arse. Then they were down on the rug, pulling at each other's clothes, zippers, eyelets, belts, straps. Their lips glided over each other's lips, eyes, ears, chin, neck, belly, thighs, kneecaps, toes. Their kisses were deep, tongue under tongue, drawing out the fluids of each other's beings. And then they were tonguing each other's parts, and he was stroking her soft pubic hair, and she was caressing his balls and arse. And then he was inside her, and they were moving to a Bach gigue, adagio, chaconne, passacaglia, the sudden stops punctuating their passion until the variations seemed to blend without a trace of constraint and the quavers and semi-quavers came faster and faster until, finally, together, locked in point and counterpoint, they felt a rush of harmony and they settled back in a pervading ground-tone of contentedness. *Oh, Bach . . . Oh, Gloria . . .*

What has happened?
Where has it gone? My need to talk drove you away.
Your ears are deaf to my speaking of love. All that remains, my love, is want.

Just before Hans Perfiger strode towards the clavichord Nathaniel saw Gloria. She was several rows down, near the aisle at the left side of the hall. It was her. The features were unmistakable: the wave of golden hair turned silver, the broad face, the Slavic nose, the widely spaced eyes. She was dressed in black, the color he always associated with Bach, and she was wearing the strand of Chinese white stones spread across her bosom, the necklace he had given her, the necklace left by Rachel that he had bought in a little Paris antique shop. She was wearing his necklace. *She still cares. Try not to give up on me and I won't give up on you, no matter what happens,* he remembered her saying. *I really care for you.* His heart was racing. *Bach and Gloria. It was a sign. God and the dead must have arranged this perfect coincidence. I must talk to her...*

He was oblivious to everything else as he left his seat to get to her. He was oblivious to the scowls of those in his way, to their shoes, to the way they squirmed and squeezed aside to let him pass. To them, he seemed an idiot on some sudden mission, picking absolutely the wrong moment to take a shit, probably, showing no respect at all for Bach or for Perfiger, who was now striding toward his clavichord.

Finally, Nathaniel reached her. She was looking ahead, seemingly unmindful of the commotion he had caused as he stooped down behind her. As he came toward her, he had settled in his mind what he would say to her. *Nothing heavy. Nothing about Stan, about how I miss her. No, Nat, old boy, lighten up. Show her how nonchalant and pleasant you can be. The old Nat...* He was bending toward her, toward the silver waves of her hair, whispering loudly over the applause now greeting the appearance of Perfiger.

"Gloria," he said, "it's Goldberg."

She turned and gazed at him, through him.

But he was still oblivious to everything but his own need to be with her. "Gloria," he said. But she had turned away.

Then he noticed the man who sat beside her. He caught his breath, rose from his crouch. His body stiffened. It was Potter. Potter the womanizer. Potter the traitor. Potter, the fucking psychiatrist traitor womanizer. Potter, the voice on the answering machine. Potter and Gloria.

"You son of a bitch," he said.

The nearby Bach lovers shook their fingers at him. They began shushing him. Perfiger sat at his clavichord, waiting for the disruption to end.

Nathaniel ignored them all. "Come on, you bastard, let's go outside," he was shouting.

"Nat, it's not what you think," Potter whispered. He turned to those around him. "He's a patient, I'm a doctor," he explained to no one in particular. "He's a little upset . . . I'll take him outside. Sorry about this disturbance."

Potter got up, told Gloria he would be back, squeezed by her into the aisle and took Nathaniel by the arm. "Come on, Nat, let's go outside and talk. You'll feel better—"

Nathaniel broke loose. "Don't you patronize me, you fucking shit."

Ushers and security police were coming toward him. There was a buzz of shushes from the audience. "Throw him out," someone across the aisle shouted. "What a vile man," a gray wig joined in. "Have some respect for Bach," another postured.

Nathaniel turned toward them. "Fuck," he said. "What's wrong with fucking? Bach knew all about fucking. He had twenty kids. That's fucking." Eyes red with anger, he gazed at Potter. "And this asshole who calls himself my friend is trying to fuck my woman." And with that he swung out at Potter and, with crazed strength, landed a blow that knocked the surprised psychiatrist to the carpet of the aisle just as the cordon of police descended on Nathaniel, grabbed him and hustled him out of the hall, the door swinging shut to the first notes of the Goldberg theme.

What happened between us drove you away. Now your love is gone.

I want to talk to you, I need to speak my love... Your ears remain deaf to me...

28

As usual, Hy Heller's account in *The Standard* was succinct, bitchy, colorful. And wrong.

The Standard's gossip columnist was also kind enough not to mention an old colleague's name:

"A protestor went for baroque Wednesday at that all-Bach concert by two East German defecting musicians at Davies. He delayed the Bach bash by shouting, 'Fugue you! Fugue you!' Before the city's next-to-best hauled him off for disorderly conduct, he took umbrage at Presidio Heights shrink Gladwyn Potter, who tried to defuse things. One blow to the chin, and Potter was down for a count of 30 Goldberg variations... And talking about shrinks, there's a new Sigmund Freud Cookbook in the stores. Repressed duck, anyone?"

The next morning, with the paper spread out before him on the breakfast table, Nathaniel noted between bites of toasted bagel that the only thing true about the paragraph was that he had indeed been booked for disorderly conduct. The *Standard*'s music critic, Orlando Fitch, had bailed him out and had gotten the city desk of both papers to kill the story on grounds of an old colleague's temporary insanity, a heart patient at that. Instead, the item went to Heller for his imaginative treatment. Newspapers, like the police, tended to look out for their own.

He spent two hours in City Jail before he was released. He could have used a credit card to bail himself out but all his credit cards were gone with his missing wallet. He didn't even have a driver's license for identification. Although he had written about jails for years, it was the first time he had been in one as an inmate. In the jail at the Hall of Justice he sat in a corner, his arms huddled about him, scarcely conscious of the others in the holding cell. He didn't want to think or be aware of anything. He was tired of the heaviness in his mind, his anger, his embarrassment, the humiliation of seeing Potter and Gloria together, his world falling apart. All he could think of was that in less than a year terrible things were happening to him, the sort of things he had once written about. *They're happening to me and I have no control over them. I'm no longer the insider, no longer the favor-giver, the helper. I'm helpless. Now I'm just one of the great unwashed mass of helpless nobodies.*

Then he thought of Stan, and the time his son had spent years ago in county jail in San Bruno. Eight months. Eight months. Two hours were depressing enough, but eight months! He thought of the rape that he had never had the courage to ask Stan about. He held his breath and shuddered. It was a wonder Stan wasn't even more screwed up than he was. Jail had not helped. If anything, the jail and the rape had helped make him suicidal.

Thinking of Stan, Nathaniel remembered how helpless he had been then too, even when he was a reporter, in talking to the judge who had sent Stan to jail. The judge, he knew, was a crook who had somehow outlasted a number of newspaper exposes, and he had wondered, with a shadow of guilt, whether it was precisely because he, Nat Dorn, was a news-paperman that Judge Shitface had put Stan behind bars. The judge had done it to his son despite a favorable probation report. *If Stan does ever kill himself,* Nathaniel thought, *I'll find that judge guilty of murder, and if I'm incurably ill, dying of a stroke, I'll get up from my deathbed, track down Judge Shitface and take him with me. Along with Gladwyn Potter.*

Before he was released he learned that Potter had come by the jail to see him. He didn't want to see Potter. Potter had tried to bail him out. He had refused. *Tell him,* he told the sergeant at the jail, *to fuck off and leave me alone.*

While alone with his thoughts, his father visited him in jail.

Boychik . . .

The anger ebbed away as he felt his father's presence.

Boychik, you can't go on like this. A crazy man you're making yourself . . . I tell you to let go the shiksa, she's not for you.

"I love her, even now."

Oh, such love. You should have your head examined, boychik.

Nathaniel had to smile. He was doing that already, going to Kaddish.

A lot good it seems to be doing you, his father said, reading his mind. *To carry on like you did, in front of all those people at the symphony, it's crazy, it's so . . . so . . .* His father groped for the right word. *So un-Jewish . . .*

"I couldn't help myself, seeing her with Potter, my friend, some friend!, and him coming to my place, helping Stan, a hypocrite with a helping hand . . . sticking a knife in my back."

Oh, boychik, boychik . . . You remind me of me. I used to get so crazy with anger, like you. It was such a waste of life. I got so angry

205

at Esther and you kids. Oh, for a lot of good reasons. Sure, a person has to get angry. But such anger! We got to let it go, such anger. My anger stayed with me. It blinded me. It cost me so much. Those precious moments of life with all of you . . .

"I don't know, Daddy, I don't know."

Who knows? Maybe your friend was just there for the concert. She likes music. He likes music. Maybe it's not what you think. I hold no brief for the shiksa, but maybe it's not what you think.

Maybe not, he thought. But now he had ruined it for good with Gloria. Who wanted a maniac?

Want yourself, boychik. Let go. Be alive for yourself. Take it from the dead . . .

"Hey, old man."

Another of the inmates, a tall pale black, was shaking his shoulder.

"You were talking to yourself," the man said.

"Oh?"

"Got a cigarette? Maybe a Chesterfield?"

No, he told him, he didn't smoke, not for ten years now. He had to worry about cancer, his heart—

"Oh, fuck," the man said. "Fuck cancer. I need a fucking *smoke.*"

The sergeant came to tell Nathaniel *The Standard*'s music critic was putting up the bail. He had to be in court that Monday for arraignment but he was free to go. He tried to remember where he had parked his car before the concert. Everything seemed gray and hazy. He felt empty. Maybe it was the beginning of letting go?

As he got up to leave, the black stood, blocking his way. "You're a strange asshole," he said. "Not a smoke on you but you got pull, two people putting up bail for you. You got pull, maybe you get me out of this shit hole."

"I got a few bucks they took from me," he told the man. "I'll leave you something for cigarettes."

The man stepped aside to let him pass. "Hey, what's your name?"

"Dorn," he said, "Nat Dorn." Then, out of habit, he added, *"The Standard* . . . I used to be with *The Standard."*

"Man, I see," the other said. "I see."

Nathaniel came to the bottom of the classifieds and put the paper aside. Golem was waiting. It was time for his walk. He had been neglecting Golem. A nice long walk along the rim of the park on Vermont Street, he decided. It was a lovely day, and it would be very good to breathe the brisk free air again.

29

Instead of turning left to the park on Vermont Street, where Golem hoped to go, he turned right. Golem hung back a moment, then joined him.

The way to the library on 20th went past Gloria's house. Her car wasn't in the driveway, he noticed, and man and dog continued down the sharp decline where the span of rooftops dropped toward the bay.

Golem kept tugging on the leash, straining to pee on the base of each tree they passed, and at one point pulled close to a doorway where he varied his aim by peeing on a rolled-up *Standard* awaiting someone's breakfast. "No, Golem, not there," Nathaniel said, "you're peeing on the hand that used to feed us." With a tug on the leash, Golem went back to peeing on the base of passing trees.

If I could pee free and easy as Golem, maybe I'd feel better. Maybe it comes down to the simple need for a good pee . . . I should call Dr. Merman, get the name of a urologist, have him look at it. That's what I should do . . .

A half block away from the library Golem lunged forward, whimpering excitedly at another dog in the distance. Nathaniel quickly realized it was not just another dog but Clara, sniffing the bushes by the side of the library door. Golem had sensed her from that distance, and now Nathaniel knew Gloria was inside the library, at any moment would appear. Although he could anticipate her displeasure in seeing him so soon after the concert debacle, he let whimpering Golem pull him forward as though he had no control over the chance encounter.

The skin of his face was burning at the thought of a sullen Gloria. He took several deep breaths, trying to calm down. Clara was barking at him, nosing at his pockets in anticipation of a snack while Golem sniffed at her haunches.

Clara's barking brought Gloria to the library door, and Golem joined in the barking, glad to smell Gloria again. "Ah, Golem, how are you, you sweet dog?" She looked at Nathaniel. His gray hair was uncombed, his beard a shag of bristles. He was wearing a worn tweed jacket, a faded yellow turtleneck sweater and nubby gray polyester pants. He looked awful, her sixty-two-year-old handsome lover. "How are you, Nat?"

Nat, at least not the formality of Nathaniel. She had called him Nat.

She was golden in the hazy light of the sun, and for a moment he was disconcerted from a hastily formed resolve to play it light. "Great," he said over the barking. He realized he was staring at her and looked away from the nimbus of her presence, the softness of that familiar white jacket she had found in a thrift shop, the silky white blouse, the homespun magenta scarf he had given her. "Lovely scarf," he said with an attempt at a smile.

Now he felt her eyes studying him. "*Your* scarf, Nat." Then, ready to leave, she added, "Take care of yourself."

He hesitated. "I know I don't look so hot, just haven't been on top of things."

She studied him again. "At least you could wear some better things, Nat. And your hair and beard . . . You're a handsome man when you take care of yourself."

Her mothering tone was welcomed. "I guess I'm becoming the original dirty old man."

"Well," she said, and turned to go.

"Any good books in there?" He nodded toward the library, trying to lighten up again and keep her from leaving.

"No," she said. "Not even a good mystery. I guess I've read them all . . . I was starting to leave when I heard the barking."

Clara and Golem were now quiet together, nosing the sidewalk in search of an edible scrap. "Golem is glad to see you," he said.

"And you, Nat?"

He smiled a lemon smile. "No."

"Well," she said, smiling.

"Gloria?" She had started to walk toward Clara.

She turned to him. "Yes?"

For a moment he had an urge to reach out and hold her. "I'd like to buy you an ice cream cone."

She looked at him warily. "Actually I was going to walk Clara to the Scoop and have a cone. No, I don't mind walking with you, Nat, but please, I'll buy my own cone."

"Sure," he said. There was a frown in his voice but he tried to relax. *So let her buy her own cone. Let feminism triumph. I can live with it.* "One Dutch almond vanilla, Dutch treat, coming up."

His forced joviality didn't last long during the walk to the neighborhood soda fountain. His show was a burden, and he began, first hesitantly and discretely, then without any stops, to let out his feelings, to fill the distance between them. He knew he shouldn't be talking so much but he couldn't help himself. All those sentences that began with *I* or *my*: "I've missed you..." "I was so crazy stupid breaking into your place, I don't blame you for being upset..." "I suppose you've heard about Stan..." "My heart's been acting up some but I think the worst is over..." "I don't know what the hell got into me when I saw you with Potter...I hope he's all right. My lawyer says they'll probably drop the whole thing. Potter told him I was his patient, that he wasn't about to press charges. Nice of him..." "I just haven't found anything to take the place of the job, not yet..." The only thing he held back on was his encounter with his dead father. *She must think I'm crazy enough.*

She listened politely, and sometimes put in a word or two. "I've heard about Stan." "Oh, Potter's all right. His dignity was a little dented, that's all."

They left the dogs leashed to a fire hydrant near the Scoop

while they got their cones. He let her pay for her own. "See," he said. "I'm flexible. I can let you have your way."

He meant the remark lightly, but as soon as he said it he realized how unfunny it might seem, even how condescending. But she seemed to take it okay. Anyway, her Dutch vanilla required her full attention. The massive scoop was starting to dribble down the sides of the sugar cone, and her tongue was busy keeping the ice cream in check.

Nathaniel licked his mocha walnut in silence as they started back up the hill, Clara and Golem trotting ahead. He noticed the sky was clouding up, like his mood. He had literally dreamed of their being together like this, easygoing, in ordinary side-by-sideness, doing something as simple as having a cappucino or eating a cone, but he had gone and spoiled things with his damned phony joviality and his heavy talkiness. "I'm sorry," he said.

"Sorry?"

"I talk too much."

"Don't be sorry for being yourself."

"I talk too much about myself."

"Well, there," she said, smiling, "you're still doing it."

"What?"

"Talking about talking too much about yourself." She sighed. "Oh, Nat," she said.

He had finished his cone while hers was still a creamy abundance. "Sometimes I wish I was someone else."

"Don't be foolish, Nat. For better or worse, we're just stuck with ourselves."

For better or worse... He was reminded of the marriage vow. *In sickness or in health, for better or for worse...* Everything had started with that, his asking her to marry him. "Gloria, I don't mean to be nosy but I have to ask you something."

"Of course you want to be nosy. That's all right, Nat. You can ask. I don't have to answer."

"Have you found someone else?" he asked, then added, "Are you seeing Potter?" Actually, he wanted to know if she was sleeping with Potter.

They had reached her gate. She let Clara in and stooped down to let her have the remainder of sugar cone. She closed the gate after her. "No, Nat," she said, "I haven't found any- one else, and I'm not sleeping with Potter. Oh, he wants to, but I don't." She started to turn toward the house. "And you, Nat, have you found someone?"

"No," he said. "I haven't found anyone. Not yet." There was a heaviness in his tone that he immediately regretted, and reaching for a lighter note, he remembered the personal ad he once wrote and had put aside. "I'm thinking of running a personal in the New York *Review of Books*," he said.

"Oh?"

The words of the personal came to mind: *Growing, graying retired newspaperman, worldly but romantic, seeks caring, sharing Bay Area woman with mind of her own* . . .

She studied him before she turned again toward her door. "You should get a lot of replies," she said.

He hesitated before answering. "You might want to reply," he said.

"I don't know about that."

As she turned to leave, her glance caught his, his eyes a stare of desire. She returned to the gate.

"Come here, Nat."

He came closer, and she reached out, the front gate be- tween them, and held him. "You did want to hold me, didn't you?" she said.

He held her with one arm, clutching her tightly. He

wanted to relax his grip on her, go easy with his damned neediness, but his other hand was holding on to the leash and Golem was straining to leave and . . .

And then she was gone.

It wasn't much, but for a moment it was everything. *Crazy,* he thought. *I'm sixty-two, more than halfway to sixty-three, and still acting like a lovesick kid who's never been laid.* He took a deep breath as he watched her fumble for her key and close the door behind her and Clara.

She had said nothing to give him hope of a distinct change, some real possibility they might be a couple again. But she had reached out and held him and he had held her—true, with one arm and a gate between them—held her close enough for him to feel the warm softness of her breasts and breathe the old erotic Gloria smell of her. *And she isn't sleeping with Potter,* he reminded himself. *Poor Potter, poor dented womanizer. I'll have to call him and apologize. I guess . . .*

Their unexpected talk over ice cream cones had been the first sign of a thaw in her coldness. At least they had begun to talk, although he felt he had talked too much, as usual. *Growing, graying,* he thought. *Well, yes, graying . . .*

He took off Golem's leash and Golem trotted ahead, stopping to raise a leg against a bush while glancing back at him.

"Stay, Golem, that's it," he said, catching up. "Good, good dog . . . Well, what do you think, my piddling friend, piddler on the roof and everywhere else?"

Golem went on peeing.

"We finally had a talk," he announced to Golem. "We held each other. You saw it, like old times. It's a start, Golem, if I really want her back. And that depends . . . Does she love me? Does she care? What do you think?"

Golem was silent except for the *shush-shush* of peeing again at a new bush.

"I don't know myself, Golem. I feel good and I feel confused, good and confused."

A snatch of doggerel formed in his mind. *It isn't much but at least I'm beginning to lighten up*, he thought.

> *Does she love me?*
> *Does she care?*
> *I think I need some underwear.*
>
> *She may not love me.*
> *She may not care.*
> *I better buy some underwear.*

He said the words aloud. "It's just doggerel, no offense," he told Golem, "but it's the first poem by Nathaniel Dorn in months." Golem ignored him.

Does she love me? Does she care? It sounded like a children's jump rope song. Ice cream and jump rope songs. *My second childhood*, he thought. *She could love me but not care. She could care but not love me.*

He noticed it had started to rain. The wetness felt good against his face. Then it began to rain harder. "Okay, piddler, let's go," he said to Golem, who was getting set to pee again. "The world is wet enough."

His heart felt younger, lighter and younger, as he and Golem hurried through the rain along 20th and down Kansas to the cul-de-sac.

He was hurrying to the rhythm of an old jump rope jingle that came to mind:

214

It's raining,
it's pouring,
the old man is snoring.
He bumped his head
on the edge of his bed
and didn't get up until morning.

By the time they were home he was unreasonably content.
As soon as he opened the door, however, he knew something
was wrong. He sensed a hush in the emptiness of the house,
as if the house was holding its breath.

30

Then the cold wet air rushed in. He noticed the shutters on
the back window in the living room were folded back. The
window to the alley, between his house and Ruthie's, was
open . . . *Somebody has been here. Somebody is here.*

Although he knew Golem was a match for any intruder,
his first impulse was to grab the long butcher knife from the
kitchen drawer, the knife he had used that morning to slice
the Tassajara country rye, icy hard from the freezer. The
jagged edge could debone an ox. Armed, he moved through
the house. First he checked the back door, then his bedroom,
then the den, holding the knife tight, holding his breath, almost hoping to confront a burglar. His movements as he
stared ahead were slow and deliberate, intent, but it was as if
he was part of a dream, acting in a daze. He tried to shake off

the feeling, to steel his alertness. But for a moment, in his mind, the unknown intruder he was stalking assumed the features of his son. Perhaps Stan was waiting in the shadows of a closet. He relaxed his grip on the knife. Then his fear and anger returned. But nobody was in the closets. Nothing had been touched, it seemed, nothing so far.

Only when he got to the attic did he notice anything missing. He had moved the TV and the stereo there to keep him company, to distract him while sorting through the memorabilia and rubbish of the past. The past was still waiting. The stereo and TV were gone.

He rushed down the attic steps, Golem ahead of him, out the front door, knife in his grip, unmindful now of the rain. He was breathing heavily. *I'm going to have a heart attack*, he thought. *That's all I need.* But the fresh wet air was invigorating. He was surprised at how well he felt. It was almost like he was covering a story for the paper and he was the first at the scene of a crime.

His tenant, the pastry chef, was home downstairs. He must have just come in. His truck was in the driveway.

Nathaniel rapped on the door until the pastry chef appeared. "I've been burglarized—"

"Oh," the chef said. "I just got here. I didn't see anyone." His tenant gazed owl-eyed at the rain coming down. "Well, it's raining," he said, laconic city dweller, resigned to the facts of urban life. Another day, another break-in.

Nathaniel noticed the knife was still in his hand. He held it awkwardly to one side, as if surprised he was holding it. It was like holding an umbrella wide open on a sunny day. "You better see if anything is missing," he said. "I better look through my daughter's place. My side window was open."

In Ruthie's driveway by the side of the garbage can he found his TV and stereo. They had been left behind inside two kingsize pillow cases, his own blue pillow cases, damp from rain. He must have been so excited that he hadn't noticed them missing from the bed. Then, turning toward Ruthie's house, he saw that the front door was wide open.

The place, usually fussy neat with a Ruthie meticulousness, was a mess. An intruder had gone through her house with a vengeance. A kitchen window had been left open. The sill was wet from rain. Dishes had been swept from the counter, spice containers knocked into the sink. Her medicine chest was open, toothbrushes thrown to the floor, perfume and lipstick and eye shadow, all the female intimacies of makeup, splattered aside. Her bedroom had been ransacked. There were no pillow cases on the torn-apart bed. The contents of her bureau drawers had been strewn over the bed and dumped on the creamy white carpeting.

Nathaniel looked for the gold necklaces bought in Jerusalem, the jewelry Rachel had left Ruthie. His eyes smarted at the thought they were stolen. It was no longer in his mind a news story that was happening to others, victims of burglaries, fire and mayhem, dished up for the breakfasts of the bored. In those days, he would empathize with the victims as he held notebook open and waited for an appropriately touching quote, some fresh slant. But the story could be put aside with his notebook, forgotten with a drink at Hanno's. *No, this is happening to me, to Ruthie, to my flesh and blood, my daughter, my own. Some little punk, shithead, fucking, goddamned, asshole dope fiend has broken into our lives . . .*

* * *

He called Ruthie at school. "I'm very busy, Daddy," she said when he was put through to her. She was in no mood for Dear Daddy. She was too busy to discuss his heartache over Gloria or Stan.

"Ruthie," he said. "It's not about Stan or Gloria. I'm at your place. Both our places. We were broken into. I don't know what they took."

She was leaving her classes right away, she said. He put the knife down on the kitchen counter and closed the window the thief must have used. The sound of his tenant's truck had driven the thief away, he decided. He called the police and waited with Golem, the dog's black snout sunk into the thickness of the cream-white carpeting.

"Oh, Golem, get your wet paws off Ruthie's carpet. *Off.*"

Golem heard the anger, sharper than usual, in Nathaniel's voice and left the room.

Nathaniel waited on the edge of the bed. In his grasp was a shot glass of Remy Martin from Ruthie's liquor cabinet. He needed something to help steady his nerves, but the brandy didn't help. The satiny taste only seemed to emphasize the shrillness of the rage he felt. His heart was racing again. He put the empty glass down on the carpet where Golem's snout had been. He felt for his pulse. There was no pulse he could find. His heart was thumping crazily. Oh, God, God, but no sound came. His throat was dry. He was dry and empty with anger. He felt violated, invaded, fucked over. In an hour he had gone from elation over seeing Gloria again to outrage over all this. He was exhausted.

Gonifs! It was his father's voice he heard. *Sometimes it's a mercy . . . a mercy to be dead . . .*

Let me hear you sigh some more, a good sigh, Kaddish had

218

said. A sigh started deep in his belly. The pain of the living and the dead was in his sigh. Oh, a good sigh.

31

Property Condition Codes: S–Stolen; R–Recovered; B–Boosted; D–Stripped; T–Towed; P–Stolen Plates; L–Lost.

S1   One gold watch with four diamonds— "Omega" $2500

S2   Five gold chains $1200

S3   Two diamonds earrings $400

Strictly routine. Not worth a paragraph in the paper. An entry in the police blotter, that's all. One of a score of break-ins on any given day in any major city. So two break-ins, next door to each other. No matter. All that was taken was a few thousand dollars' worth, probably inflated for insurance purposes, cops and papers figured. It didn't rate.

Nathaniel had called Grogan, the *Standard*'s police beat reporter. Grogan got him copies of the police reports. The reports set the tone of official matter-of-factness.

"Dorn told me and Officer Tyler #495 that he left his residence locked and secured and returned to find his valuables missing," said one of the reports. "Entry was apparently made through a side window. Crime lab notified to respond (Sgt. Purlew #834). It should also be noted that Dorn informed me that the suspects apparently left Dorn's missing stereo equipment in the next yard."

And the report on the break-in at Ruthie's: "Dorn told me and Officer Norbert #478 that she had locked and secured the premises at 8:30 hrs. Upon returning home at 16:00 hrs. she found her residence in disarray. My preliminary investigation revealed entry to have been an open kitchen window. Dorn told me that the window was shut when she left the premises. I gave Dorn an additional loss form. The crime lab has been notified."

Officers Montague Tyler and Jefferson Norbert, who responded to his call, were from Southern Station, once known as Potrero Station until property owners on the Hill hassled the city to change its name. The overflow of crime from Bayview and the Candlestick Park area, depressed parts of the station's jurisdiction, threatened property values every time a reference to Potrero Station showed up in the papers and on the TV news. Nathaniel would get needled by Terry Forman and the other *Standard* wits whenever there was a report of a district mugging or burglary.

"You live there, don't you, Nat, in that hellhole known as Potrero Hill?" Forman would say. Nathaniel, protective toward the Hill, would shrug off their barbs. In the early days, Hill property was cheap enough to buy even on a reporter's salary. Besides, the Hill was known for its generous share of sunshine, while much of the rest of the city, however expensive, remained damp and foggy; it was the reason, he decided, that the city had put the county hospital at the foot of the hill, so indigent patients could at least have the cheap warmth of sunshine. And the views were so dazzling it was a relief sometimes to pull down the shades. "You're just an envious renter," he would tell Forman.

So now it was Southern Station, a semantic answer to crime that, as usual, along with other remedies, had little effect on the frequency and anguish of a crime. Especially now that he and Ruthie were the victims.

Tyler and Norbert, whose investigation of the break-ins involved little more than writing their reports, were among the new breed of young police professionals. Young upwardly mobile police, patrol-car mobile. They reminded Nathaniel of the new crop of reporters. They were no better as cops or reporters than the old breed but they were certainly less colorful. Their most distinguishing feature, he felt, was that they spent less time in bars. Instead of alcohol to muffle the daily misery uncovered on the job, instead of hiding any hurt with an air of cynicism, the new breed of cops and reporters masked their emotions under a guise of professionalism and objectivity. Disinterested observers. *Some education, little experience, no heart.* Every time he talked with one of them, young reporter or cop, he felt as if he was shouting at someone at the other end of a tunnel, and the shouting made no difference. They looked at him blankly, as if to say: We're too polite not to appear to listen but, really, things would go a lot more smoothly if you and the other geezers just disappeared into the woodwork. On second thought, maybe it wasn't professionalism after all. Maybe they were all on their drugs of choice.

"Where were you, Mr. Dorn, when the suspect gained entry to your premises?" one of them asked.

"You mean when my place was broken into?" Nathaniel said to the other end of the tunnel. "I was walking my dog. His name is Golem."

"Whose name is Golem?"

"My dog."

"Oh, your dog's name is not necessary...Do you remember the approximate time of your departure?"

"The time we went for a walk?"

"Correct."

"Approximately one hour and forty-five minutes, give or take a few seconds." The rage in him against the shithead punk thief seeped out at the faceless cop and his faceless prose.

"So that's approximately fourteen hours?" The cop jotted something in his pad. He was a professional, all right.

Nathaniel simmered while the pointless questions went on and on. Meanwhile, any "suspect who had gained entry to their premises" was miles away, pillow cases abandoned, valuables sold. Tyler and Norbert didn't bother to check the premises for anything "the intruder" might have left behind, a cigarette butt or a missing glove, God knew what. They didn't even check the area between the houses where the intruder had to go to break in. This new breed of cop was only good for asking pointless questions and citing drivers who had parked too close to a crosswalk and making computer checks for unpaid tickets.

Gradually he simmered down. *Lighten up, Nathaniel*, he said to himself. *Sure, it's lousy, Ruthie losing Rachel's gold chains. But you both got your lives. You could have surprised that punk intruder and been killed for your trouble. These cops are just doing their daily, regular, ordinary, level least. You used to do the same. They know and you know the insurance will cover most of it.*

"Could you fellows use some coffee?" he asked, looking for Ruthie's coffeepot in the mess left by the intruder.

"No, thanks, we're almost through here," said Officer

Norbert. But Officer Tyler said he'd appreciate a glass of milk. *Milk*.

Sgt. Purlew (#834) had sent over Masters, Officer Rodney Masters (#902), the crime lab man. He was different. Yes, he could use some coffee, he said. He was also smug, but at least he was talkative.

As Nathaniel watched with Ruthie, Masters dusted the entry windows and talked. He didn't expect to find a satisfactory print, he said. "These guys are pros," he said. "Quick in, quick out. Fast turnover. And they're sure to wear gloves or cover their hands with socks."

He studied the window in Ruthie's kitchen. "This can't be jimmied," he decided. "Just make sure you keep it locked."

"It was locked," she said.

"Are you sure?" Masters said.

"I'm sure," she said.

"Are you?"

"I'm *positive*," she said.

"Well, maybe," he said. "Just make sure the windows are locked."

"Maybe I ought to move in with friends, in case they come back," Ruthie said.

"That's silly," the lab man said. "They're not going to come back. Don't inconvenience yourself. They got your jewelry. That's what they wanted. They're gone. This is no paperback mystery. They don't return to the scene of the crime."

"I've still got my TV and my stereo. They could come back for that. Or for me."

Masters had been playing up to her with his jaunty advice. Yes, she was attractive. He wouldn't mind a little bit of her.

"They're not coming back," he assured her. "Look, they left your father's stereo behind. That's nickle and dime stuff. They got the gold, that's it." Masters smiled. "And, look, honey, if you're worried about yourself, get a doublelock so the front door is locked on both sides. That way no one can get in or out unless they got both keys."

Masters glanced at Nathaniel, tossed him a winning smile. "Anyway, you got your father here to protect you. Your dad looks like he can handle things."

He moved around Golem on his way to the door. "This is your best protection, a good strong dog . . . Stubborn, head-strong and mean, ain't you, fellow?"

Golem growled.

"That's my father's dog," said Ruthie.

"Here, fellow," said Nathaniel. Golem moved toward him, continuing to mutter at Masters.

Masters paused at the front door. "Remember, a lock that needs a key from the inside. Anyone who breaks in won't be able to get out that easily." He left his card on a table by the door. "Give me a call if I can be of any more help," he told her.

The next day they changed the locks on the doors. They made sure all the windows were locked whenever they left.

Shortly after dawn, he had a dream but he couldn't recall it when he woke up. It left him uneasy. Although Gloria hadn't said it was all right to call, he wanted to tell her about the break-in and tell her to make sure her house was safe. But he didn't want to give her the impression he was looking for any sympathy, using what had happened to get her to care. Finally he did call. He told her about the break-in. "I'm so sorry," she said when he mentioned the stolen gold chains, the chains Rachel had left Ruthie. But her voice was stiff when he told her to make sure her house was safe. He was being husbandly, and she didn't want that, he thought. "Thank you for calling," she said.

Moments later the phone rang. It was Gloria. "I didn't mean to sound unfriendly," she said. "I appreciate what you told me, making sure my house is safe . . . Tell Ruthie how sorry I am."

He told her how glad he was she had called back. "I'm glad we've begun to talk again," he said.

When he hung up he thought of Ruthie, about how the day before he had met her for lunch and afterward took her to Maxferd's, the city's Tiffany of pawnbrokers, where he bought her a gold chain heavier than any of the five that had been stolen.

"It's a gift from your mother and me," he had told Ruthie. She'd been delighted as he attached the clasp and kissed the back of her neck like, it occurred to him, some sugar daddy in a hammy old movie.

"I'll wear it forever," she had said.

She had sounded so innocent in her appreciation, his dear lesbian daughter. Her delight had reminded him of those times as a two-year-old when she would play, gleeful on a summer day in the backyard, in a turkey roaster-pan Rachel had filled with water. She was small enough then to fit snugly in the pan.

"Wear it in happiness, dear Ruthie," he had said.

All this happiness, it didn't seem natural. Ruthie told him to relax, things were going to be fine.

That was the day before . . .

32

All the windows in the house were open. The door was open. All the doors. The front door. The back door. All the closet doors. I looked in Golem's closet. His eyes stared back at me. Golem got up, stretched himself, yawned, and followed me as I checked all the windows and doors. We went upstairs. The windows in the attic were all open. I began to shut them, one after another. I started to leave the attic and saw the windows I had closed were still open. I kept closing them and, as soon as my back was turned, they were open again, open everywhere I turned. I was sweating even though the attic was cold. I was in a panic. Then for a moment I stopped in my frenzy of closing windows and doors, doors and windows that wouldn't stay closed. I was looking out the bank of windows in the attic dormer. There was a plume of clouds across the dark sky to the south by the San Bruno mountains and I could see the moon behind a feather of cloud. I stood in front of the window, hoping the moon would show its full light, begging it, like it was some beacon of hope. Please moon, shine moon, please moon. And I began blowing at that feather of clouds, blowing, as if I might blow the cloud away and uncover the moon in all its full and friendly light. I was breathing in deeply and breathing out as hard as I could, exhaling every last bit of breath, every least last bit of breath. I was gasping for air. The window was wide open but there was no air. I cried out for dear life and started to choke. Then I woke up . . .

* * *

226

Awake himself, Nathaniel heard her cries. On his way to the back he flicked on the light in the kitchen. The light made the darkness through the picture window look even darker. Only when he got to the switch and turned on the backyard light could he see her. The latch on the French doors off the kitchen was stuck. He saw her through streaks in the glass clouded by his heavy breathing. The latch gave as she came over the wired sticks of fence, stumbling across the ghost-gray deck, her body white as the moon. She was convulsed with sobbing. He tried to comfort her in his arms but she drew back. "I've been raped," Ruthie mumbled through swollen lips.

She caught her breath. "He has my car." Her voice hoarse. "Don't go after him. He'll kill you. He tried to kill me. He was choking me to death. I couldn't get out of there. I couldn't get the key. Three hours. Oh, Daddy . . . Daddy."

She let him hold her.

"Don't talk," he said. He got her a robe and draped it over her shoulders. The new gold chain was gone.

"I have to call the police," she said, abruptly calm.

Nathaniel stood in the brightness of the kitchen, his arms by his side, while she talked to the police. He shook his head, trying to free his mind of shock. His mind felt amputated. He couldn't feel anger or rage. He had no feeling, only a numbness. All he knew was the sight of his daughter, her face swollen, teeth missing, mouth bleeding. She was wearing an old blue robe of his that needed washing, sitting on a familiar red kitchen chair, phone in hand, her voice metallic in its precision as she enumerated the address and the license of her car and the time the rapist left and described what she could see of him while he held a penlight shining in her eyes and beat her and raped her.

33

It was after four in the morning. Cops from the sex detail, the burglary detail and the crime lab had come and gone. They had taken Ruthie to the hospital. Nathaniel was alone with Golem.

He couldn't sleep, and Golem wouldn't leave him, staying under the kitchen table while he finished a bottle of wine to help him sleep. The shock of the rape had given way to a stirring of rage and anger, rage against her psychopathic rapist and anger toward the crime lab man, that jaunty fool who had assured them a different lock would make the house safe against an intruder's return. Masters, that was his name, had told them the kitchen window couldn't be jimmied open. Oh, no . . . Well, he would pay. The rapist would pay. He would see to that if he had to devote the rest of his life to it. He had the money from his retirement. He had the time. He still had contacts. He would see to that. Only let this awful night pass, he thought. But the wine and a half bottle of cheap brandy had no effect. He couldn't sleep.

He reached for the phone near the toaster. A voice, distant with sleep, finally answered. "Gloria," he said, "it's me, Nat. I had to call you."

"I'm asleep," she said.

"Something's happened."

"I'm sleeping, Nat . . ."

"I have to talk to you."

"I must be dreaming . . ."

"Ruthie was raped,"

"Ruthie . . . ?"

"She was raped."

"It must be some terrible dream," she said. "Must be . . ."

He was alone and awake. Golem had finally gone in the closet. Gloria had hung up, gone back to sleep. *God* . . .

A glass of brandy stood on top of the chest of drawers by his bedside. He didn't want to drink any more. All that wine and brandy, it was making him piss, a painful piss. The prostate, he had to do something about *that*. He remembered his doctor's words: "If that ticker of yours doesn't get you, your pecker will." But he didn't want to think of peckers, fucking cocks, not even his own. It made him think of the rapist who had done this to Ruthie, and, suddenly, he saw the shadowy figure pulling out an enormous black cock—he must have been black, he thought without a twinge—and come closer. He turned on a lamp to shut out the dark thought and reached for the brandy.

The streak of light gleamed in the mirrored squares on the wall by the other side of the bed. He had covered the wall with the squares once he started going with Gloria, so long ago now.

He had wanted to watch the two of them making love, her lovely breasts and behind rising in the night, with a low light on. At first, when she was the pending object of his lust, before their first intimate date, he had tried to fix a mirrored square to the ceiling over the bed. He had glued it on lightly, a tip of glue at each end, and had gotten into bed, naked, to see what he could at that distance. But the glue didn't hold, and the square came down in mid-peek and gashed his nose, and he had gone to see Gloria, that first big date, with a wide band-aid on his white-salved nose. He had tried to think of a less embarrassing explanation and then, finally, told her the truth, and she laughed and held him and they made love under his plain ordinary ceiling, and there seemed no need for mirrors overhead.

Now, brandy in hand, he looked across the bed at the mirrored wall, but the image of Gloria's body eluded him. They had begun to feel closer again, but now, hearing her sleepy responses to his need not to be alone at such a time, finally hanging up on him, she seemed further away than ever.

Then another image formed in the streaks of light in the mirrored surface of the wall. It was Ruthie. She was coming over the wired sticks of fence, stumbling across the gray-white deck, her flesh as pale as the moon, sobbing convulsively, falling into his outstretched arms. "I've been raped," she cried out again in his ears. *Oh, Ruthie . . .*

He put down the brandy and turned off the light. As he settled into his pillow, the bedroom window opposite him filled the room with a stretch of sky—the night sky darkly gray, "a dumb gray," as Gloria would call it, a gray that held no answers.

Trying to make any sense of it all was useless, he thought. He had retired from newspapering, seeking the spontaneity of an unstructured life and the tranquility of retirement, only to have his life become a living newspaper, a living hell of a newspaper. *FORMERLY DISTINGUISHED REPORTER SUF-FERS NEAR-HEART ATTACK AT DESK. BROKEN-HEARTED LOVER IN DESPAIR, ATTACKS RIVAL AT DAVIES HALL. DOPE-CRAZED SON TRIES TO JUMP TO*

*DEATH, STUMBLES AND IS SAVED: LESBIAN DAUGH-
TER IN RAPE ATTACK, FATHER SLEEPS THROUGH IT
ALL*...He wondered what next. *RETIREE'S DOG BITES
RETIREE, RETIREE BITES BACK? Only cheap jokes to force a
smile. Like the one about the holocaust victims waiting in line for the
death ovens. A specter of a man tries to force his way in line. The
skin-and-bones figure in front pushes him aside. "No, you don't," he
gasps. "I'm first, I was here before you." No, there was no recourse.
Even the dead can't help. What would daddy say? "Let go?" It was
easy for the dead to say.*

The lines by Yeats came back to him, and for a moment he
let his mind be numbed by them. *No, this was no country for
the old, no time for the young in one another's arms... No, no
country and no time. For the old or for that matter the young... It
wasn't just the prospect of nuclear holocaust. The worst thing was
humdrum daily terror, random violence waiting in the shadows, the
threat of the mean-spirited, the legion of freaks and assholes and
punks and failures mad to get something for nothing and ruin it for
everybody else, the vulnerable of all ages just trying to mind their
own lives...*

34

I was asleep when he came into my bedroom.

*He had climbed on top of me. I was pinned down. His hands were
on my shoulders. There was a white glove on his left hand...*

Nathaniel was listening as Ruthie, an oval of face showing
through her bandages, tried to recall details.

Many of Ruthie's friends, most of whom he had met before, were in her hospital room when he came to visit that afternoon after the sleepless night. He had been civil, or, in some cases, even friendly, to her lesbian friends. But it had always been something of an effort for him to be at ease in their presence. Ruthie was somehow different. She was his daughter. But their difference, the others, had remained an indefinable affront.

Now he allowed himself to feel their warmth and sympathy as they made way for him to be near Ruthie, to hold her hand as she caught her breath and told them, her father and friends, what had happened to her. He sat listening on the edge of her bed at Cedars of Tabor, where the sex detail cops had taken her early that morning.

"Lady, you sure can sleep," he said. The penlight was shining in my eyes.

I was awake. I remember my neck was stiff. I felt so afraid. He was heavy. "Please, I can't breathe," I said. "Let me breathe, and I'll do what you want."

"That's the way, lady," he said. He started to move off of me. The penlight was still in my eyes but his face was like a lit-up shadow. The sound of his voice, he must have been about twenty five, sounded like he was smiling. "You just do what I say, lady, and we're going to be all right," he said.

He moved to let me breathe and I ran from the bed. I must have bumped into a plant I have near my nightstand. I heard it crash as I ran toward the front door. But I couldn't pull the door open. I forgot the door was double-locked. I had taken the lab man's advice and locked myself inside.

Then he was on me in the darkness. His eyes seemed trained to the darkness, like an animal, like he had been trained to fight in the jungle. I tried to fight back. But he was so quick and powerful. He was slamming me with his fists. I was screaming. It wasn't only the pain. I was hoping my father would hear, that Golem would bark. But he covered my mouth. I drove my elbows into his stomach and he groaned and dropped his hands. I tried to run toward the back door. I was screaming but he held onto me and I kicked at him. I scratched at his face and bit his hand. He began punching me in the face and stomach. I fell to the floor.

"Bitch," he said. "I told you not to make trouble." Then he said, "I'm going to fuck you good. I'm going to fuck you to death."

Nathaniel wanted to tell her *enough*, no more, sleep, but like her friends he remained quiet, as though mesmerized. He was no longer dazed from lack of sleep. He was caught up in her story, all the terrible details, like a reader of a newspaper sensation, God forgive him, and he thought, relaxing his hold on her hand, all right, talk, let it out, Ruthie, let it all out.

He took his pants down and got on top of me. He tried to force my legs apart. But he had nothing down there. If I wasn't so hurt and scared I would have laughed. "I want you to give me some good head," he said.

"How can I?" I said. "You broke my jaw."

"I'll do worse than that," he said, and put his hands on my neck as if he were going to strangle me.

I asked, "Why are you doing this to me?"

"I'm being paid to do this," he said. It was like he was trying to tell me it wasn't his idea, that he wasn't really to blame. "Anyway, look at this place you got, nice furniture, pictures on the wall . . . Oh, I got a good look the last time I was here. You got everything. I got nothing."

I told him, "Look, I wasn't born with money, I had to work for

233

all I have. I don't have a mother. She died. My father's got a bad heart . . ."

All that got me was another crack in the face. "Don't try and get on my good side," he said. "I'm on to you, bitch."

Then he got up, pulled up his pants and started shining his penlight across the living room, here and there, up and down. He swung at anything nearby, knocking a lamp down, overturning my plants. "Where's your money, bitch?" he shouted. "I need money."

I told him my wallet was in the bedroom next to my answering machine. While he was in the bedroom I ran to the front door again. But I was trapped and nobody could hear my screaming. Then he was back again. I was exhausted. He dragged me towards the back of the house, near the bathroom, stood me up and slammed my head against the wall. Then he put his fist in my mouth.

He put his face up to mine in the dark. There was no smell, no heavy breathing, just a cold hatred from him. "Why don't you find a knife?" he was saying. "You want to kill me, don't you, bitch? Oh, poor baby, can't find a knife in the dark to kill this bad mother . . ."

He slapped my face hard. He was going to kill me, he said. I was bleeding, and, imagine, he got a towel from the bathroom and wiped away the blood from my face before he started punching me again. I couldn't stand. I must have collapsed. I passed out.

I found myself back in the bedroom. I heard him going through the house. Then he was back again, kicking at me, shouting, "Wake up, wake up." He was trying to kick me awake.

"The cops got the house surrounded," he said. "They're outside. I'm going to die. You're going to die. I'm going to fuck you to death."

He had me down again, pulling my legs apart, and this time he was stiff and shoved his thing inside of me.

Nathaniel gripped her hand again. *"Enough."* But she freed her hand. "Please, Daddy," she said.

Then he found some silk scarves in my room and tied my hands and

234

feet. He tied one of the scarves around my neck, pulling it tight. I told him I couldn't breathe and he relaxed his grip.

"There are no cops out there," I told him. "You can still get away. Take my car keys. They're in my purse. Just leave me, for God's sake."

In the dark, I could sense him thinking it over, whether to strangle me to death or leave. "Where's that purse?" he said. I told him again it was next to the answering machine. He had my front door keys and the keys to the car. Finally he left. But I didn't hear the door open. Then he was back again. He wanted to know which of the keys turned off the car alarm. But he didn't leave.

"Hey, you sure you don't want to come with me?" he said. "Look, I could drop you off at San Francisco General. Honest."

"Just go," I told him.

"Okay, okay," he said. "Just don't go calling the cops. Don't you tell nobody about this. If you do I'll come back. I'll kill you and your father and your brother."

Then he was gone. I freed myself and ran to my father's house next door.

She leaned back against her pillow. "The police came and found where he had forced his way in," she said. "It was the kitchen window, the one the police said couldn't be jimmied."

"Enough, Ruthie," Nathaniel said again. "It's enough, too much."

But in his mind he saw her, kept seeing her, through streaks in the French door glass, clouded by his heavy breathing, saw her coming over the wired sticks of fence, saw her stumbling across the ghost-gray deck, her body white as the moon, convulsed with sobbing, crying out to him, her father, "I've been raped."

"I'm mad I didn't pick up my lamp and try and brain

him," she was saying to the others. "Or maybe once I saw how crazy he was I should have broken my bedroom window and jumped. It's a floor up but I would have landed on the roof of my car. It's just I was so stunned. My mind was in slow motion."

"Ruthie, you did what you could," he said. "Look, you did all right. You're alive and you fought back. You fought like a tiger."

"Yes, I'm alive," she said.

He got up to go, then hesitated, looking at Ruthie. "Was he black?"

"What difference does it make?" she said. "It was like he was colorless. I couldn't tell a thing from his voice. It was an angry voice but without color, a machine voice. A mixed-up crazy psychopath with a hatred for women. Oh, he probably was black but he could have been anything, any kind of man. I couldn't see, not in the darkness or with the light blinding me."

A man, no doubt black, a black from the project, he thought. Being a man, black or any color, made him feel guilty himself. He looked at the others, lesbians, looked down on by men, many of them hurt by former husbands, disowned by fathers, brutalized physically or emotionally, finding protection among themselves, at least *some* kind of kindness.

"I'll be back, Ruthie," he said, turning to go. "I'll be back later." He looked at her friends, grateful for their presence. "I'm so glad you have such good friends to be with."

She held his hand for a moment. "Please, Daddy, please understand," she said. "I'm not blaming you for anything. You were asleep, it was hard for you to hear. Don't blame yourself."

236

He had not thought of blaming himself, but now he would have to think about it. "Just rest now, Ruthie . . . I'll be back later."

No, she didn't want that, she said. It would be dark, and for now she didn't want to hear a male voice at night. "Not even yours, Daddy," she said.

35

There was a call from Potter when he got home. The phone was ringing as he made a dash for the bathroom, desperate to relieve his bladder. He finally reached for the phone hanging from the wall near the toilet bowl.

Walking friends were walking the next morning, Potter reminded him.

"Nat?" Potter said when he heard no sound from a fellow Oofty Goofty. "You're still talking to me, aren't you? We *are* friends?"

Finally Potter's voice penetrated. "Look," Nathaniel said, "I meant to call you and tell you how bad I feel about that Davies Hall thing—"

"You did, Nat. That's all done with. Look, I shouldn't have been with Gloria anyway. It was stupid of me. Anyway, on to bigger and better walks by old Oofty Goofties."

Nathaniel couldn't even remember apologizing to Potter. He felt as though he might be losing his mind as well as his hearing. "I'm not feeling too hot," he said.

"Just the time for a good Oofty Goofty stroll," Potter said.

"Remember, we decided this time to walk from my place across the Golden Gate, all the way to the no-name bar."

"No, I can't," Nathaniel said after a moment. "I've got to be by myself. And no bridge..."

"You do sound terrible, Nat. Now what?"

"Ruthie was raped."

"Ruthie?"

"Ruthie."

Potter was silent.

"My Ruthie," Nathaniel said.

"I don't know what to say," the psychiatrist said. "Look, I'll come over. You need somebody."

"Thanks, but no. I want to be by myself."

"How about Gloria?"

"I told her. She fell asleep on me."

"She fell asleep? Gloria? I don't understand."

"I don't either. I phoned her and she was sleeping and hung up on me."

"Oh, Nat, . . . is there anything I can do, for you or Ruthie?"

"No." He hung up.

He wanted to be alone. He felt anguished and angry for Ruthie. Angry—furious at the rapist and angry at himself. Jesus. Even when Golem came to lay a massive snout on his lap or when the cats miaowed for a late afternoon snack he ignored them.

"There's nothing wrong with even a little self-pity, give in to it," Kaddish told him when she phoned to find out how he was and whether, after missing a previous session for which she would have to charge him, he would be seeing her the usual time that week.

He didn't want to, but he talked about it over the phone, about the rape, about Gloria's lack of response, about how damned helpless he felt.

"These are real things, Nathan," she told him. "Your feeling of helplessness, what does it remind you of?"

"My father. I mean, how I felt when he was angry . . . and . . ."

"And?"

"Oh, the time he and Lonnie left me alone on Broadway. I felt so goddamn helpless I was in a panic . . . And the time my mother gave away my dog, I was helpless to save him . . ."

"Or save Ruthie . . . Those are real feelings, Nathan. Acknowledge them. Feeling helpless doesn't make you any less a man. It's more than self-pity. It's *reality*. It's as real as the gas ovens or Vietnam or South Africa or AIDS. Your feelings are real."

He steadied his gaze, trying to appear to be with her.

She wanted to know about his anger. "I don't hear any anger in your voice . . . You're afraid to appear helpless. Are you afraid to be angry?"

"Of course, I'm angry," he said. "I could kill the man who did this to Ruthie. I want to find him and kill him."

"Good," said Kaddish, who he knew was as liberal-minded as he was. "It's normal to feel that way."

"He was black, I think."

"So? It's still normal . . . And Gloria?"

"I'm angry at her, all right. I'm not sure I want to see her again . . . Maybe you're right. Maybe it is time to look for someone else."

"Do what you have to do, Nathan."

Familiar words, he thought.

* * *

239

Later he took Golem for a walk. He held on to the leash as tightly as he did to his anger. As soon as they reached the mailbox on 20th and Kansas he opened the slot and thrust the letter inside, the letter with the check and the personal ad. *Growing, graying . . . seeks caring, sharing woman . . .* Mailing the letter was supposed to make him feel less helpless.

36

She appeared through a solo violin's scrim of sound. As the notes of the partita with its exuberance floated over him where he lay sprawled on the black leather couch, she came unbidden from the darkness, materializing out of the air by Bach as if summoned by the bow, like a wand, of the violinist.

Staring into the darkness, he knew that look immediately.

"You," he said. Finally, in her own sweet time, Rachel had come to him.

Her head was tilted to the right, her hair a shimmer of white like an aureole, and she was looking at him with glistening eyes and a welcoming smile. A purple-and-red woolen scarf hung jauntily from her neck, a flare of folkish color against the black velvet of her coat. He looked up from her hands, cupped together, and the brown leather purse, a near-perfect purse, always her quest in life, dangling from her left arm, and his gaze stayed with her green eyes.

You're in one of your moods, Nat, I can tell. Miserable. What's the word? Miserable and fatuous, I think that's the word . . .

240

For a moment he thought she might look for the unabridged to check on her use of the word.

"Silly or inane, unconscious, illusory," he said.

*Exactly . . . Don't sentimentalize me, please. I never want to be
anything other than I am. Don't put haloes on my head. They're not
my style.*

"How are you, Rachel?"

Dead.

"You look lovely."

*Oh, Nat. Your mind is wandering. You're thinking of an old
snapshot. Don't you remember? It was that afternoon in London, our
last trip abroad. Your cousin took us to that spot in Hempstead where
The Heath & Old Hempstead Society had put up a plaque. A tribute
to Maggie Richardson, a flower-seller for sixty years at that spot,
known from then on as Maggie's Corner. I loved the idea. I wanted
my picture taken standing under the plaque that wonderful afternoon. It's what you're seeing, Nat.*

He didn't know what to say. Too much to say. He felt like
crying.

Cry, Nat.

He did. It came from deep inside, from the pain of missing
her, for not being able to save her from death, for Stan and
Ruthie, their babies, for the pain of what they were going
through . . .

Oh, damn it, Nat, cry for yourself . . . There's no shame in it.

Kaddish had said that too. But he began to cough at her
words, a nervous cough, feeling it was such a self-indulgent
weakness to cry for himself, the loss of Gloria, the fester of
anger at Ruthie's rapist and his own powerlessness, and, and
. . . And he wondered why Golem hadn't been aroused by his
keening, propelled from his closet, until he realized that

Golem was there by his side, black snout against the black leather of the couch, breathing softly, as the Bach partita continued to play.

A good cry, Nat, Rachel was saying.

She had taken her coat off. All her clothes, he saw, were gone. They formed a drapery of light at her feet. She stood there naked. But she was whole, as he remembered her before her cancer, before the loss of her right breast.

Lovely Rachel who couldn't bear those last weeks of her life, when the cancer was spreading to her brain, couldn't bear being anything less than Rachel Dorn.

"I'll take care of you whatever happens," he had told her.

"I won't be anyone's basket case," she had said. "Not even yours, Nat."

She came home using a walker, took a week to say her goodbyes, then took the painkiller pills she had saved, just enough not to throw up, and she had died.

"You had a smile on your lips when I brought you your coffee and a sweet roll," he said.

Sure, I was smiling. I wanted to leave you with a smile, Nat. It was my decision. It helped me overcome my helplessness. I was in charge, not the cancer. I picked my time to die. It was time.

For a moment he wanted to ask her how she, an atheist, felt now that she was dead about God and an afterlife. It made him think of the Heine story about an atheist arguing with a true believer. The atheist suffers a heart attack in the middle of that heated argument over the possibility of an afterlife. He dies, then returns in spirit and says, "As I was saying . . ."

No time for any of that, Nat, she was saying. *You have so much to do, and I'm starting to fade.*

242

"I have so much to ask you."

Please, Nat, I don't want to talk about you and Gloria.

"I wanted to talk about Stan," he lied.

There's nothing to say about Stan. Only our son can say what has to be said . . . Anyway, Nat, you want to talk about Gloria, and I don't.

"I love her."

I know.

"I love you."

I'm dead.

"I don't know what to do."

It's for the living to work out, not me.

"She's not there for me . . ."

Are you there for her? Are you there for yourself, Nat?

He shook his head. He wished he could shake his head free of questions. He didn't need any more questions, not from the dead, not even from Rachel. "I just want to know if things are still possible with Gloria."

Only the two of you will find out.

"Help me, Rachel."

Help yourself, Nat . . . I'm fading, and you have so much to do.

"What can I do?"

Start with something simple. Do Ruthie's house. She's going to be back for some things even if she doesn't want to stay there. The place is a terrible mess. Plants overturned. Blood on the walls. She shouldn't have to see that when she comes home. Go over there, Nat. Clean up. You can't sleep anyway, and Bach can wait. It will be good for you, doing something necessary. It will make you feel less frantic.

Typical Rachel advice, rehabilitation counselor to the death. For Rachel, the discipline of trying to thread a needle

243

was a sure path to right living. How he'd missed her plain advice. "Don't fade, Rachel," he said.

You've got work to do.

"Don't fade."

Well, maybe a moment more, Nat. Look, change the record. Enough Bach for now. I want to dance with you.

He thought of all the old tunes they liked together. He went upstairs to the attic where he had stored the familiar records. She had followed him and stood naked in the moonlight shining through the dormer skylight.

You've changed things, she said. *Very nice, Nat. You've made it so nice. But there's still so much work to do, so much left behind, so much to throw out . . . But find a record. Pick one.*

He went through records he had not played for years. What do you play for the dead? She liked Van Morrison. "Moondance" or "Into the Mystic"? Both seemed right. Or Otis Redding. She loved to dance to Otis. Maybe "Don't Let Me Go" . . .

Put on Frankie . . .

"Frankie?"

Sinatra. One of the old favorites.

It was exactly the moment when his fingers had reached the Sinatra album, "Songs for Swingin' Lovers."

Again, downstairs, the same as years before, the old ballad spun out its snap of rhythm and sentiment, with Sinatra holding them in thrall, allowing him to imagine he was a better dancer than he was, as she, with her deft verve as ever, leaned into his arms, and they danced. He was doing his best two-step while the words caressed his ears:

> *You make me feel so young.*
> *You make me feel like spring has sprung . . .*

You and I
Are just like a couple of tots
Running across the meadows,
Picking up lots of forget-me-nots.

You make me feel so young,
You make me feel there are songs to be sung,
Bells to be rung
And wonderful flings to be flung . . .
And even when I'm old and gray
I'm going to feel the way I do today
Because you, you make me feel so young . . .

She was light in his arms as tightly as he tried to hold her, and she dipped her body into the snap and twirl of the Riddle arrangement, beaming with that joy he had last seen on her face when he released her ashes into the sea at Muir Beach and she floated until her image sprang from the ashes, arms flung out, dancing across the sky. Now in the sprung silences of Sinatra's phrasing he could hear her fading voice.

You're a lovely man, Nat . . . Why wouldn't Gloria love you?

He leaned closer to her voice, growing fainter each passing moment, and he heard a semblance of what he wanted to hear and more than he wanted to hear.

She loves you and mistrusts you, Nat. I can't blame her. It took me more than thirty years to trust you and accept you . . .

He just barely caught the drift of her last words.

The trouble is you don't accept yourself . . . Accept yourself . . . Accept . . .

She was gone. She had faded from his arms but he was still dancing, giddy with nostalgia. And he felt—what was the word?—fatuous, fatuously happy. It was *his* feeling. He was

245

the one who was alive, and it was his right to feel fatuous if he felt like it, and he felt like it. Accept yourself, she said. Well, feeling fatuous was, after all, some measure of that acceptance.

37

Before dawn, after Rachel had faded from his arms, he cleaned Ruthie's house next door. Golem followed him through the devastated rooms as he swept up dirt from the overturnd plants, scrubbed at the blotched rug in her bedroom, mixed spackle for the damaged wall where the rapist had rammed her head and wiped streaks of blood from the plasterboard.

By the time he was through he felt exhausted enough to sleep. As he closed his eyes he thought of the morning he found Rachel dead, a week after Passover. Passover was here again, only days away. A clean house for Ruthie. A clean house Rachel had to leave.

He considered himself a Jew mostly out of family nostalgia and a sense that to be anything else was a dishonor to the memory of the Holocaust victims. And some of the observances, he had to admit, held him like a rheumy-eyed grandmother cradling an infant grandson.

Passover, the spring-cleaning of the Jewish soul, was one of those observances.

Intellectually, he had difficulty with the Exodus story at

the heart of Passover. Reading the Haggadah as a boy, he could thrill with other young Jews to the picture of God smiting the oppressors of the children of Israel. God to the rescue! It was as exciting as a Superman comic book.

Drop by drop of wine during the Passover service, he could accept nine of the ten plagues visited in retribution on the Egyptians. Blood, all right. Frogs, why not? Vermin. Beasts. Cattle disease. Boils. Hail. Locusts. Darkness. Yes. But the slaying of the Egyptian firstborn? No. Not even in retribution for Pharoah's order to drown the male children of his Jewish slaves.

He still found it impossible to accept the idea of a just God, if there was one, humbling the Pharoah by passing over the Israelites and striking down only the Egyptian firstborn. That ultimate plague, to break the Pharoah's will and set the Israelites free, made him feel uneasy and even un-Jewish. After all, those firstborn were as innocent as the Jewish boys who had been thrown into the Nile. They were as innocent as the Holocaust dead.

He remembered as a twelve-year-old, before the Holocaust and before his father's death, arguing the point with his bar mitzvah teacher, who finally in despair told him he was a snotty-nosed kid who had no business judging God when he didn't know enough to wipe his own nose.

But as he grew older his appreciation grew for the humbler side of the holiday. The father in him, the poet in him, even atheist Rachel, found comfort in the annual ritual of a thorough cleaning of the house. They and Ruthie and Stan would make every inch of floor and furniture glow as they made a show of removing each crumb of unleavened bread.

Then, with family and friends gathered together for the occasion, would come the ritual of the four cups of wine, the taste of dry matzah and the bitter herb reminder of slavery, the Four Questions, the message of hope and change, the joy and sadness of such songs as Dayyeinu, and, finally, The Meal, the sumptuous gut-stuffing, stomach-oppressive overload of soup and matzah balls, chicken, fish, meat, carrot tsimmes, noodle pudding, nuts, dates, and not to forget the horseradish. Past and present merged in that belly-wrenching plenitude, that springtime dream of desert wanderers.

"No matter how awful things are,"the bar mitzvah teacher would say, "*Pesach* reminds us never to lose hope."

Never lose hope . . .

He heard the words in his dream, if it was a dream. His father spoke the words.

Never lose hope, Nathan. You've made a start by cleaning up Ruthie's house. You're a good Passover kid.

"Please, I don't need compliments. I only did what I had to do."

Do what you have to do . . . It's right.

He had no stomach for words of wisdom, not even from his father. He didn't want to be told what's right. Nothing was right. It was as if God, if He existed, had a vendetta against the Dorns. So maybe they didn't believe in Him. It was an honest disbelief.

"It's unfair," he said.

So what's fair, Nathan? That I died at fifty, that I never saw my children grow up? That your Rachel, a good woman, died young? What's fair?

"Why us?"

It's a question every Jew asks.

He wondered how God Himself would answer. Why, from

the firstborn of the Egyptians to the dead of the Holocaust, to victims everywhere, to Ruthie, did the innocent suffer? He knew how some Jews, Reformed or Orthodox, answered: Out of the plagues came reaffirmation of the power of the Eternal, your God, to go and remove one nation from the midst of another nation, with trials, with signs, with wonders, and with battle. Out of the Holocaust, after all, had come Israel . . . But how would God answer? Did any of it justify the suffering of the innocent? The suffering of Ruthie? Did any of it make sense?

I don't know, Nathan, how God would answer. I've never met the Gentleman. I'm dead, yes, but He's never consulted me. Who am I? All I know are His words: "I will put wonders in heaven and on earth."

Ruthie called to make sure he was home. She didn't want to be there alone when she came to take some clothes to Roberta's place. She would stay with her friend until she could sell the house and move elsewhere.

"Oh, Daddy, I'm so glad you cleaned things up," she told him when she saw what he had done. "I was afraid to come home . . . to be reminded."

He wanted to tell her about the dialogue with her mother, how it was Rachel who had told him to clean the house. "You know, Ruthie, I thought of Rachel," he began, but he stopped, as if the tip of his tongue was locked in his lips. He bit his lower lip, not wanting to make Ruthie feel still worse, and let the thought go.

Ruthie had turned from him and had started to look for the things she needed. She packed enough clothes for a few days. All her good jewelry was gone. "I think I'll stick with costume jewelry from the five-and-ten," she said. "It's safer."

"You'll have good things again, baby."

"That bastard took the new gold chain you got me," she said. "He ripped it from my neck."

"We'll get you another."

She wanted to know if the police has searched for clues.

"The sex detail looked. Burglary looked. I don't know what they found."

After the advice the police had given her, the incredibly ignorant advice, Ruthie wanted to look herself.

"They didn't look very hard," she said after searching the area where the bedroom plant had been overturned.

He had cleaned up and had missed it as well. It was an ammunition clip. The rapist had been armed.

She also found a cigarette in one of the ashtrays. "How could they have missed this?" she said. "This must have been his. He must have had a cigarette while I was unconscious, while he was searching the place. It's not mine. I've been off cigarettes for a month, and I never smoked Chesterfields anyway."

Nathaniel put the clip and the cigarette in an envelope and said he would turn it over to the cops.

The thought came to Nathaniel that there might be a connection between the Chesterfield and the man in jail who had asked him for a cigarette that night after Davies Hall. He had been fool enough to tell the man his name and who he was, who he had been, Dorn of *The Standard*, quick to bail out.

Ruthie was ready to leave. As he turned to follow he thought of how close she had been to being killed. She had fought for her life and saved it. Her fierceness may have gained the grudging respect of the psychopathic rapist. The madman had not used his gun. He had even stopped choking her while she continued to fight back.

Ruthie took his arm. "Don't look so sad, Daddy," she said. "It could be worse. I could be dead." She smiled. "Hey, those aren't bad odds. Here I am, over thirty, and only one psychopath in all that time."

"You're a remarkable woman," Nathaniel told her.

"What do you expect?" she said. "I'm Rachel Dorn's daughter. And yours."

38

Learn a lesson from the dead.
Don't take troubles home to bed.

The eleventh plague came with the approach of Passover, but it was a plague that brought a blessing.

April's warm morning sun was beginning to dry the cold dampness of winter from the air, and he felt a hot tub, long forsaken that winter, would be a relief from all the tension. With the springtime holiday coming, the pear tree by the deck was blossoming with the promise of pears, and a tub reminded him of the mikveh, a ritual bath, the Passover tradition of purification for some traditional Jews like Bubba, his mother's mother. He remembered her through a mist of childhood memory as a rheumy-eyed old woman in a dark shawl, speaking only Yiddish, and a good source for a dime to get into a movie.

251

He had fished out leaves and twigs from the redwood tub, the debris of passing storms that winter. He had emptied the cold water and let the tub refill before he added chlorine and a little ash to make sure it was safe. Then he had left the tub to heat up while he went to take a pee. Another difficult pee. Any time he heard the sound of water he always felt like peeing, but now peeing was a trial, and his bladder still felt full afterward. He had thought of what Rachel would say: "Oh, Nat, you can be such a fool the way you neglect something so important." *Next week*, he thought, *next week I'll do something about my prostate . . .*

Before he got into the tub he had taken the long butcher knife from the kitchen drawer and laid it within reach. The rapist might come back, and, along with Golem stretched out at the rim of the tub, Nathaniel would be ready.

Maybe I'm not that different, after all, from the ancient vengeful God of Passover, he had thought. *I would dearly love to spill that son of a bitch's blood . . .*

In his mind he had seen the rapist's blood dripping down the boards of the deck. The rapist's eyes were wide with fear. Golem was getting ready to spring at the rapist's severed neck . . .

Nathaniel's heart was racing, but the scenario of vengeance and the anticipation of a calming tub had made him feel better.

The steam of anger had drifted away, and he thought of the forgiving words of Exodus after the Israelites fled in the wake of the parting sea and the Egyptians were engulfed. Seeing the drowning Egyptians, the ministering angels had exulted.

But God silenced them, saying: "My children are drowning in the sea and you want to sing before me!"

252

Even the Egyptians received some sympathy. And the rapist? Was he, finally, to be forgiven too?

Lord, our God and God of our ancestors, just as I have removed all unleavened bread from my home and my ownership, so may it be your will that I merit the removal of the evil inclination from my heart. It was the voice of his father, Nathaniel realized.

No, I'd have to be dead before I forgive him. I'd have to be dead. It was his own voice.

Then the phone had rung. He hoped it was Gloria. She was calling to say how sorry she was not to have come over the night of the rape. He would tell her about the dialogue with Rachel, about Rachel taking her part, imagine. *Why wouldn't Gloria love you?* Rachel had said. *She loves you and mistrusts you, Nat. I can't blame her. It took me more than thirty years to trust you and accept you . . .*

The call was from Stan. He had sounded well. "No, Daddy, I don't need anything from you," he was saying. "I'm still at Emerson House . . . I'm all right. Well, free of drugs for ninety days. Not even a beer."

Stan hesitated. "Look, don't get your hopes up. I've been here before. There are no promises and no cures. At best I'll always be recovering, never cured. All I know now is I'll die if I don't change."

"Well, it's a start."

"If I make it, it's a start," Stan said.

He wanted to know how Ruthie was. He had heard about the rape from a Southern Station cop who came to question him. "He thought maybe one of my old contacts might have been behind it all."

"God, I hope not, Stan," Nathaniel said.

"I don't know," his son said. "The stuff I pulled, it's all like

253

a terrible mixed-up dream." The officer who came to see him seemed to have other leads, he said. "Something you told him, Daddy."

"Oh, Morley Ellis, you mean." It was the cop he had given the evidence Ruthie had found, the Chesterfield cigarette and the ammunition clip.

"That's the one," Stan said.

Any connection was definitely a longshot, Ellis had agreed, but he would look into it.

"They've got me working as a cook here, so I eat pretty good," Stan was saying. "How are you, Daddy?"

"Not bad . . . Passover is almost here."

"I know. I'll be cooking a Passover meal for the house. Matzah ball soup for a hundred raving dope addicts. You might want to come. I'm inviting you."

"I'll come, Stan, I will . . . Do you remember the service at all?"

"Of course. Dope hasn't completely destroyed my mind, you know." And he repeated, in Hebrew yet, remembered from his bar mitvah classes, the words of the service: "Today we are slaves, tomorrow may we be free."

Open up your mouth and breathe
Only let the kettle seethe.

He had to leave the tub to go to the bathroom. He had to pee again. The pain was the worst yet. He could see the pee coming out askew. It missed the bowl, was falling on the tip of his right bunny slipper, the slippers Gloria had gotten him for his sixtieth birthday. He stood there watching the leak, standing in a tiny puddle, seeing it was the color of blood. The bunny slipper was turning red.

And the phone by the toilet bowl was ringing. It was Gloria. He was holding his cock, nearly doubled in pain. She was asking him about Ruthie, telling him how deep a sleep she had been in that night after taking a sleeping pill, that it had struck her as unbelievable, a nightmare, and that—

"It can wait, Gloria," he said. "But, please, you have a key. Come over now . . . It seems I've just launched my own Red Sea."

Gloria called Merman. Merman called the urologist. The urologist called Cedars.

She drove him to the urologist. On the way he had an urgency to pee again, and a fear. The urgency was so great she stopped at a service station along Geary, got the key for him, opened the door to the men's room and waited while he went inside. But he came out quickly. Because nothing had come out.

He felt embarrassed when Gloria left the examination room and they put him in what looked like stirrups, with his knees drawn up like a woman giving birth. The urologist stuck a needle-like telescope up his penis and told him, as he winced, to relax while he peered up the old urinary canal.

"I don't like it," Dr. Sanford Stone said.

"What do you see?"

"Nothing," Stone said. "That's what I don't like."

Gloria had come back into the room.

"We're going to have to do a biopsy," Stone said. "There's a growth there that's blocking my view."

From the tone of the urologist's voice Nathaniel felt as if he should apologize for blocking the view. But he felt helpless to do anything. The urologist had not taken the time to let him out of the cystoscope stirrups. "Do I have to stay in this thing?" he said.

"Oh, no, of course not," the urologist said.

"I've got cancer, haven't I?" Nathaniel asked, now freed of the stirrups, the hospital gown drawn to his knees. *The final plague.*

"We'll see when we can see," the doctor said.

With a catheter attached to him to draw off the urine, Nathaniel made the rounds at Cedars of Tabor, filling up a plastic bottle and filling out the paperwork to get admitted.

Finally he and Gloria were alone in a private room on the busy urology floor. She was holding his hand. They had scarcely exchanged a word, and that was all right. He might be dying but he felt content, her hand in his. He flashed on her words from so long ago: *I'd marry you in a flash if you were dying...*

"Thank you for being here," he told her.

The silence in the room felt comfortable as he stared at her, forgetting his fear of what the results of the biopsy, set for the next morning, might be. Again, her fairness, her eyes, her nose reminded him of his mother. But different.

Glints of sunlight speckled the bed. The pattern of light kept changing as he watched her. A lovely difference.

She held his hand tighter. She kissed him. "Oh, Nat," she said. "Nat. Dear Nat."

He smiled over the wince that crossed his face when her body rubbed against his soreness.

She had noticed the wince. "Oh, Nat, I'm sorry... That poor thing has been through enough."

Norma, the night nurse, a handsome black woman, strode in, making her rounds as smoothly as a champion ice skater.

"Ah, a couple of lovebirds," she said smiling before checking the catheter. "A nice color, it's coming along."

"A good vintage," he badly joked. "Confused but interesting, needs aging."

Norma grinned. "It's very nice to see you in such a cheerful mood." She had some pills for him, including something for sleep. "You've got a big morning ahead." Then she was gone, gliding off to nurse a score of others with male troubles.

Gloria got up to leave. She kissed him again, carefully. Her eyes seemed filled with unspoken thoughts. "I'm so confused, Nat," she said. "All I know is I don't want to lose you."

> *Let ego go, that clutching beast.*
> *Time is what you have the least.*

39

The time passed in a procession of numbing daytime minutes when he felt like a pampered pincushion, and hours of tomb-like darkness, a span of daydreams and half-remembrances, remembrances and dreams as he lay in bed, the hospital bed, his mind a daze of anticipation, of dread, suspended between the demands of life and the relief of death, his energies muffled in a cotton-wool wadding of sleeping pills, pills to keep his heart from beating extra beats, pills to stave off infection, pills to take a shit.

Inderal, halcion, macrodantin, vulcolax. The words reached his mind with the intonations of mysterious writing on an ancient wall, foretelling God only knew what. *Mene, mene, tekel, upharsin . . . The destruction of a kingdom. Belshazzar. I am the Prince of Aquitane, my tower in ruins.*

There was a tangled blur of tubes attached to him, one to his arm, dripping a clear fluid, and one to his penis, a tube with a hazy hue of ruby liquid. He felt stoned. *Sanford Stone, he remembered the name. Whose name?*

His eyes tried to focus on the sun-glinting day. He made out the blur of tubes. As he moved, the warp of the topsheet rubbed against his soreness and he winced. The pain evoked a twinge of dread, a vision of Pit and Pendulum.

I am sick—sick to death. Bound, prostrate, helpless, alone on a table. Above me is a huge pendulum, the scythe of Time, like one of those antique clocks, sweeping minute by minute across my body, over my groin, my dong, closer and closer . . .

One of the nurses in the preparation room or the operation room, or intensive care, or his room, or his memory, was asking, "Any dentures, contact lenses, false eyebrows?"

A nurse was sticking him with a hypodermic needle. "Oh, a lovely vein, Mr. Dorn, just waiting to be stuck."

He had recognized the scrunchy-faced, death mask-like demeanor of the old grocer's wife, the old grocer on the hill. She was leaning over him, telling him how strange to see him there while her husband lay next door to death.

"Nothing seems to help," she was saying. "The bills are piling up and I wouldn't mind if it did any good . . . Hospitals are so expensive these days. It's cheaper to die, believe me."

Then the death mask caught herself. "Oh, but you, Mr. Dorn, God bless you, you're going to do fine."

He had drifted off to sleep, and gradually he heard a procession of voices, voice joining voice like a Bach chorale. He listened intently. He heard a guitar plucking away. Had Bach written for guitar? Vivaldi had, but Bach? And that low thrusting instrument. A saxophone? Bach had never written for saxophone. He tried to catch the words as voice after voice joined in a contrapuntal insistence, a Bach-and-blues counterpoint.

> *We're aiming to*
> *Wah-dah-do your diddly . . .*
>
> *We're aiming to*
> *Make you feel so tiddly . . .*
>
> *We're going to*
> *Wah-dah-do your diddly*
> *'til the dawn . . .*
>
> *You won't feel it*
> *'til is done . . .*
>
> *You won't know it*
> *'til is gone . . .*
>
> *Going to*
> *Wah-dah-do your diddly*
> *Whole night long . . .*

In the blur of voices and faces he wondered if the operation was over. Has my heart given out? Has my pecker fallen off? Am I dead? Will I ever make love again?

The grocer's wife was saying. "He's going to do fine, isn't

he, Gloria? Well, I'll say a prayer for him tonight at St. Teresa's."

Gloria. She was back with him. Was it dream or truth? Truth and dream, perhaps. He saw her face. Or was it his mother's face? There was so much still to be said. *To Gloria . . . to ma . . .*

And then he thought he saw the bristling mustache of Dr. Brett Z. Merman, cardiologist, punster and collector of Mark Twainiana. "How's the old pecker?" the mustache was saying. "I thought your ticker would go first. Instead it's your pecker. Tried to pull a fast one, didn't you, Nathan?"

Prostrate with prostate. Pit and the Pendulum. Poet, pee in a Poe pot. Nothing like a good clear piss. Just make sure that you don't miss.

He went back to sleep. And, woolly with drugs, he dreamt he had gone to heaven and talked with the dead.

40

It was a Cockney voice, a little arch and overdone, contrivedly knowing, as if to give the accent some extra English.

If you ask me, Nathan, heaven smells like a fish-and-chip place, she said, only she dropped the *haitch* in heaven.

He knew at once who it was, and he was in no mood for her cheery banter although he yearned to see her again.

A fish-and-chip place, she repeated.

"Please, Ma!" He was in pain. "Don't do this to me!"

Oh, Nathan, you know your mother . . . I just said that to be funny.

"Ma, please."

A little humor never hurt, dear . . . I always call him dear, he's got antlers growing from his head.

"Ma!"

It was Esther Dorn, London music hall entertainer *manqué*. Esther Dorn, as he most remembered her before her *garagul*, her Yiddish word for the upper neck, became droopy with age like an old plucked chicken. Esther Dorn, his mother.

She was alive as life and twice as nice, as she would say. She was fat and forty and *kooker-ee-koo*, her expressions, and her complexion was as red as an Adam's apple, her comparison.

"An Adam's apple isn't red," he would tell her.

"Oh, yes it is, on the inside." She always had to have the last word, his mother, the amusing last word, most likely a nonsense word. Esther Dorn, the queen of cajolery.

And there she was, funny, infuriating, loving Esther Dorn, his mother. *I thought you might like to talk to your ma a time like this, poor Nathan . . . How's your little watering can?*

The image came back to him immediately, her in bed, leaning back, making her massive belly bounce and jounce with her gyrations. "Come on," she would say to him, no more than three years old, "on with you, on Mummy's belly. I'll give you a ride, if you're good."

And on he would go, astride her belly, and she'd rotate her mounds of mummy fat, first gently, then with some abandon, holding his little hands and kicking up her legs, with him whooping in delight while she sang, as she did now, leaning over his hospital bed,

I got a man.
He's got a water can.
Also a frying pan.
I got a man . . .

All of a sudden he was back in their old apartment in The Bronx, the time he had come home from school to take Junkets for a walk. But his dog was gone. A butcher took him away, she said. Bones forever, Nathan my boy! He was in a rage, and she was trying to sing his rage away.

He laughed in spite of the pain in his pelvis, draining through the catheter. Then he caught himself. "I don't want to laugh! Please go, Ma, go if you can't stop this. I want you to go!"

I will. I'll stop, honey . . . I always call him honey, he never wipes it from his chin.

"Ma!"

Oh, Nathan, you're so angry. Oh, what a red face! Like an Adam's apple!

"Ma!"

The spitting image of my Ben . . . Angry just like your daddy used to get! Almost nothing would do to get him out of that mood. I'd have to make faces and cock one leg up. It would take a time but I'd get him out of it.

Bizarre, that rubbery face she always made, as if swallowing her chin to her nose, her eyes peering cockeyed at him, that face came closer, and he winced from the smile, the laugh, the pain that bubbled up from him.

That face came even closer.

"I don't want to laugh!"

That face grew mock-sad.

262

"Ma!"

That face . . .

"Damn it, Ma! Stop it! Stop it! I'm warning you!"

Warning me? My boy warning me? She drew back. *I come from the dead, from no life, a cold place, a cold, cold place, to visit with my son, my boy, after all these years, my boy who may be dying, and he sends me away . . .*

She seemed to be clutching a veil of vapor to her eyes, as if wiping a tear away, and he knew she was faking, and he couldn't help but smile.

See? I've gotten you to smile after all.

He remembered the last time he saw her, a winter twenty years ago. She was coming to greet him on the snowy lawn of Lonnie's place in Caldwell, where she lived. On her way to him, she picked up a handful of falling flakes, mashed it into a matzah ball of snow and hurled it toward him. An eighty-two-year-old snowball tosser! Playfully he reached down, grabbed some snow and threw a tiny wad back at her. She ran into the house and came back moments later, cupping a hand over her eye, blubbering: "Oh, I don't see my boy all these months and look what he does—blacken me eye, he does!" She had dabbed one eye with shoe polish, black as the snow was white.

Now her face began to age before him. She became thinner, even haggard, a figure in her late eighties, the time of her death. She seemed to have lost the energy for cajolery.

I died, and you weren't there, Nathan, she was saying. *All the others were—Lonnie and Jill and Rita and Janie and Paul and . . . I've missed someone. Who have I missed?*

"Me, Mama . . . I was in Europe for the paper. Rachel and Lonnie, they didn't let me know. I didn't know you were dying. How could they reach me anyway? Seven countries in thirteen days, covering the young European revolutionaries. And what could I do anyway? Ma will be dead forever by the time I got there, they figured. And me, I didn't know you were dying... I kept sending you postcards even after you had died."

Oh, keep talking, Nathan. I love the sound of your voice. Such a soothing voice, so very soothing. You know, my boy, it's cold where I am. Not even a good hot cup of tea. And no one to laugh with...

He was staring at her wrinkled face, white and solemn. "Do the dead grow older where you are?" he asked in sudden wonder.

Older, and younger when the living remember.

The questions kept coming despite his weariness and pain. "Don't they laugh in heaven? Don't you see Daddy? Don't you laugh together?"

Our laughing, it's a memory. I heard it the first time since I died when you laughed.

"Don't you get to talk to the great people of the past, maybe Shakespeare or Johann Sebastian Bach?"

What could I say to them? I don't think I'd be quite up to Shakespeare.

"Don't people make love where you are?"

She didn't speak. He thought he saw tears in her eyes. The room was silent. Deathly silent, he thought, straining his ears to hear the usual noises in the corridor.

Finally, she spoke. *Do you have somebody, Nathan?*

"I have somebody, Mama. I miss Rachel so much, but I have somebody."

You love her, I know.

"I love her, Mama . . . In a way, she's like you."

Love her, Nathan, with all your life.

Then she was silent before she spoke again. *Nathan . . .*

"Yes, mama?"

It hasn't been entirely easy, you know—my life. The babies that died before me, Alfie and Dora, and my beloved, my Ben. Oh, there was pain from the start. Remember, I told you how it was when we left Russia, coming over the border, packed in the back of a cart with strangers, my mother hiding me in her shawl and me starting to cry, and one of them threatening to strangle me to keep them from being discovered, and how my mother shoved my mouth down on her nipple to keep me quiet . . .

"I remember, Ma."

Well, I've had an appetite for opening my mouth ever since.

She laughed, his impossible, irrespressible mother, and she was fat and forty and *kooker-ee-koo* again.

It's good to laugh.

He hesitated. "Not always, Mama."

No, not always. I know what you're thinking, Nathan. You're thinking you never had the right to cry or be angry, to feel anything but happy. Oh, you did cry and you were angry, but it's true, I was always there to try and make you feel better even when I probably shouldn't have.

He let her talk, the novelty of her seriousness like a balm.

I had my own anger, you know, and what could I do with it? Your father had that territory all mapped out for himself. And you children, seven of you after Alfie died, fighting like scrungy cats and dogs. There wasn't room for me to start screaming. The landlord would have thrown us out on our ears. So I was the one to keep you all quiet and laughing. I was the pleaser . . .

She was silent a moment. *I'm sorry about Junkets. But what*

265

could I do? He was always nipping at the girls. They were terrified of him. And I did give him to a butcher. That's no story. I owed the butcher money, and he took a fancy to the dog. I couldn't tell you where the butcher lived. You'd go and get Junkets back. So all I could do was try and get your mind off your loss . . .

As she talked he was remembering the pleaser in himself, hiding his own anger, hiding from Stan's problems, trying to make peace, ready with a joke, trying to be liked. "What are you angry about, ma?"

Me? Oh, it's too late for that.

"Tell me. Were you angry at Daddy?"

Oh, at his snooty family, making out like they were better than me. And, yes, at Daddy, for sometimes siding with them. Oh, and for taking everything so serious and getting angry and getting himself sick. I had to get him out of his bad humor even when I didn't feel like it. But I loved my life with him and all of you . . . I loved my Ben. I loved him so much I couldn't hardly look at another man after he died. And I did like making love, oh, the hugging, the feeling good of Daddy inside me, the way we loved that last night . . .

He wanted to tell her about his talks with Daddy, how he loved her still in death. But that could wait. Besides, the dead know whatever the living know.

"Are you still angry, Ma?"

Only at being dead. I don't like that one bit at all. Her eyes, a gleam of moonlight making them large and bright, stared at him. *Don't you dare die, my boy. All of you, my kids and their kids, all of you still have a lot of living to do . . . You know what, my boy?*

"What, Ma?"

You won't get angry?

"I'll try not to."

I'd like to lie down on your bed. I'd like you to sit on my belly,

266

*just like when you was a little boy. Just a little jolly bounce. Gentle,
you'll see . . .*

The nurse who came before dawn found him tossing in his
sleep. But the catheter, miraculously, was in place. He had a
gentle smile on his face, and she didn't wake him.

FOUR

Youth of delight, come hither,
And see the opening morn,
Image of truth new born.
Doubt is fled, & clouds of reason,
Dark disputes & artful teazing . . .
　　　—Blake, *The Voice of the*
　　　　　　Ancient Bard

41

What in heaven or on earth could compare with the delight of reading Mozart's unexpurgated letters, with his lilt of gossip, his recititivo of plain honesty and his trill of shit-piss good spirits while listening to his *Sinfonia Concertante*, that banquet of soloist waiters following one another with dishes of melody from another world, while at the same time eating wedges of dark pumpernickel smeared with Philadelphia cream cheese and a dab of good caviar sprinkled with lemon juice, accompanied by a tart and properly chilled champagne served in the right glasses. *And* knowing, at the same time, that a biopsy shows no sign of cancer.

Gloria had come by the hospital to celebrate the good news from Dr. Sanford Stone. She had brought a picnic basket of cheer. There was a copy of the Mozart letters and along with it a portable compact disc with earphones and a feast of music. There was the *Sinfonia Concertante* with Itzak Perlman and Pinchas Zukerman, Shlomo Mintz performing Bach's *Sonatas and Partitas* for violin solo and the choir of Christchurch Cathedral Oxford singing Vivaldi's *Gloria*.

"Ah, my eclectic *shiksa*," he said.

She was sketching when he first woke up. His eyes took in the radiance of her fair looks while she busied herself in the drawing. She was drawing him.

"Don't move," she said.

"I can't. I've still got all these tubes."

He had called her the night before to tell her the news. "We jarred your blood clot loose and took a sample," Stone had said. "Negative." Not a hint of cancer.

271

What happens now, Nathaniel had asked.

"Now all we have to do is get it to work," the urologist said. "You'll be joining the great majority of men who have to have it done, usually later than sooner."

Stone had scheduled the prostate operation the morning after next. "No problem. I've done it hundreds of times, although you're one of my youngest. That's a precocious prostate you have, but we'll have you urinating in no time."

The urologist was delighted to explain the technique, how he used what amounted to a delicate apple corer that enters the urethra and scrapes away at the prostate, "an absolutely useless vestige all of us males have—the other is the appendix.... I'll be cutting through it, as if I was coring a walnut. I'll just leave the outer shell . . . You'll be able to urinate again like a young stallion."

Nathaniel wanted to ask how the operation was going to affect his love life, if he had any left, but Stone anticipated the question. "Please try and hold off for a month," Stone said. "Unless it gets out of control. Then be careful."

He was not exactly reassured. Stone was obviously proud of his handiwork and its expected results. But slips of the knife were always possible. There were always lemons in every trade. And does a used car salesman ever knock his product?

Stone caught his look of doubt. "Well, we shall see what we shall see, won't we?" he said. "I think you'll be pleasantly surprised. Now mind you, the orgasm may seem different afterwards. More of an implosion rather than an explosion. But very nice, trust me."

A worst fear, the fear of cancer, had gone. Now it was replaced by a lesser fear, perhaps, but a fear. Two fears: the fear of never being able to go on his own, without a catheter, and the fear of never being erect again, of never ever making it.

"We are a worrier, aren't we?" Stone said. "No need for that. You'll be a new man. Trust me."

And Nathaniel, after calling Gloria with the good news, faced the night with much fear and some trust. A sleeping pill helped. And now she was there, at work on her drawing, when he opened his eyes.

She showed him the sketch. He looked like a dour Pan, his beard flourishing over the edge of the bed covers, the horns and ears of a goat barely discernible, and a thermometer in his mouth, replacing the pipes of the ancient Greek god.

"Pan," he said.

"No," she said, smiling. "Bedpan."

Then they toasted each other with the tart champagne she had brought and served in Roumanian champagne glasses.

"To Mozart," he said.

"To your pecker," she said.

She was also there the morning of the operation, and in his room when Stone came by and pronounced his handiwork "just what the doctor ordered." Through the haze of inderal, halcion, macrondantin and vulcolax, Nathaniel caught Stone's appraisal of Gloria and a look of pride as the urologist gave him a knowing wink. "A new man," Stone said . . .

Gloria never missed a morning while he was at the hospital. She came with books and his mail and news of Golem and the cats. She was feeding them and taking Golem for walks. "He's such a strong dog," she said. "Driven . . ."

"Like I used to be," he said.

273

"We'll see," she said. "But he does smell better."

"I never got around to washing him, not since last Passover."

"Washed and groomed. I saw to it, Nat. That's twenty five dollars you owe me..."

She was with him the day the tube began to lose its ruby color and turn rose, pale rose and finally a blessedly normal yellow.

The next day Stone was coming to remove the catheter. A big day. Stone said he would be able to urinate on his own. The prospect seemed magical.

"I want you to do some walking today," Stone said. "You'll be going home on Passover. A new man."

As she took his arm and helped him walk through the corridor, the tube still attached to him, he held the plastic bottle and hated it.

"What are you thinking, Nat?"

He was remembering a time before, years ago, when he had wheeled Rachel through the same hospital corridors two floors above.

"I'm thinking of Rachel," he said.

When they were back in his room, he told her about his dialogue with Rachel, a dream, perhaps, in which she had taken Gloria's part. "She said she didn't blame you if you mistrusted me. It took her thirty years to learn to trust me, she said."

She had bent down to kiss him. She was ready to leave. Again her eyes betrayed unspoken thoughts.

"What are you thinking, Gloria?"

Her breath sounded like a deep sigh. "This may not be the time to say it, Nathan, but really, some things haven't

274

changed. You know, I guess I'm still angry at you and still don't trust you . . . I'm still confused."

He thought of what Rachel had said. *She loves you and mistrusts you, Nat. I can't blame her* . . . No, he couldn't blame her. Oh, he had made a show of being so helping in his helplessness, at the same time had been so full of himself there had been little room for her. And there were things she still didn't know about, untold little dirty reasons not to trust him. He thought of the time he had followed her and tapped her phone, listened to her messages. He had invaded her privacy, like some cunning rapist . . . He would have to tell her one day. But not now, not, for God's sake, with his penis still in a sling.

"You have reason not to trust me, Gloria," he said. "You have reason to be angry." He looked at her as he lay back on the raised pillow. "I understand how you feel. Look, I'm still angry with you. I still don't trust you."

He thought he saw in her eyes a flicker of acknowledgment that, no, she hadn't exactly been there for him, either. Whatever the reasons, she had rejected him and not been there, including that terrible night of the rape.

"I hope there's enough time for all this to heal," he said. "Maybe Kaddish . . ."

"Maybe time," she said.

She bent down and kissed him. That erotic Gloria aroma, suffusion of past and present, the touch of a lovely woman who loved him in her own confused way, for all his shortcomings, made him forget the overlay of antiseptic staleness, the blur of tubes, the soreness in his groin. Gloria . . .

275

42

Early the next morning Stone removed the tube. *Pfftt...* the tube went. "God," Nathaniel said, wincing.

"You're welcome," said Stone, and proceeded to tell him the standard urologist's tale.

Once upon a time a mighty leader of a desert kingdom got separated in a storm from his procession. His camel died on him during this fierce storm and he wandered for a day and a night and a day, growing more and more parched until his tongue turned gray with thirst. He felt death coming on and searched the horizon with sunken eyes for some sign of hope.

Then there, in the distance, he saw the faint figure of a man on a camel, the shadow of man and beast growing larger and larger as it came his way. Then it became clearer. Above him loomed a stranger and a huge camel slung with goatskins of water and a burden of reeds.

"Water, water," the king gasped. "My kingdom for some water."

"Oh, half your kingdom will do," the stranger said as the king took the offered goatskin and quenched his thirst.

"How generous a man you are," the king said. "I offered you all my kingdom, and you only wanted half."

"Half will do now," the stranger said, tapping the camel's burden of reeds. "One of these years you'll be older, much older, and you'll be lost in the desert again. You'll come my way, only this time you'll be dying to take a piss." He held up one of the reeds, that ancient catheter. "That's when I'll take the other half of your kingdom."

Nathaniel smiled politely. He figured Stone deserved to be indulged.

Norma, the nurse, was ending her shift. She brought him a plastic bottle with a wide mouth and a lid. She also brought him a fresh pitcher of water.

After Stone and the nurse left he put on the earphones, turned on the compact disc player and set Mozart whirling to ease the suspense of awaiting that first blessed relief.

He was sitting on the edge of the bed, his sore penis dangling in the mouth of the plastic bottle as he drank cup after cup of water while he tried to relax to Mozart. He was afraid to strain. The suspense was terrifying. He had almost drained the pitcher of water.

Then Gloria knocked and held the door ajar while she looked toward him.

And at that moment he felt the surge. He was smiling broadly as it poured out of him, a mighty Niagara. A triumphant surge of Mozart filled his ears. Mozart would have understood his exultation. *I can pee!*

Like a young stallion, he thought.

The urologist had told him to hold off for a month, unless it got out of control. Any orgasm, he had said, would be more like an implosion, not an explosion, but still very nice. Now he had that to look forward to. He had never imploded before. Well, even a hardy erection, once the soreness left, would be a pleasant surprise.

And that night, in a dream, they were together, he and Gloria. They were in an enormous hospital bed, side by side, with tubes attached to their arms and legs, making it impossible to get close, even to touch. They moved imperceptibly toward each other, across the miles of bed, straining their bodies to touch without dismantling the lifeline of tubes. He saw the pink flash of her breast, and he stretched his encumbered arm toward her, his hand extended, fingers taut to touch her softness . . .

He was in a sweat of desire when morning came and he woke up. There was an exquisite pain in his groin, and he reached down under the covers and felt himself. He was erect. He was actually erect. And despite the soreness, he smiled. He was erect, sorely erect, and life felt wonderful. An old fool and his erection . . . he thought.

His eyes were moist. He was crying and smiling. In his joy it felt as if he had never been so erect, so bursting with life. *Oh, Gloria* . . .

43

That day, the day before Passover when he would be leaving the hospital, there were calls from Kaddish, from Potter, from people at the paper, even a Brooklyn call from Stan Lee, who somehow had traced him to Cedars of Tabor.

He confided to his old friend that all his fears were not over. "I'm not exactly sure there's anything there to interest a woman," he said. *One erection, a sore one at that, doth not a man make*, he thought.

"Join the club," said Stan, and Nathaniel remembered his black friend's long battle with impotency.

"I'm not joining anything yet," Nathaniel said.

"Oh, you'll be diddling all the girls in no time, old buddy," Stan said. "You never had any trouble in old New York."

The mention of New York reminded him of the personal ad he had sent to The New York *Review of Books*. Fat envelopes of replies ought to be arriving soon, batches of replies from eager correspondents in the throes of post-menopausal lust, thrilled to have a go at "a growing, graying, retired newspaperman, worldly but romantic . . ." With his fears that he might not be able to please just one woman, a certain woman, the thought of hordes of desiring women, undoubtedly bright and desirous, made him shudder.

Stan, in his best baritone, was serenading him over the phone with a snatch from *Don Giovanni*, but he had no appetite for even a Mozartian list of the *Don*'s conquests. "Thanks, old buddy," he said without much enthusiasm when Stan ran out of breath.

Terry Forman was crestfallen with mock-sadness when he called. "What am I going to do? I'll have to junk your obituary, Dorn."

"You can read it to me," Nathaniel told him.

"Good idea," Forman said, and began reading: "Nathaniel Dorn, long the dean of *The Standard*'s obituary writers, wrote finis to his own life yesterday. He died, under circumstances too intimate for a family newspaper to recount, at the age of sixty-four, a day before becoming eligible for Medicare benefits—"

"But my birthday is two weeks away and I'll only be sixty-three, not sixty-five."

"Well, we won't be able to use this obit anyway," Forman said. "Besides, don't be such a stickler for facts. This makes a better story."

Forman was quiet a moment. "Have you seen today's *Standard*?" he asked.

"No," Nathaniel said, "I've switched to the New York Times."

"I've got a piece I'd like you to see. The cops caught a rapist on Potrero Hill . . . Grogan says it may be the one."

"I'll take a look."

"Oh, one more thing, Nat."

"No puns, please. Not in my delicate condition."

"Now that you can piss again, what are you going to do with the rest of your life?"

"I guess I'm going to take it one prostate at a time."

"Seriously."

"Any suggestions?"

"I'm doing a series on nursing homes, on abuse of the elderly. I need a decoy, someone to pass as a patient and tell all. Interested?"

"Unpaid?"

"Of course unpaid. We're talking San Francisco *Standard* . . . The Guild need never know."

"Forget it, Terry. I'm still a good union man."

"Oh, come on, Nat. I'll get some money for you."

"Well, if I don't become a full-time poet or a concert pianist I may be your man."

Again there was a moment's silence. "I miss you, Nat," Forman said. "We had good times."

"We did. Some good times."

"We were family, the bunch of us."

"Yes, Terry . . . family." He let himself feel the loss, a mix of regret and relief, but also a loss. "Look, I'll be back. I'll be seeing you at the M&M one of these days, soon as I can drive again. I'll let you buy me a drink."

"Two drinks," Terry said. "Now that you can piss again, two. And I'll buy."

Gloria brought him his mail that morning. He sifted through it while she went to the lobby for a *Standard* with Terry's signer. There were replies to his New York *Review* ad, more than a dozen already, most of them from social workers and therapists, apparently Jewish, judging from the photographs. Some of them were attractive, especially one.

But he was only interested in one particular reply, an envelope at the bottom of all the others. It was a familiar blue envelope with an imitation stamp in Gloria's hand, a sketch depicting the Greek god Pan. The note inside said: "Groping, graying admirer of Vivaldi, Bach, Mozart and Matisse seeks warm body and warm heart, preferably belonging to growing, graying, retired newspaperman. Object: being alive together."

After she returned from the lobby he put the *Standard* aside on the nightstand after glancing at Terry's story. He was pleased a rapist had been caught, some rapist, maybe Ruthie's, but the news could wait.

"I seem to be getting back to normal," he told Gloria after they returned from a walk through the urology corridors, past the open doors of those waiting for surgery, others healing. "I even finished a poem."

The evening before and that morning, he had worked on the poem begun a Passover ago. Now a new birthday was almost here, and in anticipation he had changed the title.

"On Reaching Sixty-three," she read in his scarcely decipherable scrawl. "For Gloria."

I'm still a baby shuddering to be born
at sixty-three. Sixty-three! I want to laugh . . .
Where is that damn serenity of rumored inheritance?
Instead, I've got frayed socks
and nubby memories I've half forgot.
Instead I feel the birthpangs of soul, of heart,
held back by glib illusions and compromise.
I feel the promise of so much waiting to take form.
Sixty-three! There's something wrong. Me, sixty-three? I want
*   to laugh.*
Where is that ease of mind that I'm supposed to have
at double thirty, doubled over, three score plus.
It's sheer chronology of nonsense, arithmetic gone wild.
I'm still unsure of almost everything,
unsure of God, the world and, most of all, myself,
with all my earth-deep feelings waiting to be born.
Why, I'm waiting to be born of waiting
and only sure of some memories, the touch of leaves,
my body, a lover and some friends, my dog, the dead.
They know me better than I do myself
as I turn sixty-three, waiting to be born
in the fierce light of this splendid dawn.

"Hate the handwriting," Gloria said. "Like the poem."

An intimate silence came over them. They were studying each other with a touch of amazement, a trace of a smile, a sense of relief and disbelief over all that was happening between them.

Her glance took in the blue envelope, her reply to his ad, resting on the nightstand along with the *Standard*, on top of the other replies.

"You've got a busy social life ahead of you," she said. He took her hand. "I've got my hands full already."

44

His daughter and son came on a visit together. Gloria was still there. It was late afternoon. Tomorrow was Passover, and he would be leaving the hospital.

All of them had not been together for the worst part of a year, a terrible year. They embraced, and that warm feeling of family, however illusory, or transient, felt good to Nathaniel. He had missed it so much.

"How are you, Daddy?" Ruthie asked, bending over to kiss him.

"Healing. And you, baby?"

"Trying to heal."

Nathaniel was not going to be able to share Passover at Emerson House with Stan and the other residents. So the house had allowed Stan to visit with Ruthie. He had brought along grape juice, matzahs and a thermos sample of the matzah ball soup he was making for those one hundred raving dope fiend survivors.

Norma, Nathaniel's favorite nurse, brought them paper cups and candles for an impromptu service. Nathaniel asked her to join them.

Stan, set to help conduct the service at the halfway house, had brushed up on the meaning of Passover.

"I don't exactly believe in it but it's pretty interesting," he said.

Stan seemed a far cry from the days, months ago, when he was distraught with drugs. He was not cured, he insisted. All he could do was to take things a day at a time, an hour at a time, this moment. But something was happening with Stan. It was as if a light had clicked on.

His voice was strong as he explained how matzah was a symbol of freedom, the food the free wanderers of Israel carried on their backs, eating no bread that could not be baked by the sun.

He took one of the matzahs and broke it in half. "It's a symbol of hope, but we break it as a symbol . . . a sign of . . ."

Once Nathaniel would have interrupted to help. Now he was quiet as his son searched for the right words.

". . . a sign of our imperfect ways . . . how hard it is to remain free."

Stan looked at the others and rubbed his beard, a beard shaped like his father's, and his voice took on more assurance. "I know something about that," he said.

"You're not alone there, Stan," Nathaniel said. "We all have our old habits, old fears and insecurities to break out of."

"Amen," said Gloria.

He was looking at Gloria's face, lively and glowing, and he was reminded of his dead mother's zest for life and how vivid a presence she remained in him. He turned to Ruthie, Rachel's daughter, as courageous in her ordeal as her mother had been in hers. Then to Stan, and he had a sense of his son's growing strength, and he thought of that last day of mourning months ago, mourning their son, dead in spirit, and the words of his dead father's prayer:

I thank you,
O God my Lord,
God of my fathers,
Lord of all good,
Sovereign of souls.

O God,
blessed are You
who restores souls
to the dead . . .

Stan was passing them each a cup of grape juice. Then he lit the candles as the late afternoon grew dimmer and gave one to each of them.

"The soul of a human is the lamp of the Lord, searching the deepest parts of our being," Stan said from memory. "Into the darkest shadows of our lives we carry a light searching for what is deep within."

From somewhere in the past, Nathaniel remembered learning about the Hebraic sense of redemption. The word came to him like a candle being lit: *Davhar* . . . A flaring word, a word that was more than a word, it was an act as well, a bringing forth of something long held back in the self. Someone who believed might call it the divine spark. The possibility was always there, deep inside of us, like the dead, like a pilot-light waiting to be relit, waiting for the wonder of *Davhar*, the spark of renewal and grace.

Stan had brought along the Haggadah he was going to use for the Passover service at Emerson House.

"Our God, God of our fathers," he read, "this day of the Festival of Matzah may there come to You the remembrance of us, of our fathers, of Your holy city Jerusalem, of the son

of David the Messiah and Your servant, and all Your people...

"May all of us appear before You, and may you hear with
favor and with mercy and tenderness our prayer for deliver-
ance, for happiness and life and peace."

Whether they believed or not, they were all touched, each
of them, by the music of the ancient words. They raised their
paper cups of grape juice and blessed each other. They
blessed the living and the dead.